EMPTY SPACES

empty spaces

STEPHANIE LEROUX

CONTENTS

~ one ~

1

~ two ~

Charlotte

3

~ three ~

Charlotte

7

~ four ~

Charlotte

11

~ five ~

Charlotte

15

~ six ~

Charlotte

19

~ seven ~
Glenda
23

~ eight ~
Cassidy
25

~ nine ~
Charlotte
31

~ ten ~
Cassidy
35

~ eleven ~
Charlotte
39

~ twelve ~
Glenda
43

~ thirteen ~
Cassidy
45

~ fourteen ~
Charlotte
53

~ fifteen ~
Cassidy
63

~ sixteen ~
Glenda
71

~ seventeen ~
Charlotte
77

~ eighteen ~
Cassidy
81

~ nineteen ~
Charlotte
89

~ twenty ~
Brett
97

~ twenty-one ~
Charlotte
101

~ twenty-two ~
Cassidy
109

~ twenty-three ~
Brett
113

~ twenty-four ~
Glenda
115

~ twenty-five ~
Brett
119

~ twenty-six ~
Charlotte
127

~ twenty-seven ~
Cassidy
139

~ twenty-eight ~
Charlotte
151

~ twenty-nine ~
Glenda
159

~ thirty ~
Charlotte
167

~ thirty-one ~
Brett
171

~ thirty-two ~
Charlotte
177

~ thirty-three ~
Cassidy
183

~ thirty-four ~
Glenda
193

~ thirty-five ~
Charlotte
205

~ thirty-six ~
Glenda
221

~ thirty-seven ~
Brett
227

~ thirty-eight ~
Glenda
233

~ thirty-nine ~
Cassidy
237

~ forty ~
Charlotte
251

~ forty-one ~
Brett
265

~ forty-two ~
Cassidy
273

~ forty-three ~
Glenda
277

~ forty-four ~
Charlotte
279

~ forty-five ~
Brett
285

~ forty-six ~
Charlotte
299

~ forty-seven ~
Charlotte
303

~ forty-eight ~
Glenda
313

~ forty-nine ~
Charlotte
325

~ fifty ~
Cassidy
329

~ fifty-one ~
Glenda
337

~ fifty-two ~
Charlotte
341

~ fifty-three ~
Charlotte
345

~ fifty-four ~
Charlotte
355

~ fifty-five ~
Charlotte
361

~ fifty-six ~
Charlotte
375

DEDICATION

This book is dedicated first to Vic, my beloved
Thank you for loving me beyond what I
thought was possible and never letting me
give up.

Second, to my girls –
Alivia, Isabella, Natalia, & Victoria
I'm blessed and fortunate to be called your
mom. Thank you for always encouraging me
to keep going.

And last, to my real Glenda –
I will be forever grateful for you constantly
turning my face to see how passionately God
loves me. Your love truly changed my heart.

This story was written for those hurting in silence with unspeakable pain. I pray this book helps you encounter God's unconditional love and abundant grace. Even if this book is only for *one*, the journey will have all been worth it.

First Printing, 2020

Identifiers:
ISBN 978-1-7353562-1-1 (regular edition) | ISBN 978-1-7353562-2-8 (paperback edition) | ISBN 978-1-7353562-0-4 (ebook)

~ One ~

At eighteen years old, I told my heart to stop beating for the man I believed I was going to marry. Brett McDonnell. Just speaking his name makes my heart beat painfully heavier. That torturous day set my life on an off-road course I never wanted, yet one I admit I chose.

The naive girl I had known all my life disappeared and was replaced by the indifferent one I've known ever since. At the age of thirty-two, I thought the regrets would've diminished by now, but the pain of my choices still tears me apart at any given time.

Charlotte Elizabeth Madden. Born July 6, 1979, to William and Catherine Madden. They lived just outside of Nashville, Tennessee, in a small town called Franklin. These are the simple facts of who I am, or who I once was.

My parents moved to Franklin from Lowell, Massachusetts, for a chance at a better life. As a mechanical engineer, my dad was attracted to the booming auto industry in Franklin and believed it would be the right move for our family's financial future. Hard work seemed as if it came natural to my dad. No matter how weary he arrived home from work, I'd see him get up the next day and start all over.

My mom didn't work but was busier than if she did. She was a member of every group she was invited into and even some of the ones she wasn't. She was generous with her opinion whether you asked for it or not. And according to her, it was always right.

When it came to church, she was an expert there too. The first part of her comments often started with "God would like . . ." or "God wouldn't like . . . ," especially when she was talking to me. She seemed to believe she was appointed by God to judge on His behalf.

But it was her last cruel statement to me that changed my opinion of them both. "God is disgusted by you and what you have done. I'm sure He wants nothing to do with you."

In that dark and painful moment, I wasn't sure if I was offended by her words or agreed with them.

Something in my soul broke right then from the arrows she spewed at me. Even now I can feel it. Those twenty words allowed me to let go of the God I'd tried to love for so long. I had disappointed Him, and I didn't know how I could ever repair the deep rift I created between us.

~ Two ~

CHARLOTTE

Brett's rich brown hair, light eyes and olive skin captured my attention immediately the first day of my freshman year. I wasn't just attracted to him. I was drawn to him. I found my eyes constantly drifting to look at him against my will. I would abruptly turn back when I realized where they went. I was fascinated with this boy I had never seen before.

It all started in biology class. Hesitantly walking in, the pungent smell of formaldehyde stunned my senses. As my nose adjusted, we found a two-seater, high-top lab table for us to sit at.

We started to discuss the awful odors, and suddenly the teacher started talking even louder. She caught our attention when she spoke about moving seats to have co-ed lab partners. I desperately wanted to stay where I was, but my hope died hard.

For an introvert, waiting to hear your name to be paired with a stranger was torturous, and fear set in deeper as each name was called.

"Charlotte Madden and . . ."

I barely heard who my partner was over the throbbing vibration in my chest.

". . . Brett McDonnell."

Reluctantly moving tables, I put on my backpack and brought my bad attitude along with it. When I briefly glanced up, I saw this handsome guy walking toward my table. That was the first time I saw Brett, and I was stunned. I hoped it was from coffee I had this morning during my staged attempt to seem mature. But how could I explain away the fluttering in my stomach?

"Hi, I'm Brett," he'd whispered to the side of me. "What was your name?"

Slowly turning to whisper his way, "What's my name? Charlotte. I'm Charlotte Madden." I quickly turned back.

"Nice to meet you." He slightly leaned in again. "I'm not familiar with anyone. I thought I'd introduce myself so I'd know someone."

"Me? You plan for that person to be me?" As soon as the words flew out of my mouth I wanted to reach out and grab them back. The snotty tone was awful, and I knew it.

"Okay. Maybe not." He demonstratively turned his chair and attention forward.

Why did I feel terrible and relieved at the same time? I didn't know him well enough to talk to him, but I didn't have to know him to be polite. Clearing my throat multiple times never got Mikala's attention for her to rescue me. She was so engrossed in conversation with her partner, she never even glanced my way.

How was I supposed to repair rude? I waited until there were five minutes left in class. "I'm sorry," I spilled out. "I'm shy. I rarely talk to people I don't know, and I was taken by surprise. You were just trying to be nice."

He smiled and his dimpled grin struck me. "So, you are nice. No big deal. See you tomorrow."

The shrill sound of the dismissal bell rang. I walked out with a heart that would never beat the same.

The best four years of my life began in biology class, but I often question if the joy of those four years was worth the pain of the last eighteen.

~ Three ~

CHARLOTTE

I could feel the crisp autumn wind on my face along with fresh excitement in the air. The exterior of our colonial, two-story, red-brick high school was slowly being draped with blue and gold banners announcing homecoming. The largest marquee shouted out – "Midnight in Paris – Homecoming 1995."

Waves of nausea immediately began while first reading the sign as we left school. I wasn't sure if it was the smell of fresh paint or the shock of possibly being expected to participate in this torturous ritual.

I must have been the only one affected because Mikala and Josie exuded excitement, making me even more sick. Them talking about dresses made me mentally drift from the conversation. My body was not meant to wear itchy dresses and high heels.

The JV quarterback, Nick Crossland, was Josie's hopeful date. She was plotting on how to drop obvious hints for him to ask her. Mikala couldn't decide between two possible dates. In the end, it wasn't worth talking about because she ended up not going with either one.

Sliding to the edge of her chair, Josie mischievously turned toward me and taunted, "Wait! What about you, Charlotte? We haven't heard a peep from you. Who would you want to go with?"

Not wanting to answer, I squirmed in my chair. "I haven't even thought about it. But me in a dress? That should say it all."

"Oh, please! You know Brett would ask you," Mikala teased.

I tried to stay composed. "Why would you say that? We're just lab partners—"

"Because I see him talking to you every day. He sits staring at the door when he gets to biology before you, and once you arrive, he doesn't stop studying you."

Heart be still! was distracting me in my head. I was tongue-tied and dumbfounded.

"You guys are so annoying. I know Brett is cute and nice and funny and charming. But the bottom line is this—I don't want to just date anyone. I don't even know him."

Things started to change a couple weeks after my denial. Ignoring him in biology class wasn't working, so I started making minimal eye contact with him, but it felt as if his eyes could see my vulnerability.

Something was different this one Friday. I felt it immediately as I walked into our class. People were interested in my entrance more than usual, and a serious look was cemented on Brett's face.

Trying to put the puzzle pieces together, I tried to recall if there was anything I had done or said to make this so awkward.

Was he mad at something? Was he upset? Had something happened?

My spinning mind finally was halted when I got to my table. There on my seat lay a single rose with a note attached reading, "Will you?"

Awe set in and I smiled at him shortly after. I wanted to escape or run over to Mikala, but those were not reasonable options.

Instincts surfaced and I pretended nothing was happening. Denial was starting to look great on me. Placing the rose on my desk, I slowly sat down and placed my textbook next to my gift. A folded loose-leaf paper slid its way in front of me. My false ignorance disappeared.

"Did you know the rose was from me?"

Hesitantly responding, I slid back the paper. "Yes."

Scribbling echoed and the paper appeared again. "Do you realize it's about homecoming?"

Again, I returned a curt reply. "Yes."

Perplexed, he scribed again and passed it back with the phrase, "Are you going to give me an answer or pretend this isn't happening?"

Cutting my eyes, I looked in his direction. I slightly laughed as I turned back to write on the note.

"I'm going to give you an answer."

Hearing him laugh, I couldn't stop myself from looking over at him.

I finally blurted out, "Yes."

Brett and Charlotte began after the long origami exchange. We were fourteen years old. Young and innocent, we had the world ahead of us. Becoming an attorney was his dream and writing was mine. Our personalities complemented each other so well.

We stayed away from trouble, but always managed to find fun. We kindled the type of steadfast romance you hear from grandparents. He was my best friend and the best thing to ever happen to me. And all at once, he wasn't.

~ Four ~

CHARLOTTE

October 15, 2012

Dear Diary,

I wish I could write that today was a spectacular day, but since this is my diary and I have to be honest with myself, I can't. I awoke to the alarm clock's emotionless cry and hid in the steamy shower for as long as I could.

I picked another average outfit to wear, ate the same childish brand of cereal for breakfast, and dripped a single-serve cup of coffee to drink. I checked my email, logged on to Facebook, and checked the news. Only spam filled my email, Facebook proved to be nothing exciting, and the news was depressing as always.

When I finally got to work, paperwork I had escaped from the day before was still there to welcome me. The only highlight while walking in my office was seeing my new title outside my door—Assistant Director of Operations. The projects would be more interesting, pay would be better, my personal office was bigger, and the title made me feel important. It gave me hope this new role at the Gaylord Opryland Hotel would help fill some emptiness in my life I had acquired over the years.

My mom called me today and pretended to ask how I was doing. I replied with the usual answer, and she talked past it. Did she think everything was okay, or did she just call to talk about herself? She told me all about her meetings and her friends. She elaborated on plans the Franklin Historical Society was making for Christmas in downtown. Franklin hosts "A Dickens of a Christmas" every year, and like always, she was going to play Mrs. Cratchit, Tiny Tim's mom.

She asked if I had any holiday plans this year. It felt painful she'd even asked. Why would she ask me that? I had been out of college for ten years, and this would be my tenth Thanksgiving and my tenth Christmas alone with no plans.

Was she thoughtless or careless? The difference between those words is like splitting hairs, but they make all the difference to me and my reaction. It's easier to forgive someone who is thoughtless than it is to forgive someone who is careless. So, for now, I'll call her thoughtless, although my heart knows there's a little bit of both wrapped up in that conversation.

So, Diary, I have to ask . . . How did I get here? How did I get so far down the road of life and become so unhappy? I had such big dreams and big hopes. I used to laugh and have fun.

I was thinking of Mikala and Josie the other day and remembering when we were young. We laughed until our jaws hurt from smiling so much. We even cried together occasionally. We did life together. Lately, I've been wishing to go back there and feel joy and emotion again, but those times are far gone.

Those times included another person I used to know—God. I used to think He loved me. I used to believe He had promises and plans for me. I remember the Bible verse I would always repeat—Jeremiah 29:11.

"'For I know the plans I have for you,' says the Lord. 'Plans to prosper you and not harm you. Plans to give you a hope and a future.'"

I look back and wonder what He once saw in me. I wonder if He ever loved me, because that hope left, and that future never came.

I'll take responsibility for it, though. I'll be honest. My actions were what pushed God away. I disgraced Him. I disgusted Him. I know why He doesn't want anything to do with me.

Having a chance to go back, I'd make so many different choices. I'd go back to that day in biology and never acknowledge the rose. If I could have a second chance to say no to Brett, I would. Not just for me, but for him too. How were we to know we were so wrong for each other?

I drove past a church last weekend, and for the first time in a while, an ache deep within drew me to it. I wanted to walk in and smell incense burning. I wanted to listen to the music. I wanted to smell the wood of pews. I wanted to see sunlight spread through the colorful glass-stained windows.

I began to drive into the parking lot and was tempted to get out of my car. Then, I remembered I was no longer welcome there or any other church. I'm labeled a sinner. Not an acceptable sinner who has lied, cheated or stole. I'm one whose sin was impossible to cleanse.

~ Five ~

CHARLOTTE

October 18, 2012

Dear Diary,

After our last conversation I was burdened by so much sadness. I rued and rued over what I wrote, because I finally saw my pain on paper. And that church I told you about has been taunting me to come closer every time I've passed by it.

In all the years of driving to work, I never noticed it. Yet this last week it seems to have my name in neon lights on the outside. Today, I finally pulled in, parked my car, and just stared at the church doors.

My heart was beating so fast as an unfamiliar voice whispered in my head. *Get out of the car and go!*

Then, the familiar, judgmental voice spoke up. *You know you can't go in. They won't want you once they know you.*

These voices battled in my head.

I closed my eyes, and all I could think was, *Dear Diary, what am I doing here? Is it weird I called for you? Are you the only one who really knows me?*

Fifteen minutes passed while I stared at the church with tears streaming down my face. The familiar voice was right. They wouldn't want me once they knew me.

I was more lost and torn inside than when I pulled in. The drips of tears quickly turned into a deep-cleansing cry, finally just letting it all go. Years of pain were streaming down my face.

As my tears slowed down and I caught my breath, a startling knock sounded on my window. I jumped in my seat and anxiously turned to see an older woman standing outside the car.

As I quickly tried to wipe away any proof of my sobbing, I rolled down my window. "Yes, ma'am?"

Her soft blue eyes captured mine as her soothing voice calmed me. "Sweetheart, are you okay? I'm sorry to startle you, but I saw you were upset and felt nudged to speak to you. I don't usually ask, but do you need a hug?"

A hug? Who walks up to a complete stranger and asks if they need a hug?

I was embarrassed, but not enough to blow her off completely—just enough to be uncomfortable and avoid answering such a strange question.

"I was having a hard morning and just pulled off the road for a minute. I didn't realize anyone was around. I'm okay, though. Thanks for asking."

"I'm sorry to be so intrusive, but I can see you're hurting."

On the contrary, I detected nothing related to nosiness in the woman—only concern.

"What is your name, sweetheart? I would love to pray for you."

That got my attention. "Um, Charlotte."

"My name is Glenda, but everyone calls me Ms. Glenda. This is my church. If you ever need someone to talk to, I would love to chat. We can visit here or over coffee or wherever.

"My doctor told me not to drink too many lattes, but when God brings me someone to have coffee with, coffee tastes even better.

"Charlotte, listen to me for a minute. You're a beautiful lady. Don't let anyone be careless with your heart. God loves you too much for you to hurt so deep." She winked and walked away with a knowing smile.

Her words broke through walls I'd constructed for years. Had I heard her correctly when she said the word careless? Indeed, I had.

When she'd spoken, it felt like my heart skipped a beat. I think my breathing stopped as shock was setting in. Something happened. Something shifted. But just as I was realizing something divine might have happened, battling voices returned and turned up the volume.

They started arguing about her last statement to me.

God loves you too much for you to hurt so deep.

One voice wondered if God could really still love me, but the other voice tried to remind me I already knew He didn't.

For the first time in fourteen years, there was the slightest hope He actually might.

~ Six ~

CHARLOTTE

October 25, 2012

Dear Diary,

Last week, I met Ms. Glenda. She spoke right through me, and I haven't been able to shake her sweet southern voice since. I would feel my shoulders ease with each syllable she said.

The same church drew me in again, as it had for the last few weeks, and my car steered me into the parking lot. I lingered there for a long time.

I desperately looked for words to break the ice and say hello to God, but my search ended when that awful voice reminded me of why I should stay silent. Why would He want to hear from me? Who was I to think that I could just start talking to Him as if nothing had happened between us?

Suddenly, I remembered the Bible story about Peter on his way into the temple. A crippled man sat outside the holy place, begging for money. The rest of the story was a blur.

But in this moment, I was the crippled man. I was paralyzed, sitting outside the church, too filthy to go in. The only thing I couldn't imitate was his humility to reach out for help. My pride kept me in my car where I wept alone.

Was I always going to be paralyzed? Was I going to be emotionally crippled for years to come? Was my pride going to keep me from even trying to stand up?

Visions of my world crashing in were entertaining me when I noticed Glenda had found me again. I wanted to look in the other direction, as if she would just walk by and not notice me there. I held my breath as I anticipated her tapping the glass.

The voice war started back up.

Go away. Don't come over here.

Next came, *Please knock. I'm not brave enough to come out yet.*

They were equally piercing in my head, distracting me from realizing she was approaching, and when she knocked on the window, my body startled again.

Rolling down the window, I pretended to smile.

"Hi, Charlotte. You doing okay? I saw you parked here and wanted to say hello."

I wanted to tell her everything, yet my mouth wouldn't allow it all out.

"Yes, ma'am. I'm okay." I couldn't force the truth through my lips.

She didn't seem convinced. The leftover tears in my eyes were probably her biggest clue. Her head tilted, and her eyes became more tender.

"Sweetheart, I know something is hurting in there. I don't know what it is or how deep it goes, but I can see it in your eyes. I'm still up for coffee if you ever have time."

"Thank you. Truly, thank you, but I have to get going." I couldn't say anything more.

As we were exchanging goodbyes, she gently touched my shoulder, sending chills through my body. Her touch lingered as I drove away, and sorrow rushed over me. The little girl inside me, who never wanted to be this grown-up, cried tears of pity, tears of shame, tears of regret.

Most of all, they were tears from the realization I hadn't been touched that tenderly with love for years.

~ Seven ~

GLENDA

Good morning, Lord,

Thank You for another morning to praise You. Thank You for another beautiful day to witness Your love around me. Fill me with Your love. That is the only way I can love anyone else with Your tenderness.

I want to talk to You about someone. Her name is Charlotte. She has shown up in our church parking lot the last two Thursdays. You know exactly why she was there.

Last week, You brought me to the church to bring an extra key for the youth pastor who was locked out of the building. This week, it was to bring bagels to the staff for a random treat You placed on my heart. I've walked with You long enough to know those things are never random or coincidental.

You've placed this little girl in my path. She's hurting, Lord. She's hurting more than I know and more than I can see, and I recognize pain in those beautiful eyes You created.

Lord, how can I help? I've offered coffee. I've offered conversation. Today, I barely touched her shoulder. She initially shied away from me, but then retracted back. That told me she was hurting and conflicted, wanting to be left alone and wanting to be embraced at the same time. I'm not sure what part You want me to play in her life, but I can't shake her from my thoughts.

I know You're drawing me to her for a purpose. I'm willing to be Your vessel for whatever You need. Most of all, I pray her heart is drawn to You. If she has been away from You, I pray she comes home to You.

Speaking of home, can You kiss Sarah for me? Can You tell her I miss her? It's been thirty years since I could kiss her soft rosy cheeks or stroke her silky auburn hair. Can You tell her how much her momma misses her?

Please do the same to Charles. Tell him how much I miss him and cherish our times we had together. I hope he's holding Sarah close and giving her the affection I can't.

You know how much I miss them. Being here alone has its sad times, and time alone has only gotten harder. You know I'm ready to come home to You. I'm ready to see my baby and sweetheart again.

I know You needed them for purposes I'll never understand while I stand on this earth. I know Your plan is always better than mine, but, Lord, I'm tired. I'm weary. I'll continue to praise You until the day You call me home, but today, I pray it comes sooner rather than later.

All my love,
Glenda

~ Eight ~

CASSIDY

I need this time to clear my head. Hopefully, Sydney will take a decent nap while Colin is at school, so I can actually think. I need to write this out in my dusty journal because I have so many thoughts flooding my mind. I can't sort through them all.

Two years is too long to live like this—married but still feeling alone. Sure . . . two kids and financial stress could make things tough for any couple. But why did it take me until last month to realize none of those things caused our lives to drift apart?

His parents noticed something was off-balance between him and me. They offered to watch the kids for us so we could get away for a long weekend alone.

He hesitated, making the immediate excuse that work was crazy and he couldn't get away. After his dad talked to him a while later, he mysteriously changed his mind.

Later that night, after settling into bed, he said, "My parents are going to watch the kids. They think we need time alone. I told them we were fine, but my dad gave me a speech about taking some time away with you. So, where would you want to go for a couple days? I'll go wherever you want to go."

He was being pressured into it, but my optimistic self said he would enjoy it once we arrived. We just needed to get there. He used to be the fun one. I emphasize the part of *used to be.* Aging has taken that fun side away, but I figured it was pressure of being a providing husband and father.

We live in Green Hills outside of Nashville, Tennessee, so I wanted to go be by the ocean. One of my favorite places to go is Destin, Florida. The beaches are gorgeous, and accommodations nearby are picturesque.

My favorite bed-and-breakfast was a place called "Lisbeth's B&B by the Sea." The name alone made me feel less stressed. The seven-hour drive was short enough to tolerate and long enough to change the scenery. The timing was perfectly placed, as our seven-year anniversary was right around the corner.

I needed no extra time to tell him exactly where I wanted to go. His diligent secretary, Cally, reserved a room at Lisbeth's the next day, along with a rental car to use. It was just what we needed—a weekend together to remember why we first fell in love with each other.

My optimism quickly suffocated in the car ride down. There were superficial conversations about work, stories about the kids and talks about events coming up that I needed to attend with him.

I had expected it to take a while for his tightly wound mind to relax, but even those expectations were blown open. He had become my driver as I entertained myself with music and books. His silence spoke the loudest.

Before I knew it, we were there. I walked into this turquoise room with beach décor calling me to immediate relaxation. The bed had crisp white linens contrasting pale shades of blue perfectly.

Walking out on our balcony, my senses were captivated. Breaking waves on the white sand, smells of the saltwater and cawing of the seagulls were hypnotizing.

As I went back inside, I noticed a basket of fruit, a plate of cheeses and a vase of beautiful white roses. There were seven flowers—seven blooms for seven years.

I thought he remembered our anniversary. Had he finally shown a sign he was interested in this marriage as much as I was? My excitement encouraged me to leap toward him and thank him repeatedly.

As I was thanking him, words slipped out of his mouth—words he couldn't take back.

"I didn't plan any of this. It was all Cally. Between her and my parents, I hope this turns out to be a great weekend for you. Lord knows what I'm missing to be here, so I hope you enjoy your vacation."

There it was—the raw truth, void of any feeling. I'd hoped he would've changed his mood and enjoyed himself once we were there, but hope dies hard. It was to suffice his parents and throw me a bone after all. Although I wanted to break down, something told me that would elicit no response.

Mentally, I fought like hell to stay composed. I nonchalantly walked toward the bedroom and tried to ignore the knot in my throat.

I wanted to get alone to finally exhale. After I put on my swimsuit, I grabbed one of the books I thankfully brought to read. I'd packed them just in case—just in case we ran out of conversation, just in case he had a work call, or just in case I needed something to help me fall asleep at night. My "just in case" list never included the possibility of him breaking my heart and needing to escape reality in order to avoid pain.

In an instant, I went from appreciating our dreamy seaside oasis to being relieved I had books to read so I could escape this nightmare.

I never responded to his hurtful statement, and we never spoke about it again. Our full conversations were only when his parents called about the kids or when there was something of interest on the news.

My desire to connect with him was gone, and I wanted to run back to my comfort zone at home, where I could pretend to control my pain and distract myself with the kids. Being there—alone with him—was a torturous test I was failing.

Maybe it was a blessing in disguise. I could no longer blame the distance between us on anything else. It was real, it was present, and the gap was widening. We were moving away from each other with every moment together.

That was almost a month ago. Between then and now, the empty space between us has become obvious to those close to us too.

His parents noticed first, as his mom made it clear to me when she randomly took me to lunch.

"Cassidy, is everything all right?"

"What do you mean? Yeah, everything is good."

"I mean, you and Brett."

"Oh, he's just stressed. I have the kids most of the time, so we're just going through different places in life right now. It's okay, though."

She didn't want to settle at that, but she had no choice, as I wasn't offering anything else.

The next one to notice was the hardest—my mother.

She and I took the kids to the park one afternoon, and she quickly dove in, "Cass, I know you don't want to talk about anything, because you're very private, but you've seemed very sad over the last six months, and it breaks my heart every time I look into your eyes. I'm your mom. I know when those beautiful blue eyes of yours are speaking."

Taking me by complete surprise, I had to hold back my tears with tight reins. Thank God I had sunglasses on. The little girl in me wanted to cry. I wanted to hug my mom, lean on her shoulder, lay my head in her lap, have her kiss my forehead and stroke my hair. I wanted her to tell me everything would be fine and he would one day love me again like he once had.

Yet all I could say was, "Mom, don't worry. Things are harder now with his work, but we all have seasons like this. Remember what you used to tell me? 'We all have to experience rain in order to appreciate the sunshine.'"

What I couldn't say was, *I am hurting like never before and I'm lonely even when he's right next to me.*

I felt even lonelier when we left the park. I had isolated my feelings from someone who could've comforted me.

I'm currently staring into the endless span of trees in the woods, trying to discern my options as my mind spins rapidly, like a washing machine on its final cycle. My thoughts bounce back and forth from dreaming about what my marriage should be to imagining a future alone as a single mother.

What is my plan? Am I going to accept this as my life, pretending everything is okay and adapting to the distance between us? Or am I going to stop settling for this and figure out all these feelings I'm confused about with some help? Or the hardest option of all—do I acknowledge it's over? Do I just tell him he can stop pretending he loves me and tell him he can leave?

As those words crossed my mind, my heart shattered in the aftershock. There was the truth—he was pretending to love me. And with that truth, the wall I'd created for everyone to see—the wall I'd built to hide behind—crumbled. Who had I become? Had the girl who vibrantly jumped into the marriage disappeared? And worst of all, has the man who walked into the marriage already walked out?

~ Nine ~

CHARLOTTE

November 1, 2012

Dear Diary,

I was pitying myself all week, but my sadness lifted enough to help me change my perspective.

I finally realized a wonderful woman had offered me her time, and I dismissed her. I was already convinced she'd see the real me, eventually judging me unfit to ever walk in the church again.

Yet something told me to let her make up her own mind. If she turned me away, I could handle it. I'd practiced that walk of shame plenty of times. But I was somehow optimistic that she wouldn't.

I finally felt strong enough to suffer through the pain of sharing my real story and safe enough to tell it to her. There was something about her that told my heart she might accept me anyway, but my mind couldn't fully comprehend a stranger could love me to begin with. Trying to understand how I felt more affection from this stranger than I had my own mother was even more confusing.

All this to say I went back to the church parking lot today. When I pulled up, I didn't see any cars outside the building. I got out of my car anyway. I began to take timid steps toward that beautiful piece of architecture.

The first steps were the hardest, and then it was as if my feet knew where they were supposed to go. My heart hastened and my breath slowed as I got closer to the entrance. I walked up the stairs, and with each incline, I wondered if I was making a mistake.

I reached the top of four simple steps, yet my heart raced as if I had walked up four flights of stairs. I walked toward the front doors and hesitantly grabbed the wood-carved handle. Something about the detailed texture reminded me of my childhood.

When I was a child, I would burst through our church foyer with excitement and anticipation. Here I was, years later, frozen at the entrance.

As my hand grabbed on to the handle, I took a deep breath and opened the door. The distinct smell of wooden pews surprised me. I was distracted by my emotions and didn't notice Ms. Glenda sitting in a chair, blending into the décor. My body slightly recoiled as I noticed her.

She stood up to greet me with her huge smile. She giggled as she asked, "Did you come here not expecting to see me?"

"I didn't see your car or any other car, and I haven't been in a church since . . . well, since high school," I said, almost stumbling over my words. "I was a little unsure what this would feel like."

She kept smiling. "So, tell me . . . what does it feel like?"

"To be honest, I don't know yet."

Glenda's smile grew even larger, and her eyes twinkled as though she harbored a secret. "So, are you going to take me up on my coffee offer?"

Finally, I had a good answer. "Yes, actually. I can't go today because of my schedule, but tomorrow night would be perfect for me. Would that work for you?"

"Are you saying you want to spend your Friday night with me?" She was beaming with excitement. "It would be the highlight of my week!"

As I held back unexpected tears, I tried to say *and the highlight of mine as well,* but I just couldn't spit it out.

She wanted to meet at a place called The Beanery in downtown and added they played live music there on Friday nights. Her joy brought me to smile wider than my cheeks had stretched in a while.

So, I'm going to do what I've been resisting all these years. I'm going to let her see the real Charlotte. It's scary to think that when I do, she will never see me the same.

~ Ten ~

CASSIDY

A week has passed since I first wept like a baby. I was hoping it was hormonal, but after a couple days, crying continued to creep up on me.

My best friend, Danielle, stopped by unexpectedly. I don't think I can hold all this back from her.

"Okay, what is going on? I've been calling you and you won't call me back. I came over because I know something is wrong. Are you sick? Is something wrong you can't tell me? Say it and I'll leave you alone, but I had to make sure you were alive."

Reluctantly, I opened the door wider because I knew it wasn't going to be easy to get her to leave. My aggravated tone gave texture to my short answer.

"Come in."

I knew I had just traded my privacy for a friend when she came inside and sat down. As I shared our struggle, I felt a surprising sense of relief.

"This has been the hardest thing I've ever had to walk through," exhaling while exposing the truth.

"I cry on and off. The waves of tears creep up when I picture my husband leaving me or when I imagine sharing custody of the kids and leaving them with him on weekends. My mind tortures me when I think of another woman loving him or another woman spending time with my kids as their stepmom."

"Cass, I'm so sorry. I don't even know what to say. Want me to hurt him? I'm stronger than ever when I'm pissed off." The laughter was comforting.

"I wanted to think it was all hormonal, but it's not. I'm painfully aware of what I'm losing—and grieving what I've already lost.

"I tell myself to stop thinking about it, and other times I allow myself to carry thoughts as far as I can imagine. I picture the kids' weddings. I imagine him and his wife enjoying the moment together as I sit alone, resenting that those two seats were supposed to be reserved with our names on them.

"This has happened before with us. I was in college and it was after things got serious. He ghosted and I cried constantly."

I opened an entire new treasure box of past secrets. Danielle had no idea what she was walking into when she came over.

"Cass, this goes that far back?" she asked with such surprise on her face.

"When we met in college, he had a wall around his heart, but once he and I hit it off, he was amazing. We spent all our time together, talking and laughing.

"A few months later, things got strange. We were sitting by the lake one night, listening to music, and I said something that spooked him."

Inquisitively, she asked, "What did you say?"

I slightly laughed. "I casually said, 'I love you so much,' in the middle of a conversation, and I couldn't pull it back in my mouth once I realized what I had said."

Danielle tried to not laugh, but I started laughing with her. "What did he say?" She was visibly intrigued.

"He quickly changed the subject. His American history paper was suddenly due the next day." I rolled my eyes and chuckled again.

"All I kept thinking was I wished I could've taken back those stupid words. It's not like I could've said, 'Just kidding!'

"I reluctantly apologized once we got in the car, and I told him it just came out. He just kept his eyes on the road as he drove and mumbled something like, 'It's all right,' in a way that let me know it wasn't.

"I knew something had changed when he pulled up to my apartment just by the way he parked the car and anxiously got out. He walked me to my apartment, said some parting words, and gave the most awkward half-kiss on my cheek. I remember standing there speechless as he disappeared around the corner, wondering if he'd ever come back."

"But you obviously ended up together, so what happened?"

"I cried for days. My roommates even bought me ice cream to try and comfort me. After not hearing from him for almost a week, I thought it was over. He finally showed up at my apartment. I figured he had come to break up with me in person.

"He started to apologize, but then dropped a big bomb on me. He admitted he had been in a serious relationship a couple years earlier and some stuff was still lingering. He said something along the lines of 'I loved her the best I could, and it wasn't enough. It wasn't enough to overcome what had come between us.'"

"Who was she? Did you ever figure out who he was talking about?" Danielle was more curious about who the girl was than I was at the time.

"I didn't know at the time but found out it was a girl he went to high school with. Maybe I should've ended things when I saw how consumed he was by it. But love blinded me because when I saw him crying, I was all in. All I wanted was to be the one to comfort him." With that, Danielle and I both genuinely laughed.

"I hardly remember the words he said after I saw the tears. I know he asked me to forgive him, and that he loved me. I had never loved someone and couldn't see I was taking a risk.

"I feel like that risk is now surfacing. Is he doing the same thing again and shutting me out again?"

Danielle couldn't answer any of my questions, but it helped that she was deeply sympathetic. Having her there to listen to me was a gift, because I couldn't talk to him and I couldn't be honest with our parents. I didn't realize I was grateful she showed up until she was gone.

After she left, some things I had told her started to repeat in my head. Could he still be holding on to what hurt him back then? I'd never asked him about what he shared that night nor his explanation for his behavior.

The words he'd used to describe his previous relationship's ending had come up in my thoughts over the last nine years, but I'd always been able to lay them to rest. This time, they were whipping around again in my thoughts.

He said, *My love wasn't enough to overcome what had come between us.*

That's when What had come between them? Was it distance, time, friends, family, or did something happen that he was keeping to himself?

~ Eleven ~

CHARLOTTE

November 2, 2012

Dear Diary,

Tonight, I met Ms. Glenda for coffee. I cannot think of one word to describe it. I was expecting this pious person with no emotion and all rules. My expectations were blown away.

This woman was the exact opposite. Her stories were genuine, letting me feel the way she loved so deeply with every word she said. Even her smile lit a fire in me. Her intense gaze made my soul feel nurtured. I felt loved by someone who didn't even know me.

Diary, how did she do that? There was no reservation when she told the barista she was beautiful and had gorgeous eyes. The girl was visibly touched. Even if I had thought those things about someone, I wouldn't have been able to say it to them. This woman blew my mind—from the time we ordered coffee to the time we left.

She asked all about my life—high school, college, my parents and even my grandparents. There were more questions about siblings and favorite memories.

When she asked me where I worked, her face lit up when I told her the Gaylord Opryland Hotel. She immediately asked if I was in love with the Christmas display as much as she was.

As she mentioned she used to take her daughter there every Christmas, sadness came over her face briefly, but she quickly went on and we never came back to that. As our time was coming to a close, she had one more thing to ask me.

"Charlotte, this might be a strange question, but how is your heart?"

My head tilted a little because I was confused by the strange question. "I guess I would have to say I'm generally healthy."

Her eyes softened as she began to laugh. "I'm sorry. I wasn't very clear. Not your physical heart, but the other heart. The heart that feels things and filters things. The heart that breaks when your feelings are hurt, and the heart that beats faster when a special song comes on the radio. That heart is the one I'm asking about."

Stunned, I sat there and stared down into my coffee for a while. How was I supposed to answer that? "I haven't ever thought about that. I think it's okay."

She explained that it's easy to think we're okay, but experiences stick with us and take root deep in our hearts. Our personality and perspective change when the ugly roots grab hold of our heart, often without noticing.

"I want you to really think about that question. If you come to realize anything, I'd love to talk with you about it and am available any time. But, if you don't think there's anything there, or don't want to talk about it, I understand."

All I could do was slightly nod my head repeatedly. We both started to gesture our time was up and slowly gathered our belongings. We walked each other to the parking lot, expressing what a great night we had. As we turned to say goodbye, words jumped out of my mouth.

"Ms. Glenda? Do you see something in me that would make you ask that question about my heart?"

I couldn't believe I had even asked, and when I heard my vulnerable, shaky voice, it scared me.

She turned back toward me and reached out for my wrist.

"Sweetheart, I do. I see pain in your eyes and hear a sadness in your voice. When you laugh, there's a pain holding you back from feeling the joy of it. You've been hurt, reluctant to receive love, and I've been hurting for you since the morning I met you in the church parking lot. You don't have to tell me why, but I want you to know I already love you."

She firmly hugged me and prompted tears to fall from my eyes. My walk to the car was a blur, not knowing what just happened.

How did this woman who only knew my first name see right through me? How did I let her in? How did she get past these walls that have protected me for so long?

My heart is not okay. Do I really want to see why, or can I just ignore it and keep pretending as if it's okay? Wouldn't that be the easiest thing to do? But is easy what I need right now?

~ Twelve ~

GLENDA

My Dearest Lord,

My visit with Charlotte last night was amazing. That young lady is such a delight. I found out so much about her, and she has such a good spirit within her.

At times, speaking to her reminded me of talking to Sarah. I had to pinch myself because I would feel like it was Sarah who was right in front of me. Maybe I just wished it was her. I know that makes no sense, but sometimes my heart and mind play tricks on me.

She was sad, but covered it well, as if she had learned to mask it. Her laughter seemed natural, but her beautiful eyes somehow cried out to me. When I asked about her mom, I could tell there was a void there, even though she responded positively in her response.

She grabbed my attention again when she tried to skip over her high school and college experience, then overexplained why she'd grown apart from her friends.

A boyfriend in high school was briefly mentioned, but they broke up when they went to college. I assumed they went to different schools, but when she said they went to the same college, it didn't make sense.

When she talked about him, her tone of voice was different and her eyes turned lifeless. She explained that some things had come between them, and they were too young to know how to handle it. Her lips almost quivered from holding back emotions.

God, You know what that pain is from. I pray for that sweet child of Yours. If You have more work to do that requires my help, I'm Yours and willing. If she never comes around again, I'll know You have another path for her.

As always, I'll close in praising You. I'll also ask You to kiss my Sarah and Charles for me. You know how much I've missed them lately. I'm trusting You. All I can keep saying is I trust You, God.

All my love,
Glenda

~ Thirteen ~

CASSIDY

Marriage counselor: two words married people dread.

"I made us an appointment with a counselor for us." I just blurted it out one night.

He turned toward me as if I were a demon. "I will never step foot into a therapy session with you—never!"

I held my tongue until a few minutes passed, and then I calmly responded, "I'm keeping the appointment. No matter what you choose to do, I'm going." No response was needed, so I quickly turned and left.

While walking out of that room, something shifted in me. Instead of focusing on him, I was focused on getting to the other side of what was standing in our way.

Nerves made my stomach churn at the thought of going alone, but I knew I needed to go for myself. As much as I love him, it's impossible to carry the marriage for both of us. The line where my responsibility ended was blurry, and I knew only a professional could help.

On the morning of our appointment, I left a sticky note with the time and address of the appointment on the coffee maker. He didn't mention seeing it before he left for work, and it was still on the coffee maker when I left the house for the appointment.

On my way there, I prepared myself to accept that he wouldn't be there, but it surprised me that I still had hoped I'd see his car in the parking lot when I pulled in.

I searched for him when I got out of my car and again while I hesitantly walked into the office. As I was checking in, I could hear the door open behind me. Even then, I was desperately hoping it was him and didn't want to be disappointed when I turned around.

And when I turned around, I was paralyzed—he was standing there. I had hoped he'd be there, and now that he was, I had no idea how to respond.

"Hey . . . I didn't think you'd come." As I smiled, he responded with a glare.

"I didn't think I was coming either."

His clenched jaws were twitching from anger. Wanting to break eye contact, I turned to find two seats for us to sit.

I had wished he'd show up but prepared as if he wouldn't. I built up confidence by rehearsing what I wanted to share and reminding myself what I didn't. Now with him beside me, that confidence vaporized. All I kept asking myself was, *Why did you make this appointment? Why did you stir up all these problems?*

My inner dialogue was interrupted when he turned toward me with a nasty look. "Are the kids with my mom? I assume they know we're here, right?"

His spiteful tone was maddening. I wanted to fight for our marriage, and he'd rather fight me. My emotions were surfacing, and we weren't even in the therapist's room yet.

A tall, broad man came through a door in the back of the waiting room. I was surprised because this whole time I thought Dr. Woods was a woman.

He made eye contact with us and called out, "Cassidy?"

We stood up and made our way toward him. We shook his hand as he introduced himself.

"Hello. I'm Dr. Robbie Woods. Nice to meet you both. Let's walk back to my office."

He had a wonderful smile, but no matter how nice it was, I remained shocked that the counselor was a man. As we walked, I wondered how I would tell a man how I felt. Hopelessness settled in during the short walk from the waiting room.

He opened the office door and it was gorgeous—a beautiful room with a view overlooking a pond with overgrown plants on the embankment. Wildflowers in shades of blue poked through greenery. One large leafy plant towered over five feet tall. I wanted to go hide under it instead of sitting down on his couch.

Anxiety tightened my chest and my breathing became shallow. I expected he would take my husband's side and think I was crazy too.

Every part of my body was grasping for another. My arms folded and deeply pressed into my ribs. My knees were touching and my ankles were gripping each other.

As the introductions ended, an awkward silence showed up. With it came the dreaded question, "So what brings you both in today?"

That one question quickly turned my teammate into my enemy. His body language initially spoke for him—*Oh, I don't have the problem. It's all her.*

His gesture stirred my pride. The war was about to begin. If he wanted to hang me out to dry, I could do the same. I decided to throw the first punch.

"Umm, we've been married seven years, and over the last six months to a year, we've grown distant. I've noticed major changes in our marriage.

"There's so much history and so much hurt, I'm rethinking the idea of spending an hour trying to fix something that has been eroding for years."

I didn't want to sound so cold, but I was furious. Anger had come out before I could speak my truth. I wanted to scream out that my heart was hurting—that I married my best friend, and he was gone.

But the enemy next to me didn't even flinch. I had just ripped off a layer of his skin, yet he looked untouched. I held my shoulders tight, waiting for the returned blow.

And as I was beating myself up with regret, the enemy began his counterattack.

"It was my wife's idea to come here. I think she's just going through a transition in her life with young kids and needs extra attention I can't give her right now. Truthfully, I don't think I'll ever be able to make her happy."

That wasn't even a response. He dismissed everything I said as he belittled me. I felt like a child being talked over. I shut down and turned off.

I thought I was warring for my marriage, but his comments told me I was battling alone. I'd been swinging my arms and legs, hitting nothing because no one else was in the ring.

I stared out the window with a blank gaze as I thought about who to call on the way home to ask about a good divorce attorney. That large plant outside was still calling for me to nestle under it and hide.

I didn't hear anyone talking, and it snapped me back to the present. Nothing was being said. Did I miss something?

I glanced around and then looked at Dr. Woods. His eyes vacillated between both of us, then he started to pose a question to the man next to me.

"So, you're a thirty-foot yacht at sea, strolling along, and you see Cassidy approaching you on the water. What kind of vessel is she?"

The room was silent for an extended pause. Then, I heard a smirk as he answered.

"She's a battleship with cannons ready to be fired at any minute."

I was genuinely offended, but I refused to let him see. I refused to show weakness. After all, I was a battleship, right?

The counselor opened his mouth to speak, and I prepared to answer the same question. But he responded to my husband instead.

"You see, I think that's the beginning of the problem here. You see her as a battleship.

"She is actually a sinking rowboat that is pulling up next to you, asking for help. Since you see her as a battleship, you're ready to turn and go as fast and as far as you can in the other direction."

The counselor flipped my expectations and validated me. My spirits immediately lifted, and I was finally able to breathe. But I couldn't look at my husband, because I knew he wouldn't respond well to being challenged.

The doctor wasn't finished with him.

"Do you believe in God?"

I felt oxygen leave the room. I forgot he was a Christian counselor. My husband always squirmed when God was brought up.

He pushed back a little in his seat. "Uhm, excuse me?"

The doctor raised his eyebrows. "I asked, do you believe in God?"

My husband stared at him as the pause lengthened. He let out an exaggerated breath before he answered.

"Yes, I do. I don't quite know where that came from, and I'm not quite sure the relevance, but yes, I do."

"Are you unsure of the relevance of God in our conversation, or the relevance of God in your marriage?" the doctor asked, probing deeper.

"God is relevant in my marriage, but I'm not sure it's necessary to discuss here with you." That angry response came from the attorney side of my husband, and I thought fireworks were going to go off.

I wanted to rescue both of them from a confrontation I felt coming on, but I also wanted my husband to be confronted so he could see what was happening with us.

"Are you upset with God?" the counselor challenged.

"Upset? No, I'm not upset." His face tightened and he repositioned himself in his chair aggressively. "Where are you going with all this? We're here because she's miserable. She's home with two small children while I'm working.

"I have struggles. I have stress. I'm trying to provide for them. We're here so I can figure out a way to explain it to her, and then you ask me if I'm angry with God?" He spoke deliberately and direct, and his face flushed more with each word.

"I want to know when you decided that God belonged in a box you keep on a shelf to use when it is convenient. I'm wondering if you put Him there out of anger or inconvenience, but by your tempered response, I think it's anger.

"I ask because whatever quick fixes you make will return if He isn't in the center. I don't mean to upset you. I'm just figuring out where we need to start in order to help your marriage."

The tension made my blood pressure skyrocket, but neither of them eased up.

"I asked if you believed in God because when I asked you what vessel your wife was, you described her as a vessel stronger than yours with more capacity and ability." The counselor briefly paused. "But God's Word tells us wives are a weaker vessel, and we're to live with them in an understanding way.

"Everything you've stated here leaves no room for you to begin to understand her. With her as a battleship, I'm guessing all you have room for is running from her."

That pierced my enemy's defensive posture. I watched his shoulders soften. I watched his eyes ease. There were no words. In fact, he hardly said another word the rest of the visit.

The counselor asked me a few more things, and we ended with planning to return in two weeks. My heart was grateful to witness my husband physically surrender, but I figured that was the last time we'd be there together.

We left the office and brought the cloud of tension with us. I wanted desperately to ask, *What's going on in your mind? What did you think? Are you okay with everything?* Mostly, I wanted to know if he thought we had a chance at all.

We got outside the office doors and walked toward the parking lot. We stopped, turned and just looked at each other. My body yearned to hug him or touch him, but it was clear it wasn't mutual.

"I have to get back to work," he said, breaking the silence. He turned to start walking toward his car, then stopped and faced me again. "Oh, wait, Cass? Please tell my parents I said thank you for watching the kids."

That wasn't what I wanted to hear, but I nodded. He turned and went to his car while I stood there feeling naked and raw.

As he backed his car out, I hoped he would stop and say something to me. He drove off and reality sank in. I was going back to my life with nothing changed, nothing different.

My hope had hinged on this appointment, but our relationship had just turned down an even darker road. We were further apart now than when the appointment started. There was more angst and tension in the space between us. We had more to feel and less to talk about. We both left with our walls up higher than they had ever been before.

~ Fourteen ~

CHARLOTTE

November 15, 2012

Dear Diary,

It's been two weeks since my meeting with Ms. Glenda. Since then, conversations I've had with myself have left me physically exhausted.

I think back on questions she asked me. *Charlotte, how is your heart?*

A piece of me wants to unhear that one question. Unhear? Is that even a word? No, because it's impossible to do.

I want to close that door she opened. Actually, I want to nail the door shut, forget I met her, and forget our meeting. Yet my mind won't let me because I wouldn't be able to remember how great the rest of that night was.

Part of me gets angry at her for asking that question. Who asks a question like that when you're just meeting someone? I feel like she asked me what color underwear I was wearing.

When the anger subsides, sadness sets in because she was right to ask. I'm sad. Someone did hurt me, and I'm responsible for hurting someone too.

In fact, I'm probably guilty of inflicting pain on many people. The burden is so heavy, I stop accounting for whom I've hurt and start justifying the ones I remember.

I've played mental gymnastics, flipping and switching things so I can live with them, but am I living with them well? If she can see scars, can everyone?

Maybe I should do some digging. I should start with who has damaged me. It is easier for me to dig as the victim rather than the offender.

I must ask you, should I meet with Glenda again to talk about it, or should I just process this alone? I usually want to do it alone or stuff it down, but somehow I already trust her.

I want to share everything and let judgment fall where it may. I want to explain how much I've been hurt and tell her I lost who I was fourteen years ago.

I want to reveal that my mom and I have been distanced by choice words she used when I was a broken teenager, and I want to confess that my dad's willingness to drift apart has left me aching. I want to describe how I lost the love of my life by mistake, and then four years later, I let go of the potential for love again.

I can tell her that after the dust of the drama settled, my best friends just became acquaintances. My momma and daddy became Mom and Dad. And the love of my life became a stranger.

The real question I have to ask myself is, *am I willing to have that conversation?*

So much of my past is tightly stuffed away, and I don't want to let it out. But, if I have to share some of it, how do I choose what to share and what to keep hidden?

I've begun to retrieve memories out of the dark, but the overwhelming sensations accompanying them make me push the thoughts back to where they were.

Let me share it with you first. Maybe that will soften the pain.

My high school days were like a television show. From the time Brett and I met, we clicked. We had a relationship most dream about that lasted through high school.

We hung out at school. We went to youth group and volunteered together. We went to church together. He came to every one of my soccer games. Occasionally he'd have his face and chest painted in navy blue and gold to have fun in the stands.

He wore a school sweatshirt with my name and number on the back—Madden #19. And when I had the chance, I went to all his baseball games. He was a pitcher, and I loved to watch him throw. Of course, I had a sweatshirt just like his with his last name and number—McDonnell #19. Yes, we shared that number. It was special to him, so I said I would wear it too.

We talked about our dreams and future plans. Mine involved going on to play soccer in college. My eyes were set on some great programs in North Carolina, but I was happy to go anywhere if it meant I could play.

Brett was much more academic focused. As much as he liked to play baseball, he didn't want to play in college.

The great thing about Brett and me was that just looking into each other's eyes from across the room made us both light up. He knew I was shy and I had a hard time sharing my feelings, yet he was gentle and always made it easy for me to talk to him.

He was brilliant and had a mind that worked constantly. I knew he needed someone to listen to him. He would just talk and process all the thoughts he had within, then he'd make sense of them without one response from me.

During that same time, Mikala, Josie and I were best friends. We were all involved in our church and often spent weekends together.

Brett and I always liked to be with groups of people because we knew too much alone time could lead us down a dangerous road. Our romantic chemistry was undeniable, so in order to keep it in check, we tried to minimize any tempting situation.

Let's be real for a second. We both wanted to uphold promises we'd made. When we were freshmen, it seemed so easy. In youth group, we all pledged we would hold on to our sexual innocence until we were married. It was a flag we all flew so easily. But as the romance intensified, those sexual thoughts came more often and questioned my values.

My flesh was human and hormones were raging. Friends were having casual sexual flings every couple of months, and they made it seem normal.

Even school taught us to use protection, rather than abstinence. Brett and I were the odd ones, and basically everyone knew it, friends or not. We were the "virgin couple."

Out of nowhere, something changed. I can't tell you what, when or how, but something scared us both.

I think it was February of our senior year. College coaches started contacting me after watching me at a few showcases.

A few small schools in North Carolina had noticed me, as well as one in Georgia and two in Tennessee.

Every time a different coach contacted me, Brett researched the school, including cost of attending and academic programs provided. The more schools that had declared interest, the clearer it was becoming that our idea of "forever" was possibly becoming "for right now."

Our dreams worked perfectly on paper, but they were eroding. Everyone knew a relationship that went in separate directions for college had the slightest chance of surviving. We knew that too, and something rose up in both of us because of it.

We started to long for each other, even as we sat next to each other. We started to miss what we had, even while we still had it. Our relationship became more intense. Our kisses lasted longer. Our bodies moved closer together. Our hands reached out for each other with every chance.

My mom even pulled me aside one night and asked if something had changed between us because our boundaries seemed to have shifted. Shortly after our talk, guidelines we had put in place about being alone slowly started to recede.

Fast-forward to spring break of our senior year. Brett decided to start seriously looking into Vanderbilt University. His dad and grandfather were alumni and pulling him to look in that direction. It was an amazing academic school with programs for the career path he wanted to head down.

His family was supportive of him seeking other schools, but silently hoped he would follow in their tradition. Brett dreamed of Vanderbilt since he was a young boy, but when our dreams of being together surfaced, he'd become unsure of which dream to choose.

With choices of schools I had to attend on soccer scholarships, it made that struggle even harder. Vanderbilt had showed a bit of interest in me, but communication with them dropped off. I knew chances were slim, and I had to look at other options.

I didn't have it in me to watch Brett give up his family's traditions for us to attend the same school. I had to convince him to follow his family, and he eventually knew I was right. He had to make the decision for himself—even if it took us different places.

We started talking about what a long-distance relationship would look like going to different schools in different cities. How often would we get to see each other? How could we visit each other if we couldn't stay in the same room together?

The good news was if he went to Vanderbilt, I could see him on my breaks and be able to stay at home. But those trips home would be rare because of training, games and travel. Each question bred a new question. With each uneasy answer, our fear swelled. With each surmounting fear, our faith diminished.

It was the weekend of our last spring break, and all of our friends were celebrating. Brett and I were meeting them, so I watched out the window, waiting for him to pick me up.

I grabbed my sweater. I knew I had to dress especially warm because the heat in Brett's truck only rarely worked. I'd bring a blanket most times.

Even though it was March, it was still chilly around Franklin. Trees were still bare, but a few had buds on them, as spring was around the corner.

He pulled up in his old navy Ford Bronco with thick white trim and met me in my driveway. He loved that truck.

I remember so clearly when Brett opened the door for me and our eyes met, because he seemed distant. Usually his eyes lit up when he picked me up for a date, but this time, he quickly broke our gaze and turned to get around the car. He never made eye contact again. Instead, he turned the radio up, leaving no room for conversation.

Something felt strange, and thoughts of him breaking up with me started rolling through my head. After letting my mind run wild, I decided I would just ask.

I turned down the radio. "Are you all right?"

"Yeah, everything is good, but would you mind if we headed out to Lake Hermitage before we met up with everyone at the party?"

I didn't know why, but I could see he needed to either talk about something or process something he had been thinking about.

"Sure, I don't mind, but it's really dark out there. Are you sure you're not planning to kill me and throw me in the lake?"

I tried to make him laugh, but I got a minimal response. He leaned toward me and placed his hand on my leg.

He didn't just pat me gently. He touched me on my thigh just above my knee with an intensity I didn't recognize. It felt as if he didn't want to let go.

We pulled into the park area at Lake Hermitage. With the Bronco, we could pull up pretty close to the lake, where most cars were hindered by high grass and mud.

"Are we going to be okay here? We aren't going to get stuck, right?" I was nervous because he was backing up the truck far into the thick brush.

"Yeah, we should be good here." He turned off the car and then looked down at his hands, nervously clasping his fingers.

"Charlotte, we've been together for over three years. We've spent every second together we possibly could. We've shared our ups and our downs, our highs and our lows, our crazy thoughts, our insecurities and our accomplishments, and it has all been amazing.

"But this chapter of our lives is closing, and I can't help but think we might eventually drift apart." His hands were starting to shake.

I grabbed his hands and tried to settle him. "It's all going to be okay. I've never seen you this upset. . . ."

He interrupted. "No, wait. . . . I brought you out here because I wanted to ask you something. We've always wanted to do what was right. We've always wanted to lead as an example of the life God wanted for other kids. We took a vow to wait until marriage to make love to one another. . . ." Then came the heavy gaze.

"But with circumstances of you leaving and us not being able to be together, I want to give myself to you. I want you to know you're the one who has my heart no matter where we both are. What I'm asking is . . . do you want to share all of you with me too?"

That was the bomb fear dropped right in front of us. I was shocked. I was angry to be put in that situation, yet flattered Brett felt so much for me. How was I supposed to respond?

Everything in my flesh wanted to rip my clothes off. Everything in my heart knew it was the wrong choice. I wanted to wait until we got married, and we'd already waited so long and come so far.

In the twenty seconds I hesitated with my answer, I prayed. I asked God to help me. And then tears in Brett's eyes distracted me.

I saw his fears, and something came over me, making me want to ease that for him. I knew it could mean giving up the vow we'd made, but something in me justified it by how much we loved each other.

Then, my prayer for advice turned into a plea asking for forgiveness in advance. And all I could think to say was, "Yes. I do."

Our bodies gravitated toward each other, and we began to kiss as if we were kissing for the last time.

"Wait here," he whispered.

He went to the rear of the truck and opened up the back door. He asked me to close my eyes and turn around. I heard him floundering with things and knew he was preparing something with blankets.

Finally, he came around to my door and opened it. He led me by my hand and walked me to see what he had been working on. Three red roses and two lit candles were sitting on an overturned box covered with a white cloth.

Checkered and flannel blankets were layered, and a couple pillows had been tossed on top. Tears welled up in my eyes. I didn't know if I was touched by his planning or scared of what we were sacrificing.

While I stared at the makeshift room, I began to think of reasons I shouldn't climb in, mostly scared of giving up promises I had made to wait. But his soft touch on the small of my back distracted me from hesitating any longer.

I climbed into the truck, and he followed behind me. He closed the truck's back gate and we both sat there, staring at each other with nervous smiles.

I could see Brett's eyes in the candlelight's reflection. "I love you, Charlotte Madden, and I want you to know I want to spend forever with you."

I began to happy cry but had no words.

Brett blew out the candles, and our bodies found each other in the dark.

~ Fifteen ~

CASSIDY

It has been a week since our visit to the counselor together. The hopeful beginning of healing for our marriage ended up being a catalyst for us distancing from each other further.

The night after our counseling appointment, we hardly spoke. I felt like a little kid hoping the punishment my parents decided to give me wouldn't be that bad. Waiting for another to speak is torturous.

We sat in the same bed, yet he felt miles away from me. He read through work files and I pretended to read. Thoughts about us were so pervasive, I couldn't comprehend one sentence. It was the night I needed to escape into the storyline the most, and my mind failed me.

How could we have gone to marriage counseling together in the morning and then lain next to each other as strangers that night? I tossed and turned to get to sleep. Finally, my mind shut off, and I was able to rest.

Unfortunately, that didn't last long. I woke up at four a.m. in a panic. It was that type of awakening when you remember where you are and why you were upset when you went to sleep. My heart sank. My whole body wanted to reach out and touch him, but I couldn't. I wanted to wake him up and plainly ask him if he still loved me, but that wasn't an option either.

I painfully watched him sleep for a while with tears in my eyes. I watched his face and noticed wrinkles I hadn't seen before. We weren't the same young kids who fell in love. We had both grown up and grown apart.

He was relaxed. Soon he would awake and be consumed by work again, willfully avoiding me and the kids. His work used to be a distraction from our family, and the job was only supposed to be a means to a better life. Now, the job was the better life for him, and the kids and I were the distraction.

My heart longed for something I knew was dead and gone. I couldn't lie there anymore, so I went downstairs. Should I have started washing dishes or folding laundry? Should I have watched television or tried to read the book that had already failed me?

In all those choices, nothing seemed to be the answer. I had this emptiness, as if nothing I currently knew could fill the void within.

This strange thought came to my mind once, and I hesitated. Next to the recliner, in our living room, was a basket filled with books and current magazines. Some time ago, I had placed a Bible and a devotional there my mother-in-law had given to me years before. I thought it was a good place for them but had never actually opened either one.

Over the last month, those books had grabbed my attention more than once and often crossed my mind. That night, it felt like a neon sign flashing *Read Me* pointed to the basket.

I reached down for the Bible and felt its heaviness in my hand. Not only physical weight was just as overwhelming and intimidating as the emotional weight.

What was I supposed to do with this? I felt defeated and ignorant just opening it. Then, I looked down and saw the pink leather-bound book my mother-in-law had packaged with the Bible when she'd given me the gift three years ago.

My husband's family was Christian. They were the kind that lived out their faith. I always wanted to have a piece of my mother-in-law's faith and the faith my husband once had. He was raised in a church, went to all the church groups, and had always volunteered there.

Somewhere along the way, he separated it from who he was to something he occasionally acknowledged. His mom always thought it was liberal teachers in college that turned him away from his faith, and I always secretly assumed it was me.

I was raised Catholic. We occasionally went to church on Sundays, but always went on Christmas and Easter. Christmas was always my favorite, and Midnight Mass was the ceremony I treasured most.

It wasn't the service itself. It was specifically one song—"O Holy Night." With candles burning and lights dimmed, I would hear the words ". . . Fall on your knees. Oh, hear the angels' voices. . . ."

It was an automatic trigger every year for tears to flow down my face. I always wanted to let go of my ego and just fall to my knees, not caring what others around me thought. I wanted to ask God to help me, to forgive me, and to show me who He was.

Then the song would end, my heart would stop racing, and the service would soon finish. I'd wipe away the tears, exit the building that evoked emotions, and leave my feelings behind. Christmas would pass, the new year would start, and my life would be absent of God once again. I always assumed my husband's lost faith had to do with me never finding mine.

Sitting in that chair, holding the Bible in one hand and the pink leather book in the other, I struggled with what to do. I chose the small, less intimidating book to start.

Dates were included on each page, indicating the passage to read for that day. It reminded me of paint-by-numbers I used to learn to paint when I was a child, except this would be pray-by-numbers.

I opened the book and discovered a handwritten note on the first page.

To Cassidy—the daughter-in-law I've always prayed for. May this book draw you closer to the One who loves you most. Love always, Mom.

My throat tightened as my eyes flooded. My chest squeezed together and my heart ached. I couldn't see through tears that were soaking the page I was reading.

She'd given this to me three years ago. What horrible timing I must have. I was learning how much my mother-in-law loved me as I was learning how much her son did not.

I kept flipping pages, all while doubting the power of that little book. When I reached the right day, I saw there were only two paragraphs—only two.

I wanted to laugh. How were two short paragraphs going to kindle a fire in my heart for this God I longed for ages ago?

Starting to read, my mind was blown, and my heart was paralyzed. They read as if Jesus himself were talking to me.

The message explained how some fears surface over and over again, especially fear of the future. I always project into the future and visualize myself in pain, but it said those images were lies because they didn't include Him. Since He is always with me, those lies would not come to pass.

I slammed the book closed. I felt my heart racing. That was one paragraph, and I felt someone had written those words after being in my mind over the last month. Some fears surface over and over again? They had to have seen my thoughts. Fear of my husband leaving our marriage, fear of him finding someone else, fear of my kids having a stepmom.

Then, at the end of that paragraph, it said His presence would be with me at all times. I couldn't deny the peace it gave me. It felt like warm honey in my stomach, starting to fill the emptiness, a comfort I couldn't explain. I didn't want to open the book again, yet I couldn't let it go. I pushed past the hesitation and reopened it to read the passage again.

Jesus will be with me then and here. With His help, I can cope.

I said it. I broke past the hesitation and kept going.

"Jesus, are You here with me right now? Can You help me cope?"

Tears proceeded to fall again. My face fell into my hands. I wept. I sat there and just let emotions run. I pushed back into that recliner and just curled up into myself.

The weeping continued, and it was as if I had shared my most intimate hurt and He'd heard me and consoled me. The pain slightly eased where I could catch my breath and wipe my eyes.

I looked at the bottom of that small page, and I thought the letters were parts of the Bible and the numbers referenced the page numbers. One stuck out to me—Deuteronomy 31:6.

I was desperate to figure out what that meant. I picked up the huge book that had intimidated me my entire life.

I went to the index and finally found Deuteronomy. When I opened the Bible to the page indicated, I figured it out. It was the thirty-first chapter, and six stood for the sixth verse.

"So be strong and courageous! Do not be afraid and do not panic before them. For the Lord your God will personally go ahead of you. He will neither fail you nor abandon you."

In the early morning, those words found me in my sorrow. I went downstairs afraid, even terrified, of what was ahead of me. Yet there I was with my fears comforted and that verse telling me God wouldn't fail me or abandon me.

The man I was married to for seven years had abandoned me, but this God I hardly knew wouldn't? Didn't I need to pledge allegiance or confess my sins before He would call me His own to care for?

The next few days were different for me. I read that book every day and read that verse ten times a day. I even typed it into my phone so I could read it when I felt alone.

I called my mother-in-law to thank her for the book, and she seemed so excited I had read it. It was a short and sweet conversation, but at the call's end she told me she was praying for us.

I knew the *us* she referenced wasn't our family, but our marriage. She saw the struggle. When she spoke of prayer that morning, it was more meaningful to me because I finally experienced the fruit of her prayers.

The timing of that night was perfect. I don't know that I would've made it through that week without it, because our days drew us further apart, and our nights were colder than ever. Finally, on a Sunday night, I decided to break the silence.

"Are you punishing me by not speaking to me?"

He turned slowly to look at me. A long and drawn-out pause followed, then he put his book down. "I thought I said everything I had to say in the office you took me to last week. You're going through something I can't help you with.

"I'll never be able to make you happy. I know that whack job of a counselor said something about you being a sinking rowboat, but we both know you're more powerful than that. After all, you're driving our marriage into a ditch. I would call that pretty powerful."

"A ditch?"

"Yes, a ditch. I work hard for this family, and you don't appreciate anything. I work case after case in hopes the kids have a life they can enjoy and in hopes of you having everything you want—this house, our cars, your clothes, nice purses and jewelry. They didn't just show up here."

His tone was getting nastier, and my head was beginning to tilt as if I were trying to figure out exactly what I was watching unfold.

"I worked for them, but you don't see that. You see my work as me distancing myself from you. Maybe one of us had to grow up and live in the real world with real responsibilities.

"If I'm not as affectionate as you would like me to be, I'm sorry. I can't attend to you like days when we were twenty. . . ."

Attend to me? Did he just say attend to me, as if I were his third child?

". . . Maybe it's time for you to grow up too and stop looking at everything you don't have and start being grateful for what you do have."

The tears rolled down my face, but I was expressionless. "Who are you, and why are you so damn angry at me?"

"I'm not getting sucked into this trap. You asked me a question, and my answer isn't good enough. Let's just end this conversation and settle at the fact we'll never see eye to eye. If you don't like this life, do something about it. Otherwise, don't complain to the one providing it for you."

I had never heard him talk to me like that. I had never seen that type of anger in his eyes. In so many words, it was take it or leave it.

The prideful part of me wanted to leave it. The nostalgic part of me wanted to hold on to dreams we once had together. The crazy side of me wanted to practice throwing darts at his eyes, but the wise side of me simply turned and walked away.

That night I knew I needed to go back to Dr. Woods and figure out if my perception was off. I needed to find the part of me I had lost in between our wedding and that dreadful confrontation.

It scares me that he might leave me soon, but it terrifies me even more that the joyful woman I once had been won't ever return.

~ Sixteen ~

GLENDA

I've had a long life and have had so many beautiful and amazing moments along the way. Unfortunately, great loss has often overshadowed it. As years pass on, I can't help but yearn for this race of mine to be over.

I've made up my mind to get my affairs in order, just in case You would decide to answer my prayer requesting to be home with You. I don't have much, and I don't have anyone to give it to, but I would rather give it all away to someone than allow the state to take it.

My friend Sheryl recommended I see her son. He is an estate attorney with a great reputation, so I made an appointment for this morning to begin one of the hardest processes.

I pulled up to this newly built office with amazing colonial design. I'm always fascinated when architects can create a brand-new building that looks so modern yet traditional. The red brick with white trim and white columns was gorgeous.

It reminded me so much of colleges we visited with Sarah, when she was looking for a nursing school. The colors and landscape pulled my mind back to those memories.

The office was beautiful, as it should be. It still smelled of fresh paint and new carpet. He is part of one of the biggest law firms in town—Bagwell & Campbell. I checked in and had a seat in the waiting area. Before I could open the home décor magazine that grabbed my attention, Richard came out to call for me.

"Mrs. Ryan?"

The tall young man was very handsome. His dark hair was slightly long but groomed well and combed back. He had light-brown eyes and looked more mature than I had expected.

"You can just call me Ms. Glenda. No one has called me Mrs. Ryan in years." I chuckled as I followed him down the long hallway.

We stepped through his door, and I was welcomed by a view of shaded trees with a bit of natural light making its way in.

"This is a beautiful office. I can't get over the details. The light that shines in is stunning. It almost takes my breath away."

"That's my favorite part of this place. So, we're meeting today to go over all your estate planning, correct?"

"Yes, I'm not getting any younger, and I wanted to have a plan in place in case the good Lord calls me home soon. I don't have much, but I'd like what little I do have to be used for a worthy cause. God gave me a great life, and I would like what I have to be given to my church."

Richard raised his eyebrows. "Your church?" He sounded surprised. "You don't have anyone you wanted to give it to? I was under the impression we were going to be setting up your estate for your family, but it's not my business."

"Sweetheart, all my family has gone on ahead of me."

His face changed so drastically that I felt for him. He turned bright red and pushed his chair back, as though he wanted to crawl under his desk.

"I feel awful right now. I apologize. I shouldn't have said that."

"Don't be embarrassed or apologize. I could see how you would assume that. I've been alone for quite some time, so it doesn't sting like it used to."

That is the truth. It has been so long that it wasn't very hard to just come out and tell him.

"Richard, I'm here for that exact reason. I have no one to leave it to. I was married, and I had a beautiful daughter. I had amazing parents. But they've all gone on ahead of me and I need to figure out what to do from here."

He looked like everyone does when they find out I'm a widow who lost her only child. It's the expected pity people show.

I used to need validation that the pain I was going through was as hard as it seemed. But now, after almost thirty years, it only brings me back to an identity I try to forget.

Everyone just knows me as Ms. Glenda. They don't know me as Mrs. Charles Ryan or as Sarah Ryan's mom. Those are identities I've tried to escape.

"Of course I can help you. That is exactly what I'm here for. Let's get started. I can find the paperwork around here somewhere—"

"A car accident." I cut him off because I thought I knew why he was fumbling—or at least I had a good guess. I imagined his mind was racing with questions of what happened to my family.

Richard just turned and stared at me, then froze. He appeared even more confused than before.

I repeated myself. "A car accident. My husband and daughter were killed in a car accident. That is what you were wondering, right? Instead of having questions swimming in your head, I figured I would tell you before you had to think of a clever way to ask."

He slowly rested the papers on his desk, and his body seemed to freeze.

"I don't tell many people because of the vast range of reactions, but I have to tell you. You're my advocate now."

We went on to get everything settled that day and left all I have to the church. He knew they could sell my things and keep the profit as a donation. Richard also said anything could simply be amended if I changed my mind. I'm not sure what is left to change at this point.

I left there feeling much worse than I expected to. I thought I would meet with him, get the paperwork figured out, and then be ready to ride off into the sunset to see You.

Instead, all the memories and feelings came back rushing over me like a huge wave. I don't just miss Charles and Sarah right now. I'm grieving them all over again—and I long for them.

I yearn for another passionate kiss from Charles and another suffocating hug from Sarah. They were everything to me, Lord—everything. I didn't even know who You were until I met Charles.

He taught me how to follow You. He taught Sarah even more.

She had every quality we had ever dreamed of in a child. We were so grateful for her and even more grateful when we realized she would be our only. We did all we could to raise her the way we thought You would want us to. Was all that wasted?

Charles and I had an innocent love I would've never been able to replicate. Getting married out of high school was young, but in hindsight, I'm so glad we did, because that was more time I was able to be his wife.

When we were in high school, we started as friends. It was prom time, and he asked me how he should ask this girl out he liked. It was torturous because I was in love with him at that point. I told him to make a poster and have the question written on it and give her a dozen roses. He continued with questions of exact details.

We talked about the color of roses and why it was important to ask with the right color so he didn't send the wrong message.

"If you guys are friends, yellow roses would be best. If you're in love, you should go with the red roses. But if you're stuck in the middle somewhere, maybe you should go with white."

He kept nagging me about what he should do. I almost expected him to beg me to ask this girl out for him.

"What is your favorite color for roses? I mean, what do most girls like?"

"I don't know what most girls like. I think red or bright pink. But I like blush-colored roses."

"Really? This is crazy." He wiped his brow. "There's an entire language devoted to rose colors! How's a guy supposed to know this stuff?" Charles scratched his ear, then cocked his head. "So, what does that color mean?"

"I have no clue. I just love it and want one every time I see them. I think it means sympathy or congratulations. I don't know."

My hopes of him liking me were pretty much dead and buried after that conversation. I went home and cried the hardest my heart had ever experienced.

A couple hours later, he was standing on my front step with a sign that said, *Glenda, will you be my perfect pick for prom?* In small print underneath it read, *I already asked your parents, so you can say yes, if you would like to go.*

Then I noticed the last detail that brought me to tears. He was holding a dozen blush roses while holding the sign.

That was the beginning of Charles and me. We were engaged three years later, on the eve of my high school graduation.

The next October, I wore the veil and he wore the tuxedo. We had blush roses everywhere in the church and at the reception. That color would always be special to us. Even though I didn't think the blush-colored rose had any meaning, Charles found out they meant adoration, which was fitting because we both truly adored each other.

We said *I do* in the midst of family and our closest friends. We committed to love each other in sickness and in health, in good times and in bad, until death do us part.

It was twenty-six years later that those words would be too hard for me to bear. *Until death* tore us apart and left me with an empty space.

~ Seventeen ~

CHARLOTTE

November 17, 2012

Dear Diary,

I keep thinking of that night we broke the vow we'd made together. We broke promises we'd made when fear wasn't a factor. That night we felt closer than ever.

The next day, however, we both were less talkative. The day after evoked even less conversation, and the pattern continued day after day.

We were having coffee together outside on the shop's patio, and after a few sips I realized he appeared searching—struggling—with what he wanted to say. It reminded me of the week before, when he picked me up and led us down that road we both traveled together.

A tear fell from under his sunglasses, and he tried to wipe under his eyes inconspicuously.

I panicked again, then resumed my role as his rescuer. "Are you okay? Is everything okay? Please tell me."

"I just—I just wanted to apologize to you," he said, stuttering a little. "Ever since the other night, I've been racked with guilt. Don't get me wrong. I enjoyed every moment of that night from the beginning to the end, but I have to take responsibility for putting that pressure on you and asking you to break a promise we made together. I didn't hold up my end of the promise."

He was trying to take all the blame and was really beating himself up.

"Brett, you have to see I have choices too. I chose to tell you yes. I chose to take that step with you. I chose to take your hand and walk to the back of the truck, and I chose to get in and undress. I chose to take part in everything.

"Don't put all the responsibility on your shoulders. We made a choice. If it was the wrong one, we don't go down that road again, okay?"

It turned out that wasn't our only time going against what we knew was right. The night of our senior prom and the evening before graduation, we found ourselves in the same scenario we'd promised to avoid.

Our emotions ran high when fear dangled the possibility of our dreams being snatched away, and that's when we ran down the wrong road as fast as we could.

Against all expectations, I received a call from Vanderbilt two weeks later asking me to consider joining their soccer program—Vanderbilt. I was shocked and jumping for joy. My parents were ecstatic, and his parents were just as happy for me but also for him.

Our fear of being apart had led us to make a decision that never needed to be made. Experiencing those moments together was priceless. Experiencing them too early was costly.

Summer came and we visited campus a few times. On one of our trips there, we made a big turn in the hills, and I suddenly felt nauseous. I asked Brett to pull over before I got sick all over his truck.

He swerved off the road as soon as he could, and I jumped out onto the road's shoulder and threw up immediately in the grass and wildflowers.

Brett called to me from his side of the car. "Are you okay? What's going on?"

"Yeah, I'm okay. I think it was from trying to do the crossword puzzle in the car."

I finally stood up, wiped my mouth with a napkin from his glove compartment, and got back in the car.

We got about ten minutes more up the road when I felt nausea come over me again.

"Brett, please pull off," was all I could say before he stopped again and I jumped out to repeat the same routine. I turned back and looked at him, puzzled.

"Charlie, are you okay? I'm worried about you." He sounded just as confused and concerned as I felt. "Should we just turn around and go home?"

"No, I'm fine. I think that was it."

I tried to come up with any possible reason it was happening. My mind was searching for possibilities. What was the expiration date on the milk in my cereal this morning? Was it car sickness? I usually have a super strong stomach.

Then it crossed my mind. *No, there is no way. I couldn't be. This could not even be a possibility.*

I had my period this month, right? My nerves rattled a little more because I couldn't remember when I had it last. Maybe during graduation earlier this month? Panic set in.

"Charlie, are you okay? You look like you're going to cry."

Brett prodded me for a response.

"No, I'm not okay. I think we need to buy a pregnancy test. Maybe it's just my stomach, but I can't remember the last time I had my period.

"Maybe it's just because of soccer and training. It has happened before. A test would rule it out, and we could go on and have a normal day."

That normal day never came.

~ Eighteen ~

CASSIDY

Sometimes this is how therapy goes. It heals some wounds, then exposes others you didn't realize were there. I realized that today at my first solo therapy appointment with Dr. Woods.

We talked about my husband, Brett. There was the Brett I'd been so drawn to in the beginning—lighthearted, funny—the side of him I had known when we first met.

There was also the Brett I'd heard about before we met, who was close to God and involved in church back in high school, but I never experienced that side.

But we were there to talk about the current Brett—the one I haven't recognized in quite a while.

Dr. Woods finally asked me some questions that provoked more thinking.

"Did something ever happen between you two—a major event of some sort? Was there a death or an affair?"

Nothing came to mind as I shook my head, very confused.

"No, I can't even think of anything minor."

My mind was spinning in the past while trying to engage in new questions.

"Can you remember the first time you noticed a change in his behavior?"

A door to my memory bank opened, and my stomach knotted up.

"I can remember something," I began slowly, as my mind was still processing. "It was a couple years after we got married and right after he had been hired on to a good law firm in Nashville.

"I worked in a boutique in downtown Nashville, near his firm, so we'd meet for lunch or dinner. During lunch one day I asked if he'd thought about having a baby. Our life was amazing, but I thought it was time to start thinking about a family.

"All of a sudden, he insisted he wasn't ready for kids. It was the first time I saw such an intense reaction about not being ready to have kids."

My answer hit a nerve of my own, and I became suspicious myself.

"Did you ever discuss having children before you got married?" It was an expected question from a counselor.

"Yes, of course. The conversation came up often. I would state how excited I was to have two little ones eventually running around, and he seemed to agree. I thought we were on the same page. Until that afternoon."

As I finished my explanation to Dr. Woods, I realized Brett and I actually hadn't had a conversation—he had listened to me talk about. I just thought that was what he wanted because he didn't disagree, but I guess that's what they call an assumption.

"What exactly did he say that made you see he didn't want to have kids after all?" Dr. Woods asked, prodding deeper.

"That I was rushing things because he wasn't sure he was ready for kids. He made some statement about his inability to be a decent parent. It had nothing to do with how he was raised, because his dad was an ideal father."

The counselor squinted his eyes and slightly tilted his head, as if he were processing what I had just said. "So, how did you end up having kids?"

"After that curveball of a conversation, I kept to myself a little more and I would privately break down. He would leave for work, and I'd leave a few hours later. I would get out all my sobbing after he left.

"I couldn't understand why we bought a house with two extra rooms in it if he didn't want kids. Maybe our expectations of what the rooms would be used for were completely different.

"Listening to myself, I realize I assumed a lot of things. I thought my dreams were ones we shared together. I don't know if I was wrong or his had changed."

My body was deflated by embarrassment. More discomfort came with each answer. My crossed arms were trying to hold in whatever bit of integrity I had left.

"Did you ever tell him how you felt?" He had a comforting smile as he was asking me. I think he could see I needed it.

"I was crying one night in the shower when he wasn't home because I had just found out a friend of mine was pregnant. It crushed me unexpectedly.

"I finally stepped out of the bathroom, and I found Brett sitting on our bed. He was concerned something terrible had happened. I explained to him our friend was pregnant. I told him I realized how much I wanted to be a mom but finally grasped he wasn't enthused about being a dad.

"Unfortunately, the only thing that surfaced in him was guilt. He felt terrible for me but had not changed his feelings about wanting a baby. A few weeks later, he said he was ready and would push past his fear of not being a good dad."

The more I spoke, the more I sickened myself. I hadn't realized how much I had guilted Brett into having a baby. Tears welled up in my eyes, but I didn't want them to fall.

"Did he?" With that question, my nervous habit of biting on my fingernails began.

"He did. Until I actually got pregnant with our first one. He became distant and isolated. He'd come to my doctor appointments, and his fear would scare me. He wanted the baby tested for every possible illness, deformity or other dreaded plague, almost seeming paranoid."

"Did your husband have any siblings or family members born with deformities or illnesses he could've been scared of?" Robbie asked. "Or possibly any siblings or cousins who had died while they were babies?"

With each new question, I was becoming more insecure because I had no certain answers to give.

"No, but I think his mom would've shared that with me if there were."

"Did his fears pass after the baby was born?"

"The fears of an illness or deformity passed, but a sadness set in. I thought it was the change of our life—being a dad and extra responsibilities. I thought he was sullen because of that realization."

"So, I have to ask," the counselor started. "How did you end up having another child? Was there something that changed his mind?"

"Actually, our second one was a surprise. I had been sick for a little while with an upper respiratory infection that had settled in my lungs. The doctor had prescribed antibiotics to try and cure it. I knew it affected my birth control but didn't realize how quickly.

"Surprise! I got pregnant soon after. It was a lot to process. When I told my husband, we were getting ready for bed and I started to explain the circumstances to him."

"How did he react to that news?" These short questions kept requiring long answers.

"Much worse than the first time we talked about it. He brought up all the scares of my first pregnancy as if they had happened. The paranoia returned immediately.

"He said he needed some time to think, then left for a little while. I fell asleep while he was gone, and the next morning, he woke me up and asked to talk.

"As I'm revisiting that conversation, strange comments come to mind. He mentioned the option of an abortion but said he couldn't suffer through that.

"I felt as if we had already gotten news the child was malformed and had to make a critical decision with a limited amount of time. For him, it was a decision between two bad choices, and he was debating the one he could manage."

I couldn't find any excuses for him. I left Dr. Woods's office with more fragmented thoughts in my head than when I had come. Repairing anything seemed impossible.

I went home with an uncomfortable weight of responsibility for the situation we were in. I wanted to admit it to my husband, and I thought before bed would be the best time.

"Hey, babe, can we talk for a minute? I have something I would like to apologize for." I tried to say it as nicely as possible yet imply I really needed to talk.

"Uh, sure. I have a few minutes before I need to take care of a few things for a case tomorrow," he said, slightly distracted.

I was about to say the hardest things to ever cross my lips. I was about to apologize for wanting to have my children. It felt unnatural, but it was real. My adrenaline was stirring and making my stomach cramp.

"Okay, I'll try and make this clear. Originally, you were hesitant about having children, but I thought it was a given we would start a family, and I never considered your feelings against my own. . . ."

As I was speaking, he slightly moved his pillow close to him and crossed his arms over it, not wanting to be left vulnerable.

". . . I want to apologize for that. I feel like I may have pushed you into doing something you weren't ready for. I can see how the kids have changed you, and I feel responsible for that."

Tears were trying hard to surface, but I was determined to get through this conversation without breaking down in front of him. My throat was burning, my chest was rising, my voice was changing to fight back emotion.

"It hurts me to think maybe you never wanted Colin or Sydney, but you had a right to feel that way. It makes more sense to me now why you have distanced yourself from all three of us."

He was calm and still. For a moment, I saw a glimpse of emotion in his eyes. A humanness returned to him.

"Cass, you have nothing to apologize for. It was my decision to have kids too, so don't put it all on you. I love Colin and Syd, and I wouldn't want to have a life without them in it.

"I told you six years ago, and I'll tell you the same in six more—I'm a horrible dad, and I just don't want to screw them up. It's not you or even them. It's me, and it's just how things have to be."

He showed a deep sadness I hadn't ever noticed.

"Today, Dr. Woods asked me if anything tragic or traumatic happened to you. . . ."

Brett's head practically snapped to look over at me.

"He asked you what?" He cut me off before I could even finish. "Why would he ask you that? What business is that of his?"

Brett's voice was rising and his anger emerging.

"And when the hell did our pasts start to become part of our conversation?"

He was shaking his head, and his body was unsettled. I hadn't seen him this angry—ever.

The light bulb went off in my head with a possibility I'd never considered. "Brett, look at me. Did something happen to you before I met you? Did something happen between you and Charlotte I don't know about?"

~ Nineteen ~

CHARLOTTE

"Did you and Brett break up?"

Mikala knew something was wrong when she saw me walk up to see her at the fire station. I had called her just minutes earlier, begging her to meet me.

Her face changed quickly as she saw fear on my face and that I'd been crying. Questions came immediately but I hardly had breath to answer.

"Did you guys get in a fight?"

"No."

"Is it your mom again—did she say something cruel to you?"

"No." I took a deep breath and went for it.

"Mikala, I don't know how to tell you this. . . . I'm pregnant."

Collapsing into her shoulder, the sobbing returned. I needed for someone to hold me. I was still just a little girl, sitting there scared as hell.

Mikala was dumbfounded because she didn't even know I had given my virginity to Brett months ago. I had been too ashamed to tell anyone. She actually began to cry with me and just kept looking in my eyes, searching for a clue to how she should respond.

"Charlotte, what can I do? I'll do anything you need."

She was the second person to have offered me help, and I still didn't have an answer.

Mikala kept asking, "What did Brett say?"

"He feels awful. He thinks it is all his fault and if he'd been stronger none of this would've happened. He wants to fix it, but he can't, and I don't know how he and I go on from here."

"Charlotte, you guys are going to get through this. He loves you. You guys are going to spend the rest of your lives together. Your love is strong enough to survive this."

"That is practically what Brett said, but I don't think it is."

Mikala reached out and touched my shoulder. "What are you going to do?"

"I think I'm going to consider doing what I've never wanted to do—the one thing I could never understand other women choosing."

"Charlotte, are you sure that is what you both want?"

"I think it is what I have to do for both of us."

"How will you go through with this?"

"I made an appointment already. I have to do it as soon as possible before I let anyone find out or anyone changes my mind. I can already tell the old Charlotte is gone. The cost of what we did is so much more than I ever considered."

***

When I saw the results of the pregnancy test, my world shattered right before me. We were sitting in the Vanderbilt library. We stopped on the way to buy a test, and I took it once we arrived.

Every single person I secretly disappointed came to mind, one after another. My parents, Brett's parents, my church family, my pastor, my youth pastor, my friends, my soccer coach, my Vanderbilt coach who had just given me a scholarship . . . and then the list repeated.

Tears filled my eyes as I looked at Brett and fear filled his. We both felt responsible for disappointing the other. He stood up and put his hand out for me to hold. All I could do was grab his pinky—I was hanging by a thread.

Driving home was painful. All I could do was close my eyes, hold my face, and cry. Brett kept apologizing, but I was angry with myself, not him.

Unrightfully, I was mad this was the consequence I was dealt. I knew I would never be the same, and it was then that my walls started to be built. Walls that later would keep people away so I couldn't hurt anyone again.

He was pulling into my driveway, to drop me off. As I was getting out of the car, I just looked at him and tried not to cry but tears slowly rolled down my face. He placed his hand on my forearm.

"Charlotte, I love you more than you will ever know."

I couldn't respond. I kissed him on the cheek, then got out of the car. He slowly drove away, and my heart sank, knowing we would never be the same.

I went straight to my bedroom and cried. Ironically, I saw pictures I hadn't noticed in years—pictures on my wall of me playing soccer from when I had started up to my last game of high school. Mostly, I cried for the little girl in the photo. I know she wanted so much more for me than this.

But I cried for the girl in the last picture too. What had happened to her so fast? And who was she now?

I took a shower to try and hide my tears from my mom, but I just stood there, letting the water pound on my back. I had hoped the sound of the shower would drown out the disappointment in my mind, but it didn't work. I kept trying to think of a way out of this mess.

This one word crossed my mind—no, it actually grabbed a piece of my mind and refused to let go.

Abortion.

Had it come to this? Have the baby or have an abortion?

Was I willing to go that far to save my reputation or to avoid condemnation from my mother? After all, it was her wrath that scared me more than anything else.

And in that moment, I made the decision. I was going to trade my last shred of self-respect for a permanent cloak of shame.

Those moments of passion had brought us intimacy, and now its consequences were pushing us apart with guilt. It was hard for us to look at each other when I met with Brett a couple days later, as we both felt shame for pulling the other into a situation as hard as this. I finally got the courage and told him what I chose.

Shocked and struggling to find words, he finally found his voice. "How could you make this choice all on your own?" I purposely ignored his question and spoke over him with details of where and when. He started to gaze outward and just listen.

An early Saturday appointment was the most discreet time for me to go, and that's the time I chose.

As he turned to look back at me, I saw sorrow painted over his face.

"How could you do that without even taking what I want into consideration?" Whether or not I had a right to be, I was offended.

"How can you say that? This is all about considering you! Tell me—how are you going to explain to your parents you're going to be a dad? How are we going to make this work? And how are you going to handle a child while going to law school?"

Brett was becoming just as angry as I was.

"Let me show you why this isn't just about me. The truth is, how are *you* going to explain it to your parents—who have the least ability to forgive? How are *you* going to be able to go to college and play soccer after you turn down a scholarship because of a pregnancy? How are *you* going to marry a guy who has no education and no future because all of a sudden he's a dad?

"None of that is about me. We messed up. WE MESSED UP! We let fear wreck us, but are you going to let fear take even more from us?"

I saw tears in his eyes welling up while his voice cracked with agony.

"Why can't we raise a child? Why can't we get married? I love you. What if this will be a gift in the long run? Sure, it will be hard as hell, but I'm willing to give up anything for this child. Please, I beg you to reconsider."

He didn't hold back one bit of emotion as he wiped his eyes and massaged his forehead. Everything he said was right. In fact, he was so on point, I was angry. That's when self-sabotage stepped in.

"Brett, I just don't want to. I don't know if we should even continue on after this is all over. We will never be the same. My guilt is so deep, I don't have room to love like that again."

He looked at me with so much pain in his eyes, and I stood there sterile. His focus shifted down where it remained for what felt like ten minutes, then he finally lifted his eyes.

"So, let me repeat what I think you're saying. . . . Not only have you made up your mind to not give me a chance with this child, but you're also taking away any chance of us going through this together?"

"When you say it like that, yes. That is what I'm saying."

"Okay, Charlotte." His voice was sullen. He sounded defeated. His emotions had surrendered. "You just tell me the appointment time, and I'll take you.

"I won't bother you anymore. I hope you change your mind and pray you see what I do. But I know that as much as I want to be with you and experience the ups and downs together, I can't make you want to share them with me."

He tried not to cry again but was having a hard time holding it back.

And then I threw another dagger.

"Brett, our prayers no longer mean anything. They are no good. Our word no longer means anything."

How could I believe God was even willing to listen to us anymore? We had lived our lives based around these promises we abandoned, and now he thought God was just willing to move past it and answer our prayers?

"Charlotte, of all things you have said right now, that is the saddest one of all. Whether you're aware of it or not, you were the one who brought me to know who God really was. You were the one who allowed me to learn how much He loved us."

His sadness converted back into anger and disappointment. His voice solidified, and his words were piercing.

"We made a mistake—a mistake I've asked forgiveness for repeatedly. Have you not believed the things you encouraged me to learn? Has this all been a show to please your parents, or do you have some sense of how God loves you just as much after all this as He did before it?"

"I'm not even going to entertain all that. I have enough guilt of my own. Don't put more on me and judge my faith." My head was pounding—so was my heart. "Just worry about you and your God, and I'll worry about me and mine."

Fury was boiling inside me, but I wasn't sure whom I was angry at. I was mad at Brett for loving me. I was mad at myself for what we did and for what I was about to do. I was mad at Brett for not understanding. I was mad at God because I knew He was about to hate me anyway. If I could push them all away now, the pain would be less when they all left me later.

As I walked away, I caught on to the name he used to address me—*Charlotte.* He hadn't called me that in ages. He always called me Char or Charlie. That stung just as much as everything else that was exchanged.

That horrible Saturday morning came quicker than I wanted it to. When Brett came and picked me up, he could hardly look at me. We only exchanged a couple words the whole way because he turned up the music and just looked straight ahead. The only other noise was the electronic voice of the GPS.

I had a thumping heart and shaking hands as we pulled into the clinic's parking lot. I stared straight ahead as water filled my eyes. What I was about to do would definitively end our forever.

Suddenly, I felt Brett's hand grab mine.

"Please, Charlie, please," desperately pleading with tears. "Tell me you want to change your mind and leave. Say that you're just as sad as I am and you can't bear to go through with this."

He would've done anything for me to change my mind. I noticed what he said. *Charlie . . .* He called me Charlie again. I choked up just hearing the name, but I couldn't change my mind. I just looked at him.

"I can't tell you that."

The waiting room was torturous. Brett leaned straight ahead, placed his elbows on top of his thighs, and put his head in his hands as we sat there. A few tears escaped his eyes, but I couldn't let his hurt knock down the stone wall I was just starting to build.

They called my name, and we both walked back. The prep for the procedure took longer than the procedure itself, which was all of fifteen minutes. Brett tightly held my hand, and I could feel his breathlessness the entire time.

After it all was finished, my womb was emptied, and so was my heart. Brett's tears expressed his heart was emptied too.

They gave me some medicine for pain that would last for the next day or so. That was all. The clinic was in our rearview mirror, and so was the little life we could've shared together.

Brett cried the entire way home. So did I. But we didn't cry together. It was as if there were a wall between us—both experiencing different reactions, not wanting to share them with each other.

He was driving toward my house, and it was going to take courage to get out of the truck. Hours before, I wasn't ready to give up the life inside me, but I knew I had to. And now, I wasn't ready to give up Brett, but I knew I had to do that too.

He pulled up to the house and stared outside his window. He was so angry—so hurt. As I pushed the door open, I looked at him.

"Brett, I know you don't understand this, but I need you to hear that I'm sorry. I'm sorry I hurt you. I'm sorry this is all more than I can bear. And most of all, I'm sorry you can't fix it. You're an amazing man, and someday someone will love you enough to take all this pain away. I'm just sorry I can't."

His gaze never changed. He looked like stone. I had finally hurt him as much as I was hurting. I had sabotaged our relationship intentionally. I didn't kiss him. I didn't touch him. I didn't end with an *I love you*. I punished us both and left it at that, closing the door to all we had.

~ Twenty ~

BRETT

After seven years, my wife is slowly believing I'm everything I said I'd be. We have two kids I can't engage with—two kids I'm scared of losing. I didn't deserve them. I still don't deserve them.

When I met Cassidy and knew I was about to fall in love again, I should've walked away. My past had too much of a hold on me to keep going forward, and I should've let her go before I hurt her.

Later, when I heard her deep yearning for children, my past crept up on me like a ghost. I didn't want kids. I knew I would be punished if I had them, but I couldn't walk away from her.

After losing Charlotte, I swore I would never fall in love again, but I let Cassidy change that. She loved me more than I loved myself. Fear helped me push her away, but she only pressed in more. Her love was impossible to resist, yet over the years, that is all I've done.

A month ago, when my parents offered to watch the kids so Cass and I could get away for a weekend, I really didn't want to. I knew I'd feel guilty if I didn't take them up on the offer, but I honestly didn't want to be alone with her.

I had my assistant set up a quick trip to a beach in Destin to suffice Cassidy. All I had to do was show up and smile.

I ruined it. I can admit I sabotaged it, but only to myself. I made it clear I was trying to fill an obligation by being there.

She had always pressed in when my walls had gone up, but this time she started to withdraw. I saw a hurt in her eyes I had never seen before. We both left emptier than when we arrived.

Marriage counseling was her next attempt to figure out what was happening. If I couldn't talk to her on a beautiful beach, why would she think I'd talk to her on some stranger's couch?

Guilt overcame me, and I showed up reluctantly at the last possible minute. I was angry before I even went in for having to go through the motions for her.

I was planning on being asked some simple questions and returning nonsense answers. But this counselor was more intense and picked up on my indifference. He challenged me with probing questions, but one shook me: "Are you upset with God?"

I was fuming but couldn't tell him it was God who was furious with me. The counselor tried deeper questions, but I blew them off. I was still trying to hide from the last question.

I was very defensive, posturing as if I didn't care. I acted like they were both wasting my time with minor issues—as if I were too good for the stranger to even understand me—as if Cass were crazy and just needed some attention.

Then my real emotions showed up. I saw that I was so distant from Cass, I couldn't help her—I couldn't heal her—I couldn't fix her. I couldn't convince her I loved her, and I probably couldn't convince her things hadn't changed.

The emotions felt familiar. They brought me back to the emptiness eleven years earlier. I couldn't help Charlotte—I couldn't heal her—I couldn't fix her. I couldn't convince Charlotte I loved her, and I absolutely couldn't convince Charlotte things would remain the same.

The flip side is that Cassidy could never fix *me*. I think that is the deep truth. Without realizing it, I expected Cassidy to fix me and I blamed her for not being able to. How did that even make reasonable sense?

They were my own broken pieces I never mended after Charlotte. The unbearable choices she made for us ended up defining the man I became, a shattered version of my former self.

Living without her would kill me. But, if I love her as much as I claim to, letting her go would be giving her a chance to be happy. I deserve to be miserable, but she doesn't. It's probably time for me to make that lonely sacrifice for her and the kids.

~ Twenty-One ~

CHARLOTTE

November 18, 2012

Dear Diary,

Here I am again. . . . So many emotions were stirred after my time with Glenda the other night, so I fought my instinct to hide and went back to see her today.

Her large smile was contagious as she walked toward me. After she gave me one of her nurturing embraces, she gently pulled away and asked, "Do you have some time? Want to go somewhere and chat?"

I needed to talk to her, so I got creative and made time. She suggested we go to downtown Franklin and walk around on the main street.

We exchanged simple questions as to how the other one had been over the week, and she brought up how happy she was that I'd come to see her.

"Charlotte, to be honest with you, I didn't know if I'd see you again. I thought I might have scared you away the other night, but I have to say how lucky I am that you came back."

Her voice was like the sound of soothing waves rolling up on shore. It brought me peace every time she had something to say—except that one question she had asked, of course.

"I'm glad I came too. I'll admit—I was a little intimidated to come back after our last meeting. Your last question pierced my insides like nothing has in a long time.

"I've spent the last couple weeks repeating that question. But the answer never came. I think the condition of my heart has to do with things that have been buried deep in my soul.

"I've wanted to keep them there . . . until your question made me wonder if those things are starting to poison me."

Tears rolled down my face. "Oh, Lord. I haven't even begun, and I'm crying. Can we sneak away somewhere so I don't embarrass both of us?"

"Yes, of course." Glenda's eyes were filled with compassion. "There's a park bench near the library we can go to. Oh . . . and you can never embarrass me. I've been through it all," she kindly dismissed my fear.

Our walk to the bench brought back the superficial conversation, to make the mood lighter. She asked about growing up here, what schools I had gone to, and then asked if I had gone to college. That last question came up right as we got to the bench. I purposely tried not to change the tone in my voice when answering, but I drastically failed.

"So, sit down, sweetheart. When you're ready, you can talk about whatever you choose," she said as her hand gently rubbed my back. The circulating touch was soothing.

Right then, I had to decide to share my past and possibly give up her touch or make up something and keep her affection toward me. Thankfully, the thought of continuing the superficial exterior exhausted me.

"I've never shared much of this. I've stuffed my secrets further and further down for me to go on with my life. I don't know how to start. . . ."

I just couldn't say it. I cried a little more, and then I began.

"Believe it or not, I was raised in the church. My parents loved me, but there was a piece of them always missing. It was as if they couldn't fully love me as much as my personality required, or maybe my need was normal and they were hindered by something of their own."

I kept going. "I met my boyfriend, Brett, my freshman year of high school. Ironically, we built our relationship on a foundation of virtues. He wasn't a strong believer when we met, but that changed dramatically."

Then, the conversation took the turn I'd been avoiding.

"Our senior year we both had been looking at different colleges for different things we wanted. There was only about a five percent chance of us ending up at the same college. Fear of that ninety-five percent is what killed us.

"There was a night that both of us found a moment of weakness. In my most honest transparency, I loved every moment of being close with him. I have no room to hide anything."

My body clamped up, expecting to feel her pull away from me, but she didn't flinch.

"I took a pregnancy test a few months later. The bottom line is, it was positive. I'd gotten pregnant, and my response was to put my life ahead of the one I was carrying inside."

There it was. The shameful truth had crossed my lips. Not only did I get it out, but her gentle touch remained.

"Fear of our parents' reactions and having to turn down my soccer scholarship took priority over any other thought.

"I never once considered how God would see me. I never once considered the shame that would overshadow the rest of my life. The judgment of those around me scared me more than the fear of hurting Brett, hurting God, or hurting the life within. Little did I know I'd be hurting myself just as much."

Tears continued to cover my face.

"On our drive to the clinic, both of us were shaking and crying in the car before we had to go in for my appointment. He told me we didn't have to go through with everything, but that wasn't a possibility for me. They called my name. We walked through the creepy, sterile hallway leading to a small medical room that reminded me of a run-down laboratory-type room.

"I lay down on that plastic bed, put my feet in cold stirrups, and watched them bring in a machine that looked like a crash cart. They began to work on me, and all I saw were large amounts of blood being suctioned into that machine. I looked over and saw tears falling down Brett's cheeks.

"In that moment, my sorrow and shame turned my heart to stone. That moment—that day—left an empty space that could never be filled, not only in my womb, but in my heart."

I sobbed right there, holding her hand. I couldn't catch my breath, and my pride disappeared.

Glenda hugged me, and I exhaled years of pain into her shoulder.

To some it might have been a natural thing to be emotionally vulnerable in someone else's arms. But for me, my muscles had released for the first time in years, my heart finally found comfort, and I felt as if I finally had someone to love me.

I finally caught my breath, thanking Glenda for her comfort. Then, I did what I've always done best. I allowed her a way out of my life so she could leave before I'd push her out.

"I appreciate you sitting with me, listening to my story. I understand if we can't meet again because of all this, but I just want to tell you that this was enough . . ."

Before I finished, I peered up to see tears streaming down her face. She stopped me from finishing my sentence, tenderly grabbing my forearm.

"Sweetheart, I'm so sorry for everything you have been through. I can go back down the list and individually point out each pivotal point in your story that crushed my heart. But what hurts me the most are words you aren't saying, but I can still hear them in the background.

"I know you believe God is mad at you, that He has turned His face from you. I know you believe you're unlovable. I know you believe no one will ever love you again if they know who you truly are, if they see through this facade you have created. That is what hurts me the most. The rest are just details of mistakes you have made.

"Were they serious decisions that were misguided? Of course. Did mistakes lead to consequences, which led to deeper mistakes, which led to deeper consequences—continuing to create a snowball of pain, shame and regret? Absolutely. Have we all walked through something where we thought God would never want anything to do with us ever again? I can assuredly say, *yes*!

"Your details are unique and specific to you, but your belief of God's reaction is like so many. You feel unworthy, ashamed, embarrassed, guilty, filthy, exiled, shunned, and you feel like God should turn on you.

"What is so hard to explain to someone in your shoes is God never turned away. God never stopped loving you. God never stopped seeing you as marvelous and precious. God never stopped watching each of your tears fall and feeling your heart weigh so heavy."

She was looking so deep into my eyes, I thought she could see my soul hypnotized by every word she said.

"What changed was you. Your assumption of who God was made you turn from Him in shame and guilt. Your assumption that God was similar to a human and could stop loving you was misguided. His love is unconditional and relentless. He will love you all the days of your life, no matter what you think or feel. You assumed He saw you as worthless because you had disappointed Him."

Glenda put her hand around my face, cupping it at my chin, as if she were holding something precious to her.

"He can never see you as that, because He sees you as the one He created perfectly. He sees who you will be. He sees you through the blood of Jesus, whom He sent here to suffer so He could have a relationship with His precious children—children like you who believe their sins are too heavy to forgive, too gross to get past, too vile to overlook."

She wiped away more tears and brought her hands back down to mine. She softly began to speak again.

"When you think you're disqualified, do you know what that says? It says Jesus's horrific death on that cross wasn't enough of a sacrifice for your sins. It completely negates the torture He suffered for you—for Charlotte. Think about that for a minute, really think about that."

The pause enveloped the strangest moment. What she said made sense logically. But, after years of convincing myself I was exiled from God, it didn't make sense deep within. Her sincerity pierced through many layers of pain I had allowed to build up, but it didn't break through my heart's stubborn walls.

I wanted to believe what she was saying and feel that love she described. I wanted to get past all this pain I keep holding on to. But how do you repair a relationship with a God you have turned your back on? How do you call up to heaven and say, *Hey, God, remember me? It's Charlotte. I want to ask for Your forgiveness.*

How do you begin to ask, or beg? What soft opening can you lead with and then ask for something more than you think you deserve?

At the end, Glenda spoke about something I don't even want to consider—forgiving myself. When I finally figure out how to ask God to forgive me, I'll beg until I have no breath.

But I'll never forgive myself. That'd be selfish. I already took the cowardly way out, and now I'm supposed to let myself off the hook for that? For me, it isn't even an option.

~ Twenty-Two ~

CASSIDY

"If you're looking for a way out, you don't need to go searching for one by digging up my life before we met. Don't waste time chasing after something in my past that isn't there. If you want out, just say so. I'll give you what you want."

Things have only become worse since trying to get Brett to notice our marriage was failing. I'm not sure if I regret opening my mouth. Returning to when I was secretly unhappy seems like going back to hell. Going forward and living without him seems like a nightmare as well. It's a lose-lose either way.

But I know he is hiding something. There's something he is scared to share. It's Charlotte's name that sets him off the most.

Is he still attached to her? Is he still holding on to something? How do I compete with that?

I'm his wife. I'm the mother of his two children. She was his past, but she was also his beginning. I can't compete with those memories.

My white flag is about to wave because I'm close to giving up the fight for my marriage. After all, if only one person is in the ring, is it really a fight?

This afternoon is when I realized it all. He caught me by surprise and came home early.

"The workload was light this morning." His assertive tone was awful and condescending. "Cass, sit down. I need to talk to you. I told you I'd be an awful dad. Along the way, I added being a terrible husband to my resume. I'm fully aware you deserve more than what I can give you. This is me. This is who I am. This is who I'm always going to be."

My body braced for what he was about to say.

"If you don't think you want to stay in this marriage, I understand. I'll give you whatever you want. But if you choose to stay, this is me. I'm not digging further to find more of my faults."

Anger set in as tears welled up. I was pigeonholed into having to make a decision that would relieve him either way.

"*This* is how you'd want our marriage to continue if we stayed together?"

"Yes. I'm saying I'd want things to stay the same. I'm content with this life," he said in a contemptuous tone.

"There's no way we can stay the same. You have so many walls up and refuse to let me in." The words came out firm, but my tears showed my weakness.

Infuriated, he quickly stood up and replied, "I'll leave. You can stay."

"What? You're just going to leave like that?" My heart tremored and my eyes enlarged. My world was spinning out of control. I felt the ground rumbling.

"There's no need to prolong it. You deserve to stay. You and the kids—this is your home. I'll pack up some stuff and stay at a hotel until some details are ironed out. We can tell the kids that I'm out of town for work. They probably won't even realize I'm gone."

Emotionless, he went and quickly packed his small suitcase, as if he'd planned to sabotage our conversation from the beginning.

I moved further away from our room, holding myself back from running in and begging him to stay. I finally heard him walking out of the room with his suitcase rolling behind him.

I could hear him stop at the front door. Twice I heard him call my name. I yearned to respond, but I couldn't watch him leave.

The door opened and gently closed behind him. When I heard the door shut, my body trembled. He was gone. Just like that. Running to the window, I cried as I watched his car pull away.

Half of my heart left with him.

Hours later, the phone rang, and I hoped it was him.

"Hey, Cass, I just wanted to know if there was anything you or the kids needed. I put money in your bank account as normal."

Money. That was his reason for calling. I tried to come up with anything to say.

"How is your hotel?"

"It's small, but it's just a place to sleep. I have a couple big cases, so I'll be at work late anyway."

Work. Conversation number two.

The discussion was coming to a standstill.

"Cass, are you all right?"

I don't know what response he was expecting, but he said it in a way that made my heart believe he cared, sounding as if he actually wanted to hear the answer. I answered as fast as I could without my voice cracking.

"It will get easier."

Was I supposed to tell him I cried *all* day? Was I supposed to tell him he crushed me? Was I supposed to tell him I wish I could hate him?

What I really wanted to tell him was that I wished we had never met at all.

In the end, all I said was each day would get easier, but I think I was trying to convince myself of that as well.

~ Twenty-Three ~

BRETT

My past and present are merging, and my future is plagued because of it. I have kept my life with Charlotte to myself all these years. I've buried good times in the back of my mind and the heartbreaks there as well.

My past has to stay there. I can't relive it. I can't absorb more shame and condemnation. I can't reveal my biggest failure.

At this point, I'm starting to see how she and the kids will be better off without me. I know I'm unable to be what they need. I'm hardly enough for what I need. How could I be any more for them?

It was made clear yesterday that she wasn't willing to compromise this time. I couldn't believe she was willing to let me go. Things were even worse than I'd realized.

She'd been the one who had always loved me—always stood by me. She believed in me to a fault. And now she was ready to step aside and let me go on alone.

As I was packing, I finally noticed what I was leaving, looking at the framed pictures in our room for the first time.

What was I doing? How in the hell did I get here? Worst of all, where did I have to go from here?

I choked up with the realizations, but I had to leave. Walking to the door, I called her name a couple times. I wanted to find her and tell her I was sorry, but I just left.

I walked out of my house with a suitcase, like I had a hundred times before, but that could've been the last. My secrets were suffocating me, and I didn't see a way to breathe.

As I was pulling out of the driveway, it reminded me of the last time I left all that I had behind. Only that time, someone pulled away from me and gave me no room to love them anymore. That awful day left an empty space in my heart that I haven't been able to fill.

Now I'm watching my own emptiness and pain destroy someone else. I finally can see a glimpse of why Charlotte left me so abruptly. It wasn't because she didn't love me. I finally understand that it was because she did love me, and she thought she was giving me a gift by leaving me alone.

~ Twenty-Four ~

GLENDA

Oh, Lord,

You know everything, but I want to process the details with You. I saw Your sweet girl Charlotte yesterday. I can't explain why she is so dear to me already, but I'm fond of her.

Her transparency surprised me and was more than I expected. The first time we talked, she was so guarded and closed off. It felt like she had an eight-foot wall surrounding her heart that would be hard to tear down.

Then, void of caring about my reaction, she laid down every thought and feeling about many mistakes. It was as if a dam had been building in her heart for years and it finally burst. I knew she needed me to listen more than anything else.

The hurt she and that young man went through was tragic. Your grace is sufficient to carry her beyond this pain, but I know she is just starting that journey. Your forgiveness is foreign to her right now.

When she described details of her giving into lust, her guilt was as thick as stone. Her shame was even thicker.

Their passion brought consequences she couldn't bear. She ended her pregnancy. Simultaneously, she withdrew from everyone she had once loved, protecting herself from them abandoning her first. That's when she moved as far away from You too, shielding herself from Your condemnation.

Essentially, her life has stood still from the day she made that difficult choice. She has gone through the motions for fourteen years, and any joy has vanished.

I consoled her with what I know of Your love. I had never counseled anyone after an abortion, but this child was suffocating in the ashes of her decision.

I shared that whether she wanted to believe it or not, You have loved her since she was conceived in her mother's womb and that You love her the same exact way today. There is nothing that could separate her from the love You have for her.

I believe she was blocking it from going in her heart. Her tears poured out, but I think it was more about guilt than forgiveness.

She assumed I'd judge her and eventually leave her to suffer alone. But I told her I felt no different about her in that moment than I did the first time I met her. She cried harder with that than anything.

I shared that we all make mistakes, and we all have to find our way back on our feet in order for us to move forward. The only way for her to get her feet under her again is to figure out how to receive forgiveness she has been asking for and then to learn to forgive herself.

Her response was that she would beg You to forgive her until her last breath, but forgiving herself was something she would never deserve. I told her to hold on to that word *deserve* and to let it marinate in her mind for a while. Good or bad that came from it, I just needed her to expand her mind on that word. I stopped there.

I want to tell her that none of us deserve Your love. We have it because You have chosen to give it to us unconditionally. Everything we deserve, Jesus took to that lonely cross and showed us all that Your love is greater than we'll ever comprehend. Not because we *deserve* it, but because You said we were worth it. But that's to share later.

It was heart-wrenching. Her guilt has her locked in chains she can't even see, and she won't allow herself to be loved either. I can show her my love. I can show her Your love. But ultimately, I'll never make her able to receive it. That is something only You can give her.

Lord, I ask that You show me the next step to take with her. I thank You for letting me be a part of her healing process on her journey back to You.

Maybe you left me here for something as powerful as this. I wonder if You will allow this to be my last piece of work for You. Is this the end of my race? After all this time—in blessings and tragedies—will I be able to stand before You and hear You say, "Well done, my faithful servant. You have finished your race with faith"?

The finish line is approaching, and I know I can keep going if that is what You need. But I wait to heal voids in my heart that have been left empty for so long. As always, please give Charles and Sarah a kiss and a hug that can last until I see them again. My heart is so lonesome for them. But I know Your grace is sufficient for me. I know I believe that . . . but, Lord, please help my unbelief.

All my love,
Glenda

~ Twenty-Five ~

BRETT

I was raised by a dad who would do anything for me, and my first hint of a child and I was powerless to help it. After all, it was a life we both created that she decided to take. In fact, it was my baby that I could do nothing to save.

I stood next to her and watched that life I treasured be extracted as if it were waste suctioned through a disposal. My heart shattered during the ten-minute span it took for my baby to be lifeless. I was angry—and sorrowful.

I couldn't understand how I could love someone so much and hate them at the same time. I left there weak and debilitated. I felt like I was being torn from limb to limb and more tearing was ahead.

I couldn't even look at Charlotte when I dropped her off at home following the appointment. As she was getting out, she said a few things, and I worked so hard to not listen. There was only one piece that I heard and has stayed with me all these years.

". . . and most of all, I'm sorry that you can't fix it."

I drove away and never turned down that street again. I never heard her voice address me again. I never saw that smile of hers again.

In an instant, it all had changed. It was like a death, except the person was only dead to me. I had seen her or talked to her daily for four years—and then nothing. My parents knew I was distraught, but they didn't know the depths of it.

They comforted me more than I deserved. My mom made my favorite meals, and my dad offered to spend time with me. The more they reached out to console me, the more I noticed their ability to be amazing parents. The shame thickened for not being able to save my own child.

My life was never the same after that. I immersed myself in studying. It felt amazing to finally feel successful after all the mental self-mutilation. At other times, guilt piled on because it seemed my life was benefiting at the cost of something so tragic.

I promised myself a few things when I left for Vanderbilt. The first was to leave all this heartbreak behind. It was over. Nothing could change what happened. No number of tears could erase the pain.

The second thing was that I could never bring up Charlotte's name again, no matter how much I wanted to. That person was a stranger to me—dead to me. I didn't want to ask about her, nor did I want to hear anything about her.

The final thing was that if I were to ever run into her, I would go on as if I had no idea who she was. She didn't want me in her life, and it was the last gift I could give to her.

My first test of my strength was at a gas station in town, right before I left for school. I saw her car pull in. I actually wanted to stop the hose from pumping, get in my car, and subtly drive away. But I was paralyzed.

My deepest feelings urged me to just say hello, look into her eyes, and see if any feelings for me had returned. The fear that they hadn't kept me still. She pulled up to a pump parallel with mine, where I could see her reflection in the mirror.

Charlotte got out of the car and put her hair into a bun on the top of her head. She turned around, then stopped suddenly, seeing me pump gas a few feet away. Without saying a word, she quickly turned away.

My tank was full, but I stayed there as if it were still going. I wanted to see how this was going to end. I stared at her through the reflection, and after I adjusted my focus, I realized she was doing the same into her window.

Oddly, we both just locked eyes through the reflections. There were no smiles exchanged—no one turned to actually acknowledge the other. It was empty and cold.

I let the stare last as long as I could bear, then looked away. I put the nozzle back on the pump and never glanced back at her. If I had any hope left for her to change her mind, it died that day.

I would ask myself at times if this education was worth trading the life of my child. I know it wasn't my ultimate decision, but I would spin my mind asking myself if there was anything I could've done to stop it.

Those questions that began with the words *what if I had . . .* kept me up late at night for so long. Sometimes I would have dreams about seeing the child running ahead of me. I would be chasing it through a thick forest, but I could never catch up. I would awake to my heart pounding. I wondered if Charlotte had the same nightmares.

We didn't cross paths again until months later at a friend's party. I never figured out the connection—how we were both invited—but she showed up with some teammates.

I'd recently begun seeing a girl in one of my classes. Madison was fun and beautiful, and dating was something I needed to do to get past Charlotte. Madison was helping me do that.

That night it made me feel completely awkward. I had never been with another girl besides Charlotte in five years, and she happened to be there and see me. Joey said he could tell she was surprised to see me but stunned to see me with another girl.

I felt terrible, but after a couple days, I realized that she was the one who wanted nothing to do with *me*. She had pushed me out of her life and shut that door. No matter how hard or how many times I knocked, the door never even cracked open.

I had to move on. I had to have a life where I didn't look in the rearview mirror every day. It was hard to remember that her feelings were none of my business anymore.

She had grown apart from most of her friends we'd grown up with. One night, I overheard Mikala and Josie complaining to Joey. They were frustrated that they had hardly seen Charlotte since she had left for school.

The surprising part was that Joey defended her. He explained how busy she was with soccer and school. He also told them to give her a little slack because every time he ran into her, she didn't seem like the same person they had all known.

The way he protected her in that conversation made the hairs on the back of my neck stand up. I forgot that he'd known her so much longer than I did, but how far did his feelings for Charlotte actually go?

I found out three years later. We were at a party, and the same thing happened as the first party I saw her at, except this time I was with Cassidy.

She left. She disappeared. And Joey decided to try and run after her. I was surprised at how pissed I was.

"You're leaving me to go run after my ex-girlfriend?"

"What? I haven't heard you refer to her as your ex-girlfriend in three years, and now you want to pull some 'bro-code' crap?"

I could tell Joey was just as mad as I was.

"I know you like her more than just a friend. I know you're trying to rescue her from whatever she's upset about. Let me just say that whatever is going on with Charlotte isn't any of your business."

He completely turned toward me and slowly walked closer to me to make sure that I heard every word he said.

"What the hell are you even talking about? I'm her friend. I've been her friend, and I'll always be her friend. I'm also your friend. I've been your friend, and I'll always be your friend." His face was stonelike. His voice was steady and deep.

"Whatever happened between you two has always stayed between you two. I don't know why you're trying to have me choose sides three years later. I don't get it, but I'm sorry. I won't."

He was going to try and repair an injury I caused. He left to rescue the same girl I had tried to rescue three years earlier. When Joey walked out that door, he chose Charlotte and took my trust with him.

I tried all I could not to think about the two of them the rest of the night. Cassidy asked me a few times if everything was all right, and I just told her that Joey was upset about an ex-girlfriend. I wasn't ready to have that difficult conversation with Cass.

But from that night forward, I felt as if nothing was pulling me back anymore. There was no nagging interest in wondering if Charlotte and I could ever work things out. Emotionally, I finally let go of her that night.

From then forward, all I could see was Cassidy. It was as if she were my remedy. Her ability to care for me and try to make me smile was the perfect prescription for an emptiness that I had been trying to fill.

There was one point when I realized Cassidy and I were getting really serious, and I freaked out. I almost sabotaged it, but I couldn't let her go.

I shared just enough about a *former* relationship, not mentioning Charlotte's name. I shared that it ended horribly and I was now scared to hurt her. But she didn't care and was confident I wouldn't. I'm sure she wishes she could go back to that night and change her answer.

The part I was really wrong about was that I thought she could love me enough to fix all wounds I had left over from Charlotte. Cassidy helped, but it's hard to get past scar tissue. Those wounds weren't for her to fix. They were for me to heal, and I never had the chance to do it the right way.

I never sat Charlotte down and asked her hard questions. I never asked her for forgiveness, and I never worked to forgive her. I realize now that I have an eighteen-year-old's wounded heart inside this thirty-three-year-old body.

I never ran into Charlotte again after that night she disappeared. I had seen her picture in the school paper a couple more times, but I never saw her again. She was a ghost that haunted me at times. I would see cars that I thought were hers and peer in to see if it was her. I would walk by the soccer training center and suddenly realize that I could run into her there, but it never happened.

I would look on the buses I would ride to campus, but a chance meeting never occurred. I would hear her name in conversations. One I regret listening in on is when I overheard that she and Joey were dating.

I nailed it. His view of her as a friend at some point changed, and her view of him must have changed too.

How do you have a friendship with a guy who likes your ex-girlfriend, while you're trying to deny she even exists? My roommate, Nick, stayed in touch with Joey, so we still saw each other occasionally. I eventually heard that he and Charlotte had broken up. It was right before graduation, so I've always been curious as to what happened.

It's just another piece of unanswered trivia I put into my jar of questions I have for her if we were to ever meet again. That would probably be the worst thing that could happen to me right now. My marriage is in ruins. Running into my ex-girlfriend who practically destroyed any chance at a normal relationship would be horrible.

Or would it be? Is that where I need to go? Do I need to go back to where the pain came from? Is it too late for closure? I'm so lost. I don't know if it would help me to repair damage I've done to Cassidy or if it would completely destroy her.

How would I even find Charlotte?

~ Twenty-Six ~

CHARLOTTE

December 4, 2012

Dear Diary,

It's been some time since I wrote anything to you. I met with Glenda about a week before Thanksgiving. Ever since then, thoughts have been flooding my mind over and over and over again. I've relived the memories. The pain and sorrow still overwhelm me.

I went to my parents' house for Thanksgiving, and although our relationship has somewhat reconciled over the years, I don't know if I can ever feel worthy in their presence. I always have this cloud of guilt and shame looming over me because of their subtle comments. I know what they mean and the intention behind them.

After dinner, I returned to my place, and the accumulation of present and past pain overcame me. I lost it. I sobbed for hours. I tried to watch funny movies to make me laugh and forget what I was feeling, but tears kept coming. I tried a different rationale and watched something sad. I thought if I was going to cry anyway, a depressing movie would make my tear reservoir empty out faster.

That was wrong. Our bodies seem to have an abundant number of tears available on demand. The statement *I have no tears left to cry* is very dramatic but not entirely true. I would change it to something like, *I wish I had no more tears to cry, because I'm running out of Kleenex and my entire face is bright red and puffy*. It doesn't have quite the same sullen effect, but it is much more accurate.

Thoughts had rented space in my mind for this entire time, and I haven't made them leave. I'd thought about meeting with Glenda again, but I'd already shared so much with her. How much more could I open up? How much more of my past was I going to expose to her?

I'm only ready to write it here. I've said enough to her, and I have no one else. I need to process, and you always help. I have to go back there again.

The memory of that awful morning with Brett was torturous. From the time he'd dropped me off until the time I awoke the next morning, my mind and body were in turmoil. I hated hurting him. I wish I hadn't seen hurt in his eyes after he'd dropped me off. I struggled knowing that I didn't have the ability to help him understand.

As the day moved on, it was hard to look in the mirror. I would see my tear-soaked face, then tell the girl staring back that she had no right to feel sorry for herself. She had put herself in this position, and these were the consequences. No amount of pity could make her whole again.

Torturous aching and throbbing would come and go in my lower abdomen, preoccupying my thoughts. As cramping consumed my body, all I could envision was that whatever was in my womb that morning was gone.

Through tears, my soul grieved the innocence I had just given up, but my throbbing abdomen panged from what it had just lost.

No amount of medication cut through the suffering. It would lower the intensity at times, but deep bouts of discomfort still came and went. Countless pads were used to capture blood that was shed.

I had to hide used ones in a garbage bag in my closet. If my mom were to see the amount of blood shed, she'd think I was hemorrhaging.

I was warned by the nurse how much blood there would be as my body continued to cleanse itself. It was responding as if I were having a miscarriage. I was so naive. I didn't even know what a miscarriage was.

I had to come up with an excuse for my mom, so I told her I'd gotten my period and seemed to be sick at the same time. I lay in bed for the rest of the evening and wrestled mentally and physically.

Bleeding slowed down significantly the next day, but I still got out of going to church with my parents. She wasn't totally convinced it was my health. She assumed it was about Brett and me breaking up. I'd completely forgotten the chance of me running into him there. That would've been ironic.

A week passed, and I was starting to get my feet up under me. I didn't think it could get worse, but I was wrong. My life flipped completely out of control.

I was coming home after hanging out with Mikala and Josie, and something felt strange as I walked up to my house. It was a premonition to what was waiting behind the front door.

As I walked in, my mother was sitting at the dining room table. The scowl on her face made hairs on the back of my neck stand up. She held something that was amber colored, but I couldn't tell what it was, because she was moving it around.

As I got closer, she held it up. "Can I ask you what this is?"

My throat closed in fear, and my adrenaline pumped faster than I had ever felt. I had played in the State Cup Championship and never felt a rush like this. How was I supposed to respond? I had nothing to say that would make this conversation end well.

"Uhhhh, I don't know. What is it?"

Out of the corner of my eye, I saw my dad come toward me. I didn't have time to brace myself, because I didn't expect what was next.

My dad loved me. My dad had always been my ally. My dad had always held a special place in my heart. My dad had always believed in me.

But that day, my dad reached his hand away from his body and smacked my face so hard, I immediately grabbed my cheek with both hands. I looked up, devastated.

"Don't you lie to your mother, and don't you lie to me, dammit! You start explaining yourself right now."

"What do you want me to explain?" I asked through painful tears.

He came at me again, and I screamed for him to stop.

"Stop!! Please, no! Please!"

He tried to smack my face again, but I dropped to my knees. I sat there, crouched over my knees with my hands on my face.

"Go to your room. Go to your room now! I don't even want to look at you. You make me sick." My mom's choice words were just as painful as his hand.

I got up as fast as I could and ran to my room. My world crashed down all around me. I was a month away from going to college but debated leaving right then.

I was summoned to the living room by my parents. I imagined crawling out the window to avoid what was coming. She had just turned into a monster in front of me, and I knew she was capable of doing it all over again. I knew it wouldn't end well.

"We need you to sit down," my mother said, pointing to the couch. Her tone sounded as if she were talking to a juvenile delinquent. I sat down and stayed silent.

"We know what you did, Charlotte. We know what you and Brett both did.

"I don't want you to say one word. I gave you a chance to talk when you came in this house, and you chose to lie, so now I don't trust another word that will spill out of your foul mouth."

Her voice was filled with hatred and condemnation.

"What you both did is beyond any standard that your father and I have ever set for you. The thought of my only daughter getting caught up and having sex after all that I've done to provide a virtuous life for you makes me sick to my stomach. But that wasn't enough.

"I found this pill bottle in your room. I couldn't figure out what it was for, since I hadn't taken you to a doctor in quite some time. I read the information, and I saw it was a current prescription from a doctor I had never heard of.

"So, I thought I'd make a phone call, and when they answered, they mentioned the name of their clinic. I had never heard of it before. I was wondering if it was a place where you had to go for college physicals. So, I took it upon myself to do a little research."

She was on a roll and getting more dramatic and sarcastic as she went.

"And wouldn't you be surprised to know that it was an abortion clinic? Yeah, I was surprised too. That little girl who had taken it upon herself to lie with a boy—who had no business knowing her that intimately—now decided the consequence of that terrible decision wasn't worth enduring. So, she had an abortion.

"She decided to kill the baby that she and her precious boyfriend had accidentally created."

At this point, my head was hanging in shame, and I flooded the floor with tears below me. My mother just kept going with such anger and revulsion.

"They just said that it would be easier than actually having to live out the days with that child. They disposed of the inconvenience and thought their lives would just go on as usual.

"I've news for you, little girl. Your life is about to get real right now. I need you to hear this, so I need you to look at me."

I lifted my head and tried to focus my eyes through the tears so I could see her.

"I'm so deeply ashamed of you. I'm disgusted at how you have disrespected me. All that I've given to you. All that I've offered you, and you return the favor with this. I need you to know that I'm going to let you stay here until you leave for college.

"But when you leave, I don't want you to think you're welcome back here. When you leave, you will live with big-girl decisions you seem to be able to make. I want nothing to do with you. And in case you have stopped to wonder, I want to let you know that God probably wants nothing to do with you either."

I just sat there. If there were a word that was a combination of filth, shame, guilt, condemned, isolated and abandoned, that would describe how I felt on that couch. That heart of stone that had emerged a few weeks before now had stone walls around it.

Where does an eighteen-year-old girl go from there? Where do you turn when the two people who promised to love you more than anything in the world disown you for shaming *them*? The mom who gave birth to me was so disgraced that she was willing to trade those eighteen years in exchange for a life without me.

My dad, who was my biggest fan, had smacked me harder than I had ever felt, and then he sat there in silence as my mother shredded me to pieces. Not one of them asked about me. Not one asked what led me to this point. Not one asked me where my life had taken a wrong turn. Not one could tell me they loved me beyond my mistakes.

I thought I was taught that God's love was unconditional, but there must be a list of things that don't apply. So, tell me—where was I expected to turn? Where was I expected to go?

I know Glenda tries to share with me how much God loves me, but I heard words out of my mother's mouth fourteen years ago, and they've been etched on my heart ever since.

I want nothing to do with you, and God wants nothing to do with you either.

I went to small group once more to see if I could find courage to ask for help, but I just kept hearing my mom's voice in my head telling me I no longer belonged there.

After that night, I never went back to small group again. After that week, I never went back to church. A few youth pastors reached out and contacted me to see how I was, since I'd been away so long. I told them I was busy going away to college, so they emailed me names of churches. I stared at the information for a while, then deleted it. They wouldn't have wanted me either.

It was over. My faith was gone.

It has been fourteen years since then, but that pain will never be erased. Out of everything, it is that pain caused by my parents that hurts most.

About a year after I was in college, my parents and I reconnected, but it wasn't a true reconciliation. It was early into my second year, before the soccer season started. I had just finished up an early morning soccer training and was going back to my apartment to get ready for classes.

As I was leaving the soccer stadium, I noticed a man standing in front of his car, just waiting there for someone. I continued to my car, until I heard someone say my name.

"Charlotte?"

I turned slowly and looked at the man again. I was shocked to see it was my dad. I couldn't find one word to say.

Did he come to chastise me some more? Did he want to smack me again? What could he possibly want from me after they exiled me? I was at a loss for words, except one.

"Yes?" That was my word—a word and a sentence in one.

"Can I please talk to you?"

I could now see his eyes and how much emotion he had behind them. I was curious if he'd come to give me horrible news or something else.

"Is everything okay?" I asked with as little emotion as possible.

"Yes, I just wanted to try and talk to you."

"You know, I just can't right now. You haven't phoned or answered my calls for a year—an entire year. Now, you show up out of nowhere and expect me to listen to you make excuses as to how you could abandon your only daughter because she didn't turn out how you wanted her to?

"All I can say is that I'm sorry I didn't end up being whom you thought I should've been. I'm sorry that I wasn't good enough for you. I can't undo my past, and I also can't forget the words that you and Mom spoke to me in the midst of all my failures.

"That's all I've left to say. So, if you don't mind, I need to leave so I can make it to class on time."

I turned away, holding back tears. I walked to my car and drove home that morning. I didn't look in the rearview mirror. I just moved forward, shaking.

As I turned the corner, realization set in that my dad had come to see me, and I had turned him away. My heart broke because I couldn't grasp how my life had come to be so unrecognizable. Just writing the words now makes me cry.

My parents didn't speak to me for a year—a year. My parents didn't have any contact with me for more than twelve months. I was so filthy that my parents wanted nothing to do with me that entire time.

My dad came back to school a week later and left a note on my car. He had asked me if I could just give him an afternoon where we could talk and he could ask me for forgiveness. He left his cell phone number, as if I didn't have it in my phone. As if I still didn't pull it out to call him after every game or any big news I received.

I made the all-conference team as a freshman, and I remember wanting to call him. It was like a punch in the stomach when I grabbed my phone to call and remembered he didn't want me to call anymore. But each milestone or award became a little easier to stomach not having anyone to call. Things were just getting bearable, and now he wanted to talk.

I had to think about it, but in all of my pondering, I realized that the entire time that my mom was berating me, she kept telling me what I did to her, not *them*. All she kept saying was *I, I, I—me, me, me.*

It was never about them. It was about me embarrassing her. It was about me inconveniencing her. It was about me giving her a bad reputation. The only thing she needed my dad for were physical blows. She did the verbal slaying. And a year later, it was only my dad who had come to reconcile.

I couldn't meet with him. Not out of revenge, but because I couldn't emotionally. I wrote him a letter a few weeks later telling him that I wasn't ready to talk but that I loved him, and a day had never gone by that I didn't think of him. That was all I could say.

There was so much going on in my life, and I knew that if I gave in to talking to him, all of my pain would resurface and take center stage in my mind again. Soccer training had begun, and I was working so hard to keep my starting spot. New recruits come in every year, and they can knock you out just as fast as you've earned it.

The second most impactful stress was the relationship between Brett and me. We had always dreamed of going away to college together. Now that it was a reality, it wasn't a dream at all.

After breaking up, we hardly spoke. I ran into him on campus a couple times and turned away.

He went on to date other girls through college. At first, I was shocked because I wasn't prepared for it when I first saw it. I was relieved at the same time because I knew he was able to move past pain I'd caused him.

I kept holding out hope that we could one day resolve things, yet I knew that there was no way to bridge the deep ravine I placed between us. But fear crept up when I thought that the new girlfriend could possibly be the one to take my place in dreams we had planned together.

This went on for two years. With soccer, I wasn't out that much, so awkward exchanges were occasional. When I did go out, I was always with my teammates.

I wasn't ready to date again, and I never understood how he was. I guess we all go through things differently. He kept moving forward. I chose to stand still.

Things took a turn my junior year. Soccer season had ended, and trainings were reduced to a few times a week. This was when we could make a slight return to a social life.

That spring, my teammate Victoria heard about a Mardi Gras party that was off campus. I had a feeling Brett would probably be there. My instinct was correct. He was there with some of his friends from high school, most of whom I knew.

Although running into him wasn't a new occurrence, this time was different. This time he was with a different girl. It was obvious they were a couple. My body froze, and my blood rushed.

She seemed to be the opposite of me—blonde, skinny and fashionably dressed. I saw her smiling and looking at him as if he were a god. Then, I saw them lean into each other and watched him kiss her as if no one else were around.

I wanted to throw up. I wanted to cry. I wanted to run.

After I got my heart to stop racing and my eyes to stop staring, I made my way out the back door, seeming as if I were just checking out the rest of the party. I slipped out the side of the house, got in my car, and headed home.

I didn't think my heart had anything left to break, so I don't know how it hurt so bad to see him. I don't think I realized how much I still loved him—how much I still thought he was the one for me.

At that moment, I looked at the life around me and wondered if it was worth all that I had given up. Sadly, it wasn't at all. Soccer was my life, and at that point, the only absolute thing in my life at all. It was something I clung to and hated all at the same time. I hated it because it was only a game, yet it was my everything.

If I didn't have that, I would've been lost. I had no relationship with my parents. I had no relationship with Brett. I had no relationship with my church. I had no relationship with God, and if I could've had a choice, I would've chosen not to have a relationship with myself.

I didn't recognize who I had become. Just a few years before, I saw my life going in a completely opposite direction. But one night changed the direction of it all.

I cried when I got home, but not the type of weeping I had become accustomed to over the years. It was a slow stream of constant tears. It was a grieving cry. I mourned the hopeful girl I had lost. I wish I could go back and warn her, allowing her life to be different, but that's impossible.

She's gone.

~ Twenty-Seven ~

CASSIDY

"We know something is wrong between you and Brett." Nancy had come by to see the kids. She had called and asked if it was okay to stop by, and I never hesitated to say yes. She was her normal self on the phone, but I didn't realize she knew so much.

"We respect the fact that you two are keeping your relationship matters private."

She moved a little closer to me, and her face tensed up. I quickly anticipated where this conversation was heading.

"But, as your parents, it's torturous to stay silent when we see you two drowning. We've called him multiple times because we sensed something was wrong, but he won't return our calls. The kids told us they hadn't seen their daddy lately, and pieces add up to us being in the dark about whatever is going on between you two.

"I know he's my son, but you're just as much a part of me as he is. Is there anything you can tell us? If you don't want to, I can respect that and mind my own business. I'm just concerned and needed to ask."

I didn't know how to respond. It has been three weeks. Three weeks since Brett has been gone. I can say it has been the most difficult and foreign time in my life.

I knew my face couldn't stay straight, and I felt as if I were suddenly naked. I didn't expect her to be so direct. I'd always known her to hint at things she knew, but never to inquire so bluntly.

So, that is exactly what I disclosed.

"I don't know what to tell you. I don't know how to respond," I said as I stared at her.

She looked flustered and then appeared to gather her thoughts. "I'll do as I said and respect the fact that you don't want to reveal anything."

"No, it isn't that at all. I truly don't know what to tell you."

I was being honest. It wasn't that I didn't have anything to tell her—I just didn't know what to tell her. The more I reveal to her, the more of a reality it becomes.

"Can you just start where you feel comfortable?"

"It goes so far back. The bottom line is this—Brett moved out three weeks ago. That's why the kids haven't seen him. That's probably why he isn't returning your calls. That's why you sensed something was wrong. Your instincts were right."

And with that, my tears slowly started to fall.

"I wish I weren't the one to tell you. I feel ashamed that we've gotten this far off course. Our marriage has been circling the drain for quite a while, but I couldn't admit it to myself. I couldn't let it be true. I had excuse after excuse.

"Then it came to a breaking point when I needed some questions answered. He refused to let me in, and his response to that was shutting me out altogether. He was done.

"It wasn't until he left that I realized I could be done with it all too. I've chased him for years to be closer to me—to be closer to us—and the more I pursued, the more he pulled away. It has been mentally and emotionally exhausting.

"About two weeks after he left, I knew I couldn't run after him anymore. I had to face where we were in that moment and let it be. When I finally let it go, I felt my body exhale."

While describing it to her, I could feel my body release the strife all over again.

"I love that man more than anything else I've ever had in my life, but I can't make him love me. Sometimes, when you love someone, you have to give them what they've been asking for all along. I finally got that when he left. He wants to be left alone, and I'm giving him what he wants."

She was devastated. You could see it all over her face. Tears in her eyes lingered, waiting to fall as she whispered, "I'm so, so sorry, Cass."

I wasn't expecting her to have such an immediate reaction, and I definitely wasn't expecting such deep empathy. She walked over and gave me a mother's hug. I rested my head on hers and let love she had for me sink in to comfort the emptiness within me.

The moment went on for a while, and the conversation continued back and forth, but in the end, she wanted me to know how much they loved me and how they wanted to be there to help me with the kids when I needed it.

"Is there anything we can do for you—for you both?" Nancy's eyes were filled with compassion, and her gentle voice soothed my aching heart. "I obviously want to talk to my son and see what he's doing."

"Please don't bring up our talk. I feel like you should've heard it from him first. I probably shouldn't have admitted to anything."

Guilt set in that I had just played his mom against him. That wasn't what I intended.

"His dad felt something wasn't right a couple months ago."

"That's when Brett decided to take me on that weekend getaway that didn't go so well. That was actually the catalyst of where we are now."

After Nancy left, I wasn't sure if I felt better or worse for sharing it all with her. I had shared my deepest feelings and almost wanted to take it all back.

I was angry, I was grieving, I was relieved, all within minutes of each other. The questions spun like a hamster wheel.

How could he have left us so easily? How am I ever going to get over the dreams I had for us? Why would I want him to come back?

And then the questions would recycle, only rephrased.

The bottom line I landed on—I could only change me. I was wise enough to know that nothing I said or did could make him love me any differently.

I kept going to counseling. If there was ever a time that I needed to go, it was now.

I had started to see myself as a failure as a wife and as a mother. I had a failed marriage that I wasn't able to make work, and now my kids were going to be products of a divorced household. My confidence had been dwindling for a while, but this emptied the bin.

"Cassie, you keep blaming yourself for all of this. I've heard you asking what you did wrong or what you could've done differently. I hear you blaming yourself for your moods or emotions that might have ignited some of his.

"But truth is, we're all flawed and responsible for our own mistakes. You keep looking at Brett through the lens of your brokenness instead of looking at him as a separate individual.

"There's nothing you could've done or said that would make you responsible for his decisions. But just saying that isn't going to get you to where you need to stay.

"If someone were to ask you what type of crisis you found yourself in right now, I'm guessing you would reply that you were in a marriage crisis."

"Yeah, I'd say that."

"From my perspective, that's secondary to your confidence crisis."

"Of course I have a confidence issue. We've been married for seven years, and he's pecked away at it for at least half the time.

"I know I'm partly responsible because of wanting to please him. When I didn't succeed, a piece of me fell away. After time, anything you consistently chip at erodes.

"So, I would agree, but that seemed obvious and more of a symptom of marital problems to me. No?"

He went to grab a sip of his coffee, and when he put it down, he took off his glasses and leaned forward toward me.

"I'm here to give you the truth and not to just nod my head and agree with you, so that is what I'll do.

"Your confidence in yourself really has nothing to do with him. When we have confidence at one time and then find ourselves without it, we handed it over. It was never taken from us. Can you see where I'm going?"

At that point, I just wanted the session to be over. I knew something hard was coming because my body tensed up.

"He has done things that have communicated to you that the confidence you had in yourself was overvalued, and so you gave some away. This was continual until there was nothing left to give.

"I believe that's where you're at today. You've come to the end of being able to give any more of yourself away. Yet that phrasing is dangerous. It puts you in a victim position. The dreaded 'victim robe' I refer to it as." He shifted in his chair. "I'll explain."

"Okay?" I braced myself. Would I appreciate what I'd hear next? Or would it put me more on the defensive?

"The uniqueness of a robe is that it covers you and shields you. A victim robe can do that for us. It can make excuses for our behavior, or it can allow ourselves to sulk.

"Pity parties are lonely after a while, but the victim robe's shielding feels so good. So good, in fact, that we often forget it is a robe. After a while, it becomes part of us."

I was afraid of what he was about to say. I had just started to settle into my robe, and I anticipated he was going to make me pull it off.

"The clarity I want to show you today is this. The other beauty of a robe is that it's supposed to be a temporary cover that we can take off when we choose.

"That is my challenge to you. Although you feel right now that your confidence was taken away, I challenge you to take off the robe and see that you have given it away. I challenge you to see that there is something within you that believes you don't deserve to get that confidence back."

"I don't even know what to say. That just felt like a kick in the gut. I wanted to come in here and have you say what was wrong with him, and here I sit staring at you because you showed me what was wrong within me. That stings."

My eyes had filled with tears again. There was a sudden realization that he was right, and I was so upset that he was.

"Let me be real with you and start with how this applies to your life. You can meet with some of your friends and tell them about your encounters with Brett. They can all feel for you and be there for you. Some will encourage you to be angry and bitter. Some will be angry and bitter on your behalf.

"Then, there are friends you need in your life who will be upset for you. Yet they'll still believe in God's power to heal both of you and restore your marriage. They'll pray when you can't. Those are the friends you need."

The problem was, I didn't have any of those. Another unavailable remedy.

"I'll give you a Bible scripture later to refer to, but let me go on. Your enabling friends and other outsiders are going to allow you to wear this victim robe for as long as you want. You could probably end up being seventy years old and tell this story, and the person on the other side of the conversation would feel sorrow for you.

"But the testimony of a believer is how you live your life *in spite of* all who have hurt you, in spite of pain you have been through. Your life begins to be an example of God's unfailing love. Your life begins to be an example of how Christ can turn all things meant to harm you into things that will bless you."

My life as an example? I'm completely falling apart right in front of him. And he thinks my life can be an example?

"This is when you can take off the robe. I call this, laying the robe at the feet of the One who sacrificed His life so that you wouldn't have to wear one at all."

The heavy session led me into what I would describe as silent weeping. I was trying so hard to hold it in. My chest was rising and lowering, and I couldn't control my shallow breathing.

I turned to look out the window instead of at him because I was embarrassed. There were so many pieces to my humiliation. He had shown me all my mistakes I've made along the way, and I couldn't take the introspection.

He just sat there and waited for my response while I waited for my internal panic attack to subside.

"This is hard to swallow." I rubbed my damp, shaking hands on my slacks, then clutched them together in my lap. "I'm a pretty up-front person, and I'm going to tell you what I'm thinking.

"I know what you're saying is true, but it's painful. I know I should take you up on your unofficial challenge, but there's another part that I have to admit."

Just speak the truth, Cassidy.

"Sitting in this robe feels so much better than having to look in the mirror. I don't know if I'm ready to take it off just yet. Those are my honest thoughts."

"That is actually a great thing to hear. I believe you're stronger than you know and wiser than you believe. When the time is right and you have grieved all you can, I believe you'll want to remove the robe."

If only I could see myself that way.

"Let's say that somewhere in the future I would want to rise to the challenge. How would I even begin?"

"You can't start until you learn how much God loves you. I can tell you all about Him. I can tell you about times I've experienced Him. But when you experience Him for yourself, that is when your life will change."

Experience Him? What does that even mean?

"He doesn't care for you like your closest relative or spouse or child. He has an overwhelming love for you. Just by talking to you, I know that you're unaware of how deep and wide that love goes."

A change came over him as he spoke to me about God loving me. His face eased and his voice softened. I saw this gentle man in front of me passionately talking about a love I've never heard of.

"When I was first coming to have a relationship with God, I was in a similar place. There was a lady at my church, and I remember her giving me advice to take a Bible concordance and look up the word *love*. She called it a word study, as a matter of fact. She said to go through the entire Bible and learn about God's love and how much He loved me alone."

A concordance? What are all these words?

"It was the best advice I had ever received. So now, I pass it on to you. I suggest you do the same. I'm going to leave it there for now, Cassidy. I know your mind is reeling and you're exhausted."

I nodded my head yes and left with a soaked face and swollen eyes. That was three days ago. I believe that might have been my emotional rock bottom.

That night, I continuously tried recalling where I had gone wrong. How had I given away my confidence? Would Brett have stayed if I had kept my self-worth? I started to think that everyone had been able to see this all along except me.

Washing dishes the next morning, I started recalling everything over again. It had somewhat lulled me into a deeper and consistent sadness. Anger and bitterness had taken a back seat to my self-loathing.

Then, sunlight started to kiss my forehead. It was like any other morning where the sun's rays would break through openings in the trees and lightly shine on me, except this time it felt like they were going directly onto my face.

I looked up, and it felt warm and soothing. I closed my eyes, then opened them again and realized that it was still just shining right there. Something in me woke up, and I felt tingling all throughout my body. Heat covered my entire body, as though wrapped in a soft blanket.

I knew that was God. There was no doubt. That was my first personal encounter with Him, and He arrived as my comforter at my most sullen time.

After the sunrays left, I knew that I would be all right, but that morning sparked my curiosity as to how I could experience that same feeling again. Calling Brett's mom was the first thing that came to mind.

"Nancy?"

"Hey, Cass! How are you? How are the little ones?"

"We're all doing all right, but I was calling to ask a question. It's kind of strange for me, so bear with me."

"All right. What is it, Cass?"

"How do I take a step toward God? I have the books you have given me, and I have a Bible, but opening them isn't easy for me. I feel like they are talking in 'Christianese,' and I can't understand the language.

"You're a great source of wisdom, but with everything going on, I think I need to take a step out on a limb and talk to someone. Do you understand?"

"Cass, I don't know where to begin. . . "

"I'm sorry if I hurt your—"

"No, don't be. That is not my reason for being caught off guard. I'm so happy to have this conversation with you, and I wasn't expecting it at all.

"Now, let me think." Nancy paused for a moment, followed by a deep breath. "How would you feel about meeting for coffee with a staff member from our church? She is an excellent source of wisdom and has been through a thing or two herself where she might be able to relate. She is much younger than me and would probably be more relevant to you."

"How do I reach out to her? What do I say? Hi, my name is Cass, and I'm looking for God. Can you help me find Him?" The laughter from that broke up the intensity of the moment.

"That would be one approach. You can just call and tell her who you are. See if she wouldn't mind meeting with you soon so you could ask her a few questions. If you'd like, I could call her for you, but I wouldn't know what you would want me to share and what you would rather keep to yourself."

"I'll call her. In fact, I'll try to reach her today." A germ of hope sprouted within that I might actually connect with another woman who could help me. "Can you give me her info?"

"Absolutely. Her name is Trish Bellamy. She is amazing and does so much for women's events at our church. Her number is . . ."

I got off the call with Nancy and placed the phone on the coffee table in front of me, then stared at it as if waiting for it to make the first move. I looked at the neon-orange sticky note with Trish's number on it.

Who was this lady? Nancy liked her, but what if I didn't? What was wrong with me to even imagine meeting a stranger for coffee and asking her how to "know" God? I'd been to church, I'd heard prayers, and I'd skimmed through Christianese books. None of it appealed to me.

But now, in probably the worst time of my life, the sun shines and provokes me to find out who He is? How could I even translate that into normal thinking? Talking about a troubled marriage is ten times easier than telling a stranger that God found me through a window while I was doing dishes.

I waited to call. I went and tended to the kids and waited again. I made dinner, gave the kids a bath, and put them to bed. I walked by that stupid sticky note nine more times. In the end, my pride got to me. I just couldn't do it.

~ Twenty-Eight ~

CHARLOTTE

December 6, 2012

Dear Diary,

There is more I need to share. . . . Someone I wasn't ready to talk about, but he's part of my full story.

During my difficult times in college, there was one friend who could see that I was struggling. It was Joe. We'd been friends since elementary school, but he had been Brett's best friend through high school.

Things changed between Joe and me after the breakup. Joe never knew why Brett and I broke up. Our moral compasses had broken, and one of our best friends had no clue. It was hard for him to understand why things changed so drastically.

Neither of us spoke to one another nor spoke about each other. It was just over. As if we had never known each other to begin with.

Joe stopped me at the campus coffee shop one morning, just before classes started our first fall semester. He asked if I was okay. There was something in the tone of his question.

"Yes, I'm good. How about you?"

"Ever since you and Brett broke up, you have been isolating yourself. Josie and Mikala say they never see you anymore, and whenever I see you, it seems you're trying to avoid me." Joe took a gulp of coffee, despite steam rising from the cup, then wiped his brow. "And this part might not seem like my business, but you seem sad."

"Sad? I don't know what you mean by that. Maybe I'm just stressed with school and soccer starting at the same time. I have reasons to be a bit preoccupied.

"And Josie and Mikala have both been home and hanging out, but I've had to be here for soccer training. I train twice a day, and I'm exhausted to do anything else. Our lives are already going in different directions. That's all."

By his perplexed look, I knew he wasn't buying it.

"That's all true, but there is one piece that doesn't fit. All of this started before you even left for school. You stopped coming to youth group and church. Hell, we were surprised you even showed up to graduation. This isn't something that is college related."

I was shocked by his audacity to call me out right there.

"I appreciate your concern, if that is what you call this, but I'm okay. I'm busy with soccer and getting used to it here. I'm having a hard time adjusting to all of it, and you stopping me like this doesn't help.

"I don't know a lot of people here, but I'm trying to get to know my teammates. I'm not outgoing, so it has been a challenge. And as for church, who knows? Maybe it was a subconscious thing, since I knew I was leaving."

I crossed my fingers and hoped he wouldn't press me anymore. I didn't want to break down right there, and I could feel the emotions starting to close my throat.

"I understand if you don't want to open up to me. But I just wanted to let you know that I see it, and so do Josie and Mikala. If you need to talk, please know that I'm here for you whenever you might need a friend."

"Joey, I appreciate you reaching out, but I promise I'm okay. There's nothing wrong and really nothing to talk about. Brett and I are over, so it is awkward between all of us. And the church piece is between God and me. We'll have to work that out."

"You know I'll always be here for you, right? We've been friends since elementary school. I'm going to keep tabs on you. Maybe you need a big brother on campus." He said it with a laugh, but I knew that he meant it.

As nice as that sounded, I thought his first allegiance was to Brett. I didn't expect him to follow through, but he was very intentional in reaching out. He would call occasionally to see how everything was going or to ask if I wanted a ride home on some weekends.

I always had an excuse for staying at school. He didn't know going home wasn't an option for me anymore. He'd ask if we could meet for lunch or dinner. I had a list of reasons why I couldn't meet up with him, but after a while, my list ran out.

Listening to his life was pleasing to me. He'd talk about his classes, his dorm, his roommates, parties, girls he kind of liked. Those conversations let me smile.

Accidentally mentioning Brett's name would happen occasionally, but he would try and talk past it quickly. He brought up being back home and at our church. Those stories made me tense up because I longed for what he still had.

We became closer as time went on. Joe and some of his buddies would come to my soccer games, and their presence helped me play more relaxed. It was nice to have a section of support. It felt like a little bit of the life I used to know.

Through those times shared, Joe had somehow become closer with my teammates too. A couple of them had a crush on him. Isabella asked me if I minded her being interested in him. Over and over again I would tell them all that he was like a big brother to me. He had taken my friend Alivia out a couple times, but there were no sparks between them.

That fateful spring night, when I saw Brett with his girlfriend at the party, is when things changed for Joe and me. I was stuck. I needed Joe around me to make me feel safe, but I pushed him away out of respect for him and Brett.

Hurting Joe wasn't my goal, but it was an unintended consequence.

Joe came up and sat next to me. "Everything okay?"

"Oh . . . yeah . . . everything is fine . . ."

"Hmm, not convinced, but I know you saw that Brett is here with someone."

"Yeah, no biggie."

Victoria was the only friend who knew about us. She knew we'd dated for a long time and that I thought he was the one. She understood it was hard for me to talk about.

Whenever we ran into him, I could tell that she was checking me over to make sure I was okay. She'd never ask, but she'd always do something kind to show me she would protect me.

That night she did the same.

"Hey, you want to get out of here? I can get the girls and go if you'd like. It's a little 'crowded.'"

She gave me a wink as she said it, knowing it wasn't crowded at all. She was giving me an escape, since Brett was there.

"I'm good. It's a great party, and we haven't been out in so long. I think the team needs to let off some tension and just hang out."

"Okay, but if you change your mind just give me the sign."

"All right . . ." I said, with a slight chuckle.

Fifteen minutes later is when I made my escape home. Victoria and Joe called me before I even made it through my front door.

I didn't want to answer, but I owed it to them to let them know I was safe. I answered Victoria's call and told her I'd gotten sick but didn't want to take them from the party, so I just left. She knew exactly why I left, but she played it off in the brief conversation.

After he couldn't get through to me, Joe asked her where I'd gone. They both knew I'd lied to get out of there. Shortly after, he left a message.

"Charlotte, this is Joe. You know that already because you purposely didn't pick up. Please answer your phone."

He called again, but I still couldn't pick up. I cried myself to sleep with my phone next to me, but it never rang again. I'd succeeded again at isolating myself.

Natalia came in my room that night to wake me because someone was at the door. Completely unclear of who could've shown up, I quickly went to the door in my sweatpants and T-shirt. There was Joe, leaning up against the wall.

"Charlotte, hey. I felt bad and wanted to check on you, since your phone isn't working."

"Why? What happened?" I was so out of it. I had no idea what he was talking about.

"Yeah, Char. It's you I'm concerned about. I know why you left tonight. You weren't sick. It was because of Brett and Cassidy. I should've warned you he had a new girlfriend, and I'm sorry I didn't."

It took me a second to focus and remember what had happened, and once it all came back to me, my heart dropped again.

"Joe, that wasn't it. I must've eaten something . . ."

As I was searching for my excuse, tears in my eyes interrupted me and my voice was silenced. I turned my face away from him to hide. I'd done so well at holding it in, and I fell apart right in front of him.

"Charlotte, it's okay. I understand . . ."

"No, there's nothing to understand. I just don't feel good." I was trying to say that nothing was wrong as my bottom lip quivered and my eyes closed to hold back tears.

"Charlotte, stop! Just stop! Let it go."

"Joe, there's nothing to let go of . . ."

And then I surrendered to the sorrow that overcame me. Stepping into his outstretched arms, I let all my pent-up emotions run free. He had no idea how long I'd been holding them in.

"Charlotte, I told you that you could talk to me. Why haven't you?"

"You'd never understand. I just can't. I'm sorry. But I appreciate you coming to check on me.

"Brett has moved on, and it hurt me a little bit. That is all. I wasn't expecting it, but it will be fine tomorrow. What is that line everyone says? 'This too shall pass.'"

"All right, Charlie. If you don't want to tell me what's going on, I'll respect that. I get the hint. You keep pushing me away, so I'll leave you alone, but I'm your friend. I'd never judge you."

"I wish that was enough to make me open up."

"Okay, I get it. I'll leave it alone."

He gave me a hug, I gave him a "thank you," and he left.

Crying resumed on cue when the door closed. I bent over and sobbed. I couldn't do it anymore. I couldn't pretend anymore. I didn't want to go back to my room and try to forget everything all over again. And then, a thought grabbed hold of me, and I realized that I didn't want him to leave.

Swinging the door open, I rushed to where we'd been standing. Joe was gone. I raced down the staircase that emptied into the parking lot. I looked everywhere, but I couldn't see him there either.

I was telling myself that I had messed up again, when a car backing out of its parking spot caught my eye. I recognized it and immediately took off running toward it.

I made it before he took off and banged on the window. He suddenly stopped when I startled him. I ran around to the driver's side, and he rolled down his window.

"Don't leave!" I begged. "Please stay."

After hesitating, he didn't respond. Rolling up his window, he pulled back in and turned off the car. As he got out of the car, he turned to look at me, appearing slightly confused.

"You were right. I could use a friend."

It was the first time in ages that I purposely humbled myself, and it had been just as long since I found relief. I'd wanted someone to share my secrets with for so long, but now I was scared to let them out.

We made ourselves comfortable in the living room. Joe sitting on the couch and me curled up in the lounge chair. I looked for a blanket desperately. I already felt exposed and wanted anything to cover me.

We sat there for a minute with an awkward pause. He was waiting for me to say something, and I was waiting for my breath to return.

"I don't know where to start" was all I could seem to get out at first. "It feels like there is so much, and yet I have no words right now."

"Charlotte, I didn't come here to pry. I just know something's wrong. You don't have to tell me anything. If you just need me to sit here and say nothing, that's fine with me."

That was exactly what I wanted.

"Yes, that's it. I just need you to be here. Can we watch a funny movie and not talk about anything?"

"If that is what you'd like, that is what we'll do."

When I realized he meant what he said, I exhaled twenty pounds of fear. We found a classic movie we both found amusing, and after thirty minutes, the film took me to a superficial reality. It was exactly where I wanted to be.

We must've fallen asleep during the movie because I woke up in my chair from music playing while credits rolled. At that point, I contemplated waking Joe up from the couch so he could head home, or falling back to sleep, since I didn't want him to leave.

It wasn't a romantic desire. It was for security. When he was around, I felt calm and my life didn't feel empty. I turned off the television and chose to fall back asleep in my chair.

I woke up first the next morning. I decided coffee brewing would be the least awkward way to wake him, since it would be the smell and not me.

The plan worked, and when he realized where he was, he apologized for falling asleep. I graciously accepted his apology as if I didn't have a part in making sure he stayed.

I poured him a cup of coffee, and we talked a little more about the movie. There was a lull in the conversation where he was able to gesture that he was going to gather his things.

"Charlotte, I'm going to head out. I don't want to scare your roommates when they wake up or have them telling stories," he joked.

Joe stood up and looked for his keys. He walked toward me awkwardly, so I stood up for him to give me a hug. As we embraced, he reminded me to reach out to him whenever I needed a friend.

Unexpected emotions arose in my throat, and I had to hold back tears. I stared at him as he was leaving. I felt like my gaze was grabbing ahold of him. And something in his eyes changed as well.

~ Twenty-Nine ~

GLENDA

"Hey, Charlie. It's me, Glenda. You probably already knew that. I came to check on you and sit with you a little while. I brought you some flowers that I thought you would like. They are the blush ones that I always bring for you.

"I want to know how you are, but that is an answer that I'll never get. I want to know if you miss me like I miss you, but that, too, I'll never know. I know there is no pain in heaven, so I'm guessing loneliness doesn't exist there either.

"Earth doesn't offer a way to escape missing you, so I'll always long for you. I can't wait until the day I see your precious smile again. It's been so long and hard, and my strength is fading. I've always pleaded with Him to take me home to be with you, and He has obviously not wanted to oblige.

"Lately, though, I've been wholeheartedly asking Him for my race to be finished. I have run and given it my all. My two most precious things in my life were taken from me, and I went on for thirty more years, despite the empty seats at my dinner table.

"I've asked that He take me to be with you before next spring. I just don't want to go through another anniversary of your accident. I don't want to relive it all over again.

"I think about the call I received. Then I relive going to the coroner's office, identifying your bodies and seeing shards of glass embedded in your swollen face. After that, it gets hazy because I don't even remember how I got home.

"I think about nights I woke up screaming because I thought it was all a dream, only to wake up and find out that it was worse than any nightmare. At least in a nightmare, no matter how deep into it you go, you have to wake up from it. This one has never ended. It has faded a bit, but it never ends.

"I often wonder if that man lives with the same pain I do. He never knew either of you, but your deaths took away years of his life. I think back sometimes and remember what I was doing when I got that horrific call.

"I'd just finished scrubbing the floor. Both of you were gone, and those were the best times for me to get work done. I wanted you to come back to a sparkling home . . . when you returned.

"The phone rang, and I almost didn't answer it. I knew you couldn't have been there yet, so whoever was calling wasn't important. I picked it up anyway, and my life changed in that moment.

"I rewind a bit before that and think back to what his night was like before the accident. I imagine what he could've possibly been doing. I remember his attorney talking about 'emotional distress.'

"His wife had left him during that time. The irony, right? He loses his family and takes mine.

"Nonetheless, I wonder where he was drinking. Was he home, sitting in front of a TV or looking at a broken family picture? Was he at a local bar, one that was open during the day for regular attendees?

"At what point did he forget to stop drinking? When he grabbed his car keys, did he even consider that he could change so many people's lives forever?

"Was there a bartender who let him leave after drinking so much? Was there anyone who could've taken his keys and called a cab? It was just one turn, one slip of the wheel, and one moment of contact that changed me from a wife to a widow.

"Through the years, I've forgiven Jason. I've prayed thousands of prayers asking for God to help me offer grace to that young man I still see sitting in the defendant's chair. He was twenty-four. He was demonstratively shaken up. I knew he wasn't a terrible man, but for the sole reason that he had deemed me a widow and childless, he was evil to me.

"During the trial, he seemed to become more and more emotionally distressed. In the end, the jury recommended sentencing, but the judge was responsible for handing out the appropriate consequence. Before sentencing, I was asked if I wanted to get on the stand and give my testimony.

"I wanted to get up there and tell him what an idiot and reckless fool he was. I needed to say that he took you from me, the only love my heart had ever known. I imagined me expressing pain of him taking Sarah from me, my only child who was more precious to me than anything I had ever held in my hands.

"I wished I could've screamed he belonged in hell with every other murderer out there. I yearned to sternly tell him that his wife was right to leave him and that he didn't deserve to be with anyone else for the rest of his life.

"Then after all that spun around in my head, I came out here to you. After telling you everything I wanted to say, I could hear what you would say to me.

"Glenda, he made a mistake. He didn't mean to hurt me, he didn't mean to hurt Sarah, and he didn't mean to hurt you. His life was terrible, but now he will have to live with this for the rest of his life. Do you need to punish him more?

"All I could scream was, 'Yes! Yes, I do!' But my temperament settled, and I remembered who I was. That person wanting revenge wasn't whom I had been all my life. That wasn't the woman you had married. That wasn't the mother or example I would've wanted to be to Sarah. So, I rethought what I would say, and I rehearsed it to you.

"I knew you would approve, and so I went forward with speaking what we had agreed on. So, I told him the truth. I told him things that I had wanted to say and things I wanted to feel.

"And then I told him who I was. I was a God-loving child. I was your wife. I was Sarah's mom. But what would define what my future held was to sit there and tell him that I forgave him.

"I sobbed. I didn't want to tell him that. I didn't want to let him off the hook with no punishment, but I knew that God had blessed me with over twenty years of great memories with the two of you, and that was enough to sustain me. Punishing him over and over with my words and in my mind would only diminish those memories.

"The day I left the courtroom, I felt like I had lost an opportunity for revenge that I would never get back. Yet, as I sit here talking to you, have I fully forgiven him? Have I ever let it go? I might need to revisit this with God. I was reading a book that a friend recommended, and it said something that has stuck with me for weeks.

"'You know that you have completely forgiven someone when you ask God to withhold punishment for what they've done to you.'

"My throat closed when I read that. Was I ready to let Jason completely off the hook? Would my forgiveness be complete when I ask God to withhold punishment from him for what he did to you? For what he did to Sarah? For ruining the last thirty years of my life?

"Charlie, I just don't think I can. I just can't. Is this really happening? Is this something that I must do? I can't. No one can expect this of me. I have every right to refuse to do it.

"God, I'm begging You. Please don't ask me to. Please. This is where I get angry. He kills my Charlie, he takes my Sarah, he ruins my life, and you're about to ask me to go through more pain?

"Charlie and Sarah are safe with You. Jason is serving his time. But me, I've had to be resilient while my faith and strength have been tested every day for the last thirty years.

"I'm old. I'm tired. I don't want to do more work. I don't want to dig up this pain anymore. Haven't I forgiven him enough? This is unbelievable. There has to be a way for me to get out of having to do this. This isn't fair.

"Charlie, can you please help me? I'm assuming you're one of my guardian angels. Can you please ask God to bring me home to you? This is all too much. Just from this conversation, I know God is asking me to forgive Jason completely, and I just can't. I'm not strong enough. I'm incapable of that kind of forgiveness.

"Can't God decide Jason's fate on His own? Isn't He the ultimate judge? Why do I have to plead for this man's salvation? I just want to be with you. I'm sorry that I came here babbling and sobbing again, but I'm just finished.

"The irony is that I hear so many people saying how Christianity is a crutch or an easy life. This is no crutch and it's hard as hell.

"I've been trying to be obedient to God. I've been meeting with a girl named Charlotte. Ironically, her nickname is Charlie. She is the perfect combination of you and Sarah.

"Sarah, she has so many qualities that I believe you would have if you'd lived out your life. She is beautiful. She has hair almost the same unique amber color that you have—or had—or maybe still have.

"Charlie, she shares your nickname. Time with her has a strange way of making me feel as if I'm with you both. If I were to say that out loud to someone, they'd probably think I was losing my mind, but I believe God brought her to me as a gift.

"She would never think that of herself, but she is a precious gift to me. She has been through so much heartache and has so many lies built up in her head. I wish I could pull her out of her entanglement, but the truth is, her freedom is only between her and God.

"I can reveal things about God to her only so far, and then she has to meet Him herself. As you can tell, I'm still working on my relationship with God, so I can only reveal to her what has been revealed to me as of yet.

"Even more irony in all this is that I'm going to have to teach her about forgiveness. How can I fully teach her when I can't fully understand it myself?

"They say the hardest lesson to learn is one that you thought you already learned. I think that is what is going on here. I think I'm about to relearn a lesson that I thought I had passed. I see now that I'm not just helping her with forgiveness. I'm mirroring her journey of forgiveness.

"Lord, if this is what You want from me, I'll try. But I know without a shadow of a doubt that I cannot do this without You.

"Please, Lord, be easy on me through this. I'm weary, but I want to finish the race for You and with You, no matter the cost.

"Oh, Charlie, I can't believe I committed to this and no one is here to help me. Please, please pray for me. I don't want to leave you this time. I want to stay here all day. I know that I can't because it is getting dark, but if I could, I would.

"I imagine you here with me. I imagine you sitting here with your arms around me. I've missed it for so long that I'll do all I can to believe that I can still feel your touch.

"Until I return, know that you always have had my heart, and I leave another piece of what I have left with you tonight. I love you, Charlie. Take care of my girl."

"I love you, Sarah. I miss you more than I can say. Take care of your daddy for me. Hug him for me, since I no longer can."

~ Thirty ~

CHARLOTTE

God?

It's me, Charlotte. This feels so awkward—reaching out to you. I'm not sure if you even want to hear from me with all the terrible ways I disappointed You.

You know I've been meeting with Glenda and she's been telling me that You might still want a relationship with me and might possibly still love me.

She said it much more confidently, but I'm still having a hard time wrapping my head around it. I'm sitting here in the ruins of my bad decisions. It has been almost fifteen years since I've turned to face You, and I don't even know where to begin. I just know this—my heart is empty, and there is nothing that can fill it. My heart is desiring companionship and comfort, but what I think it's yearning for the most is . . . You.

I recently remembered something. When I was in high school, I heard a sermon at my church that stuck with me. It said that You designed us to need You. You created us from Your breath. You formed us to have a need for you so deep that nothing else could ever satisfy it. I finally believe that is why I have this dry place within me.

That is what pushed me to try to reconcile what was left of our relationship. I could choose to believe that my need for You was true and face the disappointment You have in me, or I could resist it and go on living the rest of my life empty.

I can't stand living like this anymore. So, I'm here. I don't know what else to do. I cry tears of regret and pain. Tears that know You must be let down by all that I've done. You know what they are. Speaking of them to You feels impossible, yet You watched every step along the way.

I stepped out of my promise to You when Brett and I had made love that fateful night. My consequence was the pregnancy. That is when I slid so far out of control, I didn't recognize myself or anything around me. I put my head down and went forward with what I thought I had to do.

Looking back, I went ahead with something that could've made my life easier. But the cost of that decision was far more than I could bear. I lost everything that mattered to me. Everything.

The only thing that was there for me as a constant was a simple game I had played my whole life. How is that even sensible to say? I don't know how to admit that soccer held me together, but rhythm and routine of it all kept my feet moving forward, even when I didn't want them to move at all.

How do I look to You and ask You to forgive me for taking the life of a child You gave me—gave us? I thought I could handle doing it to myself, but one thing that has tortured me over the years is the image of Brett's face while he was begging me not to go through with it. I took his child as well. In the moment, I couldn't see past my own pain to visit his.

I don't blame him for hating me. Part of me pushing him out of my life was a defense against how horrible I felt about doing that to him. The other part was knowing that I no longer deserved him.

He was willing to change his entire life to have a future with me, with all three of us. But I couldn't let go of my pride and what everyone would think—my parents, his parents, my church, my pastors, my teachers, my future coaches. I couldn't think about giving up my education and scholarship, and I definitely couldn't think about Brett missing out on his education either.

As years have passed, I've seen that they were all lies. We would've made it. We would've gone after our dreams together. We would've supported each other to get things that we needed. I would've supported him through law school, even if I had to sacrifice my own education. But that would only have been clear to me if he and I had lived on an island with no one else around to disappoint.

Some would say it's water under the bridge and I need to move on. My truth is, I'm drowning in the undertow of raging water without any bridge in sight.

So, I come to You with what I have left of my heart, and I ask You to forgive me. I don't know what to do next, but I'm sorry. If there is something I need to do to get a second chance, please show me. And if my ways have carried me too far away from You, I absolutely understand.

Truly,
Charlotte

~ Thirty-One ~

BRETT

My mind would not stop spinning. An idea occurred to me, and my thoughts have been ravaged by it ever since. All this mess seems to be leading back to something I never dealt with years ago. It all points back to Charlotte and not putting any closure to our circumstances.

All of that damage seemed to fade to black. It was like those movies where you wait for a reasonable conclusion that would make sense of the film, but credits start rolling and you're left confused instead.

My college English professor would ask me to take a story and give it an alternate ending. Now I was trying to convince myself to do the same for real life. But how would I even begin that process of rewinding?

I couldn't return to the lake. I couldn't go back to the Vandy library. I couldn't go back to the abortion clinic, and I couldn't revisit that day I dropped Charlotte off at her house for the last time. I would have to go back to the person, not places.

How would I find Charlotte? How would I reach out to her even if I found her? I could check the Internet. She might be on Facebook. I could create an alternate identity to protect Cassidy from suspecting anything. But would Charlotte even know it was me?

I wanted to get creative. I wanted to think of something that she and I used to talk about together. I could use our jersey number. Could I use old nicknames, like Charlie or Mac? I would just have to hope that she would accept the friend request.

CharlieMac19 was a good alternate name. She might catch on. I created the page and searched for her. I finally found her after entering names I thought she might use, then remembered her middle name.

There she was—Charlotte Elizabeth. I stared at my computer. Was reaching out to her worth the risk of hurting—or even possibly losing—Cass?

My only justification for either scenario was that I had to dig myself out of this mess, and it kept leading me back to everything in my rearview mirror. I almost pressed the button, and then I suddenly shut my laptop out of fear.

I wanted to make sure I had prepared myself mentally for any consequences. I walked back over to the computer, opened it up, and the screen for a friend request was still open. I pressed send.

Adrenaline rushed through my body. It was more powerful than when I would ask for three shots of espresso in my coffee after pulling all-nighters at work. I did it. It was out there.

Once again, I had made myself vulnerable to her. The proverbial ball was in her court. I sat there and stared to see if she would accept.

With every passing minute, my heart beat harder. Hope of her responding took over every thought. I checked every thirty minutes, then about every hour to see if she'd accepted.

A day passed without any response. I wasn't familiar with how social media worked and how often people interacted, but I'd always been under the impression that it was immediate.

The only familiarity I had with that sort of stuff was back in college when "instant message" on AOL was the huge thing. You could see on your computer when the person you were trying to talk to was online. When they signed off, you'd hear the sound of a squeaky door closing.

I was so engrossed in finding out if she would respond and why it might be taking her so long that I did research on the Internet. Looking back, I can laugh at how ridiculous it was, but in the moment, I was so obsessed that I couldn't mentally pull out of the zone I was in.

My probing entailed how often women checked their Facebook accounts. My fact-finding results only made me feel worse. It stated that people had it as an app on their phone and they received alerts for new friend requests.

It also said that on average, women checked their accounts at least ten to fifteen times per day. That shocked me. Not only because of their obsession with looking, but that it had been over a day since I tried to connect with Charlotte, which meant she could've potentially seen my request over ten times and ignored it.

My research led me to find one more crazy detail about Facebook. You can "poke" someone you're not "friends" with yet to get their attention and let them know you see them or have found them. So, after another day of no answer, I did it. I "poked" her. I hate that phrase, but that is what I did.

A couple days later, I was at work and I checked my faux account. I had two alerts. One was a notification that she had accepted my friend request, and the other was a notification that I had a message. My pulse raced again.

Who is this?

That was all the message said. What was I supposed to say to her? I was so confused about how to respond. I had done all I could to find and contact her, but I had never once stopped to consider what I would say if she accepted my friend request.

I wanted to collect my thoughts for a decent response, but I didn't want to let too much time pass either. I started to panic. I had to sit and go back to the inner conversations I'd had with myself to find out the real reason for contacting her. This wasn't for entertainment—it was for a purpose. I just had to keep my eyes on what I set out to accomplish. My response was nothing profound.

Brett

That was all I could come up with. Either she would entertain more of a discourse or shut me out altogether. I was interested to see her response, thinking I might get a feel for her temperature. It wasn't long before I got her reply.

Why?

Yes, that was all that I got and probably exactly what I expected from her. She was usually a girl of few words in an awkward situation. Now, I had to move forward and express what I needed to.

Yes, hello to you as well. Trust me, this is as strange for me to write this as it is for you to receive it. I'm going to put myself out there and see how it goes.

I've come across some obstacles recently, and I've been trying to figure out where they came from and how to move them out of my way. I think and then process and think some more.

But every time, it leads back to our history—back to events that happened between the two of us. The words that were left unspoken are ones that trip me the most.

I just wanted to know if you would be willing to meet up and give me a chance to talk with you. I know that nothing we would possibly discuss would change anything in the past or change anything now. I just need some things answered in my own head so I can move past these potholes in my way.

If you can't because of a relationship you're in, or even if you just don't want to, I understand. I'll find another way to figure things out. I don't want you to think that you have to. I only wanted the chance because you're the only one who knows details that seem to keep playing in my head. Take all the time you need to think about it.

Brett

There it was. I did it. I said it. I asked. That was all I could do for now. It was up to her to respond, and I would wait as long as I could.

I needed to be prepared for both a yes and a no. If she said no or didn't respond at all, I knew that I had to move on and try to find the fossils of my past alone.

But if she said yes, what would I ask? What questions had I placed in that mental jar of mine over the years? None were easy. I guess I could start with more recent ones and lead into those more historic.

Why did you disappear from everyone after your senior year of college?

Why did you leave that party that I saw you at last? Was it my fault?

Why did you break up with Joey?

Why did you date Joey?

Why did you always stare at me so coldly whenever we ran into each other?

Why have you seemed to hate me so much?

What did I do that hurt you enough to push me away?
Why were you so angry with me?
What could I have done differently to help you?
What could I have done differently to keep you?
How was following your dream of playing soccer?
Was what we did worth it?
How have you moved past it? Because I don't know how.

Those are questions that sting. Just thinking about them makes me sick. The amount of questions let me see how hurt I still am.

Dammit, I wish I weren't. I'm entangled in the space between now and then. I don't see how to move forward out of this web I've woven for myself.

I need to break free. I need to feel alive again. Not just for me, but for Cassidy.

~ Thirty-Two ~

CHARLOTTE

December 9, 2012

Dear Diary,

Oh, there is so much to tell you. Where do I start? If you thought I was insane before, I feel twice as crazy now.

So, here is the first part. I recently reached out to God. I wrote to Him on pages before this one.

Anyway, I asked if there was a way for me to reconcile with Him. I admitted all the things I'd done wrong when I was younger, and also those done to Brett.

I asked God to show me if there was a way for Him to love me again. Of course, I haven't heard anything yet, but I don't expect Him to just come running to me. It took my parents almost a year to want me back in their lives—well, at least my dad.

That is a huge thing in itself, but then there is more. I was on Facebook yesterday at work, and I had a friend request. I didn't know the name, so I just left it alone. I looked around my feed for a while and then went on to do some other work.

While I was contacting some vendors for our hotel's Christmas extravaganza, I clicked back on Facebook for a second to scroll around while I was on hold. The friend request popped up again, and this time, the name CharlieMac19 stuck out.

"Charlie" was my nickname of course, but "Mac" was Brett's in college—a play on his last name, McDonnell. We shared number nineteen in high school.

When the caller took me off hold, our conversation pulled me away from the computer. I was rushing around the hotel for appointments I had that day. While I was talking to one of our contracted business managers, the name went through my head again—CharlieMac19.

I could hardly pay attention after that, but I worked hard to refocus. I finally rushed back to my office, shut the door, and pulled up Facebook again. I accepted the request and sent back a simple note.

Who is this?

Simple and to the point. I sat back in my chair and started to go back to work. I didn't expect an answer so soon. The answer I got was one I was expecting, yet I was shocked that I was right.

Brett

After all these years, he'd found me and was attempting to communicate.

Why?

I'd heard a long time ago that he'd proposed to the girl I saw him with at the party. I'm pretty sure her name was Cassidy or Cassy. I assumed they'd gotten married.

So, I was confused. Maybe it was someone pretending to be him. I looked for some mutual friends, but there were none. In fact, there were no friends at all and no picture, so it felt a little suspect.

When he responded to my question asking why he wanted to reach out to me, I knew it was him. In short, he said unsettled things from our past are stumbling blocks for him right now. Having no one else who understands the details, he asked if we could meet so he could ask me some things.

I was immediately breathless. I was shocked, stunned. My boss called, asking me to come down to her office. My initial reaction was no, because I was in the middle of an emotional disaster.

I walked down anyway and worked to stay focused on the conversation. I don't think she sensed I was distracted from directions she was giving. But I finished the rest of the day in a cloud of questions and scenarios.

What am I supposed to say? Isn't he married? Why would he want to talk now? What if I were to have all those old feelings flood back? What if I weren't able to hold back my real emotions this time?

Should I ignore it? Deactivate my account? Run from him again? Or sit in front of him and tell him the ways I was wrong and ask for his forgiveness?

No matter how much I convinced myself to not respond, my mind couldn't stop thinking of possible responses.

When I got home last night, questions still went round and round and fought for space in my mind. Finally, I sat down and thought it through. I had to ask myself some questions. For example, *what did I really want in the end?*

Did I want to see him? Probably. *Did I want to help him?* A little, but helping him meant I'd be giving up another piece of me. I knew he needed to hear me say I'd made a mistake and that I was sorry for putting him through something so terrible.

Did I want to ignore him and hurt him again? No. *Did I want him to know that I wasn't in a relationship after all this time? Did I want him to know, that because of our past, I wasn't sure if I could ever love again?*

I can't believe I said that. I don't want to admit that. So, thinking it through made me realize that I owed it to him to answer, and I owed it to myself to resolve as much of this as I could. I'm ready to move on. I'm ready to get out of this sewage I've been drowning in. So, I responded.

Brett,

Obviously, this is awkward for me also. It is quite surprising to hear from you after all this time. Actually, that's an understatement. You said you wanted to meet, and after thinking about it, I would be willing to do so. I'm not sure how it will help after all these years, but I believe I owe you a chance to say what you have to say.

I'll tell you that there is no relationship holding me back from meeting you, but I'm quite convinced that there is one on your end that might make this a bad idea for you. Please reconsider if that is the case. There is no need for more people to get hurt and tangled in this web. If your situation is uncomplicated and you can meet, great. I would like to keep it private and distant. The last thing I need is for anyone to see us together. Rumors travel fast around here, and for some reason they always find their way back to haunt me. I'll wait to hear from you and see if there is a time that works for both of us.

Charlotte

I told him I'd meet him. I told him I was willing to talk to him. I'm a little stunned. I'm not even sure if that was the right thing to do.

Deep down inside, I believe he's married. The sad part is that I believe I'd still meet with him even if he was.

Not because of a relationship interest, but to oblige his request. Who was I to take moral high ground with him now?

I should ask Glenda, though. No, I can't ask her. I've put so much on her plate already. I told her what a mess my past had been. I was enjoying my time with her helping me heal from that.

If she knew I was putting myself in harm's way again, I know she'd convince me I was wrong and talk me out of it. If I know it's wrong, why am I doing this? My assumptions could be completely wrong, and there could be no one else getting hurt.

If we did meet, where would we find a place comfortable for me? I don't want anyone to even have a small chance of seeing me with him. My parents seem to know everyone in town. The last thing I would need is for my mother to find out that we met.

I don't know why I keep thinking the confederate graveyard might be a good place to meet. It's usually only filled with people visiting Franklin, and during weekdays, it's always practically empty. But would it be morbid to even suggest that? I can't think of anywhere else that would offer a public, yet private, setting. I'm going for it. It's just as strange as the idea of us meeting, so maybe it's the perfect fit.

Charlotte,

I don't know how to answer you. All I can say is this. I'm willing to meet to resolve things I thought time would heal but hasn't.

If you're still willing to get together, I can meet any time that's easy for you and at any place you feel comfortable with. I'm not doing this to try and reconnect, so I don't want you to think I have those intentions. This is simply to resolve some things in my head.

Brett

His response made me more comfortable with the idea of seeing him again. I still didn't want to tell anyone. I was justifying meeting with him instead of paying attention to my instinct to say no.

After a few more exchanges, we planned on meeting there at 8:30 a.m. on Thursday. I can't believe this is about to happen. With him resurfacing, so many things are swirling around in my mind again.

Just as I was trying to get past everything that had been weighing me down, he shows up out of nowhere, and my mind is flooded with guilt again.

Meeting with him will either bring me deeper into that shame or help me see a way out. At this point, I'm desperate for any possibility of hope.

~ Thirty-Three ~

CASSIDY

"Hi, Cassidy. I'm Trish. Nice to meet you."

She had a beautiful smile, and I could tell that she and Nancy must share the same recipe for their "cup of joy" in the morning. It exuded from her. This was Nancy's friend, and I wanted to be careful with my words.

"Nice to meet you."

We spoke about what specialized overpriced latte we were going to get and finally ordered. I hesitantly followed her to sit down at the table. Thankfully she knew how to start the conversation.

"I'm sure this is awkward for you, so let me start. Just tell me a little about you and your husband."

She was serious. Although she was smiling, I knew she wanted to get straight to business. I shared details about how long we'd been married, how we met and how we got to this place. I was expecting her first response.

"Have you guys tried counseling?"

My body tensed up as more personal questions began.

"Yes, we went together once or twice, but I've gone alone since Brett left."

The phrase . . . *alone since Brett left* . . . kicked me.

"Did the counselor offer you help?"

"I don't think he had much of a chance to. Brett only went a couple times, and then it became clear that Brett refused to come back. From there, it became more personal help for me. When I say help, I should say that loosely. He has challenged me in ways that have caught me off guard."

"How so?"

It felt like she was pulling out my most personal secrets with a rope. She'd ask, and with little hesitation I would reveal the answer. I obviously was comfortable with her.

"I thought he was going to listen to me and teach me how to handle my broken marriage. Instead, he started to draw my attention to what he sees as the bigger crisis in my life. That is my huge void of confidence.

"He upset me with what he said, but I knew he was right. Have you ever had someone tell you something, and you knew there was something right about what they were telling you, but you wanted it to be wrong?"

Trish nodded her head and sarcastically laughed, "Way too many times."

"That is how I felt last time we met. I started to explain that my lack of confidence had to do with our marriage, and over time, Brett chipped away at it, leaving me with partially functioning self-esteem.

"The counselor didn't agree. He said that confidence and esteem are never taken from us—that they are given away. So, according to him, over nine years, I was giving away the parts I needed to keep."

Trish's eyes widened and she leaned slightly in toward me. I could tell in her eyes that she was fully engaged. "That had to have been hard to hear. Talk about stinging you with the truth. Wow!"

"Exactly. But what I didn't understand was how to ask for it back. Do I call him and ask for him to return it? Since I gave it to him, do I just take it back? It was strange to leave a counseling session feeling so confused."

She laughed as I tried to lighten the mood.

"I have to laugh when you asked if you should call him and ask for it back. But your counselor sounds wise and kind enough to not let you stay stuck.

"Sometimes we just want those we're talking with to be agreeable and sympathize with our plights. He could've told you all that because he does sympathize and understand your situation, even though it doesn't feel that way."

Great. She seemed to be just like the counselor, except she laughed more often.

"I guess that's a good way to look at it. I'm just sitting here whining to you. I've been babbling when what I've wanted is to hear what you have to say."

"You're in a hard spot, and I would have to guess that when your counselor told you those things about yourself, you felt that he was against you."

She spoke what I was wanting to keep inside. Tears began to swell in my eyes, and I questioned my agreement to meet at a public place. As if life weren't handing me enough humiliation, I was now in a coffee shop crying to a total stranger.

"Cassidy, I'm sorry you're hurting. I really am. Don't worry about the tears."

"I'm sorry. I tried to hold it back. Everything has been building up for so long, and it all decided to pour out right now."

Trish toyed with her coffee cup. I could tell she wanted to comfort me with a hug but tried with words instead.

"I had an idea of what I was going to say, but I don't think today is a good time to talk about it. I think we can discuss it later, when things settle a little bit."

I didn't want to hear it later. I wanted to pile it on right then. Maybe it would help me figure out all that I was feeling.

"Please share. I need it." Maybe I was asking too much of her. "I'm open to whatever you have to say."

Oh, crap. What did I just say that I wanted? Now that her mouth was opening, my body prepared for the blow.

"I come from the approach your counselor does, and I don't want to come across as another person against you."

"I can handle it. It might hurt a little bit, but it is worth it at this point."

"Okay." Trish chewed on her lower lip for a moment, then took a deep breath. "Let me ask you something. Before you and Brett met, what was your confidence based on? It's a strange question, I know, but try and answer it."

"Uhhhh . . . I was a good daughter for my parents. I didn't get in much trouble. I got good grades in high school and college. I graduated with an education degree. I was a pretty good person overall."

Those were things I spit out, but after searching for an answer, I didn't have one.

"What has changed since then that you don't feel as good about yourself?"

"I'm a mom now. Raising kids never seems to provide many opportunities to let you know if you're doing a good job. My role as a wife has made me completely question if I'm doing that well. My parents and I have a good relationship, but we don't communicate as much as we used to. I just don't have anything in my life right now that stands out showing that I'm good at anything."

Just hearing myself say that made me want to cry. What was I good at?

"What I'm hearing you say is that your self-esteem or self-confidence comes from what you're able to do well?"

"Simply stated, it seems that would be right. Isn't that how esteem operates?"

"Not always. So, if you can't do things well, you have no value? You have no worth?"

"I would hate to say yes, but yes would be the honest answer."

"Do you believe in God?"

I knew the twist was coming. She was about to play the God card.

"Yes, I believe. I know He's out there."

"What do you believe about Him?"

"That's hard to answer. I believe He's always watching. I believe He's aware of everything.

"Sometimes I believe He loves me. Other times I believe He's disappointed in me.

"I was raised in a way that told me the more I did right, the happier God would be with me. Now that I've done so many things the wrong way, I can't imagine where I must stand with Him."

Trish tried to hold it back, but her eyes sympathized for me. She had more compassion for me in that statement than she had the entire conversation.

"In my unprofessional opinion, your self-worth was traded for those lies, having nothing to do with anyone else. Maybe people played a role in forming your opinion of yourself, but ultimately you assumed God's opinion of you was the same as yours.

"When you described God, my heart was heavy. You described Him as a judge or a professor. Someone who had high expectations of you, and if you didn't live up to them, you would fail or be punished based on the significance of the failure."

My shoulders dropped. Was I supposed to think anything different?

"If you could imagine the exact opposite of that description, that would be much closer to the characteristics of God. If you can get rid of lies about who God is and correct your perspective of His character, your self-esteem and confidence would rise in a way you have never experienced.

"And I believe that what is happening in your marriage is a tool by which God is using to bring you closer to Him and show you who He is in ways that only He can.

"Not to hurt you, but the exact opposite—to show you how much you're loved. To show you that if you knew how much He loved you and cared for you, you would only need to focus on Him and all else will be well."

I sank deeper into my chair. I exhaled frustration and tried to breathe in hope.

"I don't want to say this, but I know you're right. I've never heard those words before or thought of anything that way, but my stomach is fluttering, and something is telling me that I need to listen to what you're saying.

"I have to share this one thing. I've never experienced anything like what I'm about to tell you, and maybe you will say I'm crazy."

"I've heard a lot of crazy, so test me."

"A couple days after I went to the counselor, I was devastated. I believe that I was more upset that day than when I started going to see the therapist to begin with. I cried on and off for days.

"This one morning, I was doing dishes and looking out the window. I think I was looking at the kids' playground we had gotten for them last Christmas, and I started thinking about upcoming holidays. I began to get even more depressed when I questioned if the kids would even have their parents together for Christmas.

"Sunshine came through the trees, as it always does, and then the rays seemed to touch my face. It wasn't the type of sunshine that forced you to cover your eyes because of its brightness. It felt soft and warm."

I was looking for a reaction from her, but her face was still anxiously engaged. I then took a leap of faith and shared my crazy.

"My body froze a bit. I closed my eyes. Relief fell over my heart, and heat on my face warmed my soul. It felt so strange. I opened my eyes, and the sun still shone on me. The trees moved with a slight breeze, but the motion never obstructed the sunshine.

"I just stood there, looking out that window, knowing for the first time I was experiencing something of God that I've never encountered before. Because of that, I reached out to Nancy, who led me to you. I was expecting to be corrected and be told my ways are flawed. I wasn't expecting this."

I did it. I shared. I felt breathless. I had let out months of air and weeks' worth of thoughts that had been swirling around in my head with no answers. But there was an internal instinct that things were moving toward something that was going to lead me to healing. I had no idea how, but I knew that I was eventually going to be okay.

By this one meeting with Trish that God led me to, the cloud of confusion had begun to lift. He had let me see the full circle of information revealed to me. I had been hurt and discouraged in the process, but when it was put together like a jigsaw puzzle, I was grateful for what God had shown me.

Trish offered to meet again for coffee, and she also suggested going to a Bible study. I could learn more and connect with some other women.

I'd have the opportunity to meet new friends who'd have advice after going through similar experiences. I'd also get to learn about God and the intimidating Bible.

But the real reason was that they had childcare, and I'd get a couple hours to just sit. I know that probably wasn't the right reason, but honesty is honesty, and that was my truth.

My first study was the week after meeting Trish. The ladies there seemed to have it all together, but they were kind and made me feel so welcome the minute I stepped foot inside.

The lady who hosted the group at her beautiful house had the warmest smile and most comforting hug. The atmosphere was relaxing and comfortable.

I tried to be open-minded, yet cynicism crept into my thoughts after we gathered in her living room and sat in a stereotypical support circle.

Do you really think these ladies live like this? Are they happy all the time? If so, they must have amazing marriages and sit around reading the Bible all day. They all are nice, but I doubt they really like me. They don't even know me, yet they greeted me with more excitement than my friends do. It has to be fake just to make me feel good.

I just realized I didn't even check out anything about this group before I came. What if this is a cult? What if they are just wanting me to join their group to gain another cult member?

I finally had to tell my mind to shut up and give the study a chance. New habits were hard to start, and new friends were even harder to make. Trying to do both at once was a little overwhelming.

The study started, and the teacher was captivating. She was so sincere, that I wanted to pay attention. It felt as if she were teaching me alone in that full room. She spoke of something I had never heard of before.

That would be an obvious statement, since I hardly know anything about the Bible, but she spoke about Noah and the ark. Who hasn't heard that story? It is almost the most popular nursery-room theme—the ark, two animals of every kind, the rainbow, the dove with the branch, the flood.

I would've never thought it would be used to open my eyes to see God from a different angle. She started with the obvious. Noah was building an ark. Then came details I'd never known.

It had never rained. Noah was building a boat for a flood, but it had never rained, not one drip.

How does one hear God so clearly that he knew to make something for an event that had never happened before? On top of it, God gave him directions a little at a time. He never gave Noah the full picture of what was happening or why it was happening. He only listened to what God had commanded him to do.

God gave him specific measurements, and he created it to those specs. God told him the exact type of wood to use, and Noah traveled far to get the exact materials.

People he had known his entire life taunted and teased Noah about his crazy idea. They thought it was nonsense. They ridiculed him for his relentless faith of something no one else could understand.

That information was enough to send me home with my mind blown. Would I ever be able to hear God's voice like that?

After the teaching, there was an opportunity for listeners to discuss how they related to the message. My mind had already been overwhelmed by the lesson, but the discussion brought more surprises.

The women weren't as perfect as I had assumed. They had rough marriages, some falling apart right before them. Others had children addicted to drugs.

More than one had been through abuse. A few had illnesses they weren't sure they were going to recover from. Yet, their dispositions never hinted at any struggles.

How did these women walk through horrible fires with smiles on their faces? They all astonished me.

Many knew God. Many heard God's voice. Many were walking through hell on earth yet believed beyond any doubt that God was with them. How in the hell did they know that? How were they making it?

Meeting for two hours a week wasn't the answer. Even if you threw in another hour and a half on the weekends for church, that wasn't the answer either. It wasn't where they met together—it was Who they met with when they were alone.

Culture had taught me that I should change course when things started to get hard and my own happiness was in jeopardy. It taught me to seek those things that made me feel good, as life is short, and we all must enjoy what we can.

These women stood in opposition of what culture had taught me. Mind blown once again.

The gathering ended, and I went to pick up my Sydney. Her hug was the security I needed in that moment. She was the only piece of me that stayed the same after that morning. Everything else seemed to be flipped over.

All I knew was that God was doing something, and it was going to be good. Something was also telling me that I was going to need the women I'd met that day in the near future. But, as to what that meant, I didn't have a clue.

~ Thirty-Four ~

GLENDA

My Lord,

I come to You this morning, and I don't even know where to begin. I don't know if I should just apologize and ask for forgiveness or try to defend myself.

Ultimately, I'll ask for forgiveness anyway. You know everything about me, so You already know my answer. At seventy-five years old, I would think that I would be over trying to justify my actions, but I must be stubborn.

A couple days ago, I went to visit Charles and Sarah. I spent the afternoon and part of the evening with them. I was missing them so much. These last thirty years without them have been difficult, but I don't have to tell You. You know my heart more than I do.

What I do have to tell You is that this last year has been more painful than others. I might be miscalculating because I'm so far removed from the first few years, but as for the last ten, this one has been the most agonizing.

I'm seventy-five years old. I'm all alone. I have no family left to enjoy things with. The family I have now is a combination of people I've met since being alone.

My parents have passed, and I watched them struggle with their last breaths. They died within two years of each other. My mother first. Her funeral evoked emotions I didn't believe I had left.

My mom was there for me like no other after the accident. She came and lived with me for months. She would bring me food and check on me.

There were days I refused to get out of bed and days I tried not to, but she would demand I do something. She knew if I didn't start to put one foot in front of the other, I might never move forward.

She lay with me. She cried with me. She rubbed my head as if I were a child.

At her funeral, I realized that through her eyes, I was still a child, and though I had suffered great loss, there was nothing she could do to take the pain away.

I never had to experience that with my own child. Sarah had been through some trials, but nothing agonizing that I'd taken upon myself to fix. Any hurt I felt for Sarah was only mine.

I was sad she wouldn't experience dreams I thought she'd reach. I was sad that she'd never be a mom. I was sad that her dream to be a nurse would never happen. I was sad that she'd never walk down the aisle as a beautiful bride.

I had dreams a mom foresees when she first holds her baby girl, but most of those would never take place. That was sadness that only I held for her, a cruel sadness named grief.

After my mom passed, grief came to visit again. I didn't know who I would talk to. Who would have lunch and coffee dates with me? Who would go to the movies with me?

It was just my dad and me after she left us. He loved me so much. My dad always protected me, always looked out for me, and always wanted me to be happy.

He knew Charles loved me, and that's why he loved Charles. He never paid attention to anything else, except for how the man I'd chosen treated me. Dad didn't care if my husband was smart or talented or wealthy or anything else. He just wanted to know that the man he was giving me to loved me as much as he did.

Communication was my weak link with my dad. My mom usually filled in the gaps of our relationship. With her gone, we both felt lost, but my dad and I eventually figured it out.

One day I visited my dad, and he seemed upset. It had been a while since my mom had passed. After settling into a conversation, he said some things I'll never forget.

"Glenda, I need to talk to you. I need you to hear me. I want to tell you that I'm sorry."

His face dropped and he could hardly even look at me. He looked like he was hurting.

"Daddy, you don't need to apologize for anything. What are you talking about?"

He moved up to the edge of his seat cushion, leaning over toward me.

"Glenda, just let me finish. I want to tell you that I'm sorry for not being there for you after the accident. I should've been there for you, and I wasn't."

Tears started to fill his eyes, and he was trying to control his voice from breaking.

"Your mom went and spent all that time with you. I knew you needed your mother, but the truth is that I was scared to watch you suffer and not be able to do anything to stop it.

"I'm your dad, your protector. I was supposed to be able to make the pain stop. I was supposed to bandage all your wounds and fight off anyone who hurt you."

He couldn't stop the tears, and I couldn't stand to see him suffering. I grabbed his aged hand as he continued.

"After the accident and that horrible pain, I had no bandage to offer you. I had no one to fight on your behalf. I just had to bear the knowledge of your suffering, and there was nothing I could do about it.

"I would talk to your mom and ask how you were doing. She told me about days you wouldn't get out of bed. She'd be excited when those days were interrupted by you going outside for a walk. But they were followed by many more when you would avoid the sun again."

He stopped for a minute to just cry. I started to join him, just hearing how sorry he was.

"Sometimes, she and I would sit on the phone and cry. Neither of us knew what to do for you. Neither of us could bring them back for you. We couldn't rewind that day and make sure it ended up differently.

"The difference between her and me was that she could be there for you and stay with you. She could face the pain and walk through it with you.

"I was too scared to. I was too selfish to let go of my pride and break down with you. I still wanted to be strong for you, but I knew I couldn't if I was there. For that, I'm sorry. If there's one thing in this life I regret, that's it."

He stopped again and leaned in to hug me. I embraced him and tried to hug him enough to let him know it was okay. He kept crying in my shoulder until he resumed with what he wanted to say. He sat back and began again.

"I just want you to know that I love you. You're precious to me. You have always been my baby girl. You have treated me with love and kindness like no other. You're always patient with me, and you always take such good care of me. I just wish that I could've done the same for you when you needed me most. . . ."

Tears flooded my dad's face, and inconsolable crying came again. I tried and tried to explain to him that I knew he was there for me. I knew he loved me. Just because he wasn't there physically didn't mean that I didn't know he was hurting for me.

My mom had told me then that my dad was in agony just knowing I was hurting. I knew my dad enough to know that if there would've been something he could've done to change the situation, he would have. But there was nothing he could've done. There was nothing anyone could've done.

He got up out of his chair and moved toward the hutch that was near him. He reached into a drawer and pulled out a small gift.

"Here. I want you to have this."

"What is it?"

"A gift. Open it."

The aged navy-blue box was tarnished. The mechanism to open it was tight. When I finally got it open, I saw a tarnished silver heart-shaped locket. I was stunned. I couldn't think of the last time my dad had actually given me a gift from him alone.

"Thank you, Daddy. It's beautiful." I started to put it on, and he stopped me.

"It isn't meant to be just a necklace. I was reading something the other day. I think it was a newspaper or a magazine article. I don't remember it all exactly, but what I do recall is that a woman was telling her story of a tragedy she'd experienced. Her words and details immediately made me think of you and all that you've been through.

"She said happy memories comforted her, but one thing in particular helped her daily. She spoke of a locket that she wore with her loved ones' pictures in it. When she would get upset, she would touch the locket or open it to see their faces. She said it didn't erase her grief, but it filled in just a little bit of emptiness that she reserved for them. It stuck with me.

"Shortly after hearing this, I was in this antique store, looking for one of those old cast-iron model cars I always like to look at, and right in front of me was this beautiful locket. I immediately remembered the story and wanted it for you. I released the latch, and it swung open beautifully."

I was holding the beautiful locket but crying because my daddy had loved me so much that he wanted to help relieve my pain.

"So, that's the meaning behind it, and I want you to have it—for whenever you might experience a moment of grieving. It's the least I could do for you after all these years."

It was the most meaningful thing he had ever done, and I treasured that necklace. When I got home later, I found perfect pictures of Charles and Sarah and slid them inside. In a strange way, when I put the necklace on, it felt like my dad's arms were wrapping around me too. It was a precious gift and a memorable moment.

That conversation ended up being one that would bring us closer together—and one of the last. He passed away two weeks later. That conversation was a gift that You gave me before You took another piece of my heart to heaven. That necklace was a beautiful gift that would always allow me to remember my dad's love for me.

That funeral was harder than my mom's. Not because my dad meant more, but because his death represented the end of my family.

Michael Anthony James was the end of one side of my family tree. Charles Joseph Ryan was the end of the other. My dad's death represented the end of my lineage. There was no one left except me, and I didn't want to be there either.

I used to think about people in hospitals fighting for their lives. I would offer to instantly trade places with them so I could go on to be with my family in heaven. But that wasn't Your plan for me. Your plan was for me to stay here, living out the purpose of my lineage.

So, back to where I was talking about my visit to see Charles. While I was there, I was talking to him and Sarah. I was telling him how I was ready to come see him. If I worked hard at it, I could feel his arms around me at times.

Then, we began to talk about something I don't often talk about at all. I purposely push it out of my mind any chance I get. We began to talk about the accident. I began to recall the surrounding circumstances of losing my family.

I hadn't gone to that dark place in a while, but for some reason, it all came flooding back when I went to see Charles this time.

I remembered the details again. Pulling up to the scene of flashing lights and horrific wreckage, I heard crying, but had no idea where it was coming from. I remember officers asking for my name, warning me to stay back, seeing blankets dropped over two masses that I assumed were deceased bodies. I never guessed for a minute they belonged to me.

I believed that mine would've been the ones in the ambulance, racing away for help, but they weren't. They were eventually brought to the hospital with dreaded white sheets over their bodies.

I was distraught. So much was taken from me. Everything that my world revolved around was gone.

Yes, my mother came to help, and what a blessing that was, but she wasn't Charles. It wasn't my husband holding me at night as we fell asleep. It wasn't Sarah who would sit with me in the morning and have coffee.

My house was empty. Nothing in the home changed, yet it was empty. There was no laughter. There was no joy.

I became so angry at that driver. His selfish act punished me. Our lives had never crossed paths, yet I paid for his recklessness.

I didn't care about his circumstances. I didn't care about reasons people would say why he was drinking. That wasn't my problem. I wasn't going to allow what he had done to be minimized by the why behind it.

He drank—then drank some more. Jason took his keys and got behind the wheel of his car. Then he crashed his vehicle into Charles and Sarah, taking their lives. The man stole my husband's and daughter's last breaths, but he lived. And the story stops there.

I thought of every defiling act that I could've done to that young man. I didn't care if I embarrassed myself. But reasoning would set in, and I'd pull my thoughts together. I walked around angry, bitter and disenchanted for months.

At the trial's beginning, I thought if I stared at him long enough, his eyes would catch fire. Like when we were kids playing with science. If we held a magnifying glass up to a leaf and let the sun radiate on it long enough, the heat would eventually get hot enough to make the leaf burn. My glare was so intense, I thought I'd be able to make something singe on him.

He was charged with two counts of vehicular manslaughter. During the trial, he cried almost every day. I wanted to tell him he had no right to feel sorry for himself. I didn't want to feel any pity for him, and I definitely didn't want the jury to either.

About halfway through the trial, I remember crying on my knees at the edge of my bed. I was so destroyed. I asked You how this young man could be so reckless in taking Charles and Sarah from me.

I asked You what I could've done differently that day for them to never have encountered him. If there was nothing that could've changed the timing, could I have made a different decision to go along with them? I wondered if we all could've perished together instead of me slowly dying a little bit every day without them.

And then You spoke. You told me it wasn't Jason who took them. It was You.

Everything in life passes through Your hands, even the most painful parts. Nothing that I could've done would've changed anything. Their time was done here. They'd run the race You'd set out for them.

Resentment I felt toward that young man lightened, but the hurt I experienced from Your words took my breath away. In my most raw emotions, You asked me to forgive him. Forgive him? Forgive *him*? I swore I heard You wrong.

I was so angry. I had met You on my knees for Your comfort. Instead, You challenged me. In that one encounter, I heard that not only had You planned their time to leave me, but that I needed to forgive the man who helped You take them.

I couldn't even stay in Your presence. I was so angry. I don't have to tell You, because You already knew. My anger toward Jason was redirected toward You.

It made no sense to me. How could I be angry at God? The God who had seen me through so much and blessed me my whole life. All of that was erased because I didn't trust You any longer. How could I?

What punishment did You have for me next? What tragedy was waiting around the next corner? Then I grieved three relationships—Charles, Sarah and You. My husband and daughter would never be able to engage with me again, but You were different.

I missed my time in Your presence. I missed praying to You and leaning on You. I missed You showing me Your truths and revelations. I missed being used by You for Your purpose. Yet, I knew that You were always there waiting for me to come back to You.

You never left. Only I did. I remember my friend coming to see me because she was worried about me. She knew my faith had weakened and struggled. She came over and brought coffee for me. We sat for a while and tried to talk about superficial things, but she couldn't leave it there.

She asked if God had been good to me before the accident. Of course You had. She asked me if I had trusted You before the accident, and You know I did. She then asked me what had changed. I didn't answer. She said her grandmother had told her something once that had always helped her, and she hoped it would do the same for me.

"God is either good or He isn't. You either trust Him or you don't."

I didn't respond. I didn't say a word. I stared off and cried. She hugged me and comforted me, but I was still speechless.

I thanked her and told her I needed to be alone. I pulled up my feet into my chair, wrapped my arms around my legs, and cried into my knees with my head bowed.

Then, I heard You whisper, "Bring your anger to me, the same way you used to bring your gratitude. I'm bigger than your anger. I can walk with you through this the same way I'll walk with you through everything else."

That was one of the hardest days, but one of the best. I could feel my body surrender to the fact that You were God and I was not. Your ways are higher than my ways, and Your thoughts are higher than my thoughts. You loved me, and You would never harm me, and if harm would come my way, You would deliver me through it.

I've always heard that the hardest lesson to learn is one you thought you already knew. I know what You're wanting me to revisit, and I can hardly write the word down. I have a harder time even saying it—forgiveness.

So, what are You asking of me? Why is it that when I ask You a question, deep down inside I have the answer, but I don't want to acknowledge it? I thought I forgave him. I thought I had passed this point. I laid it down at the cross over and over again until the pain went away. Are you calling me to forgive deeper? This is so painful.

Lord, I ask You . . . Lord, help me ask You . . . Lord, I ask You to let Jason off the hook for what he did. I ask that justice he might face be surrendered by my petition.

Oh, my gosh! I can't believe I said that. I can't believe I wrote that. I asked You to set him free.

I've held my tongue and refrained from revenge for so long because I knew that in due time You would bring me justice. I knew that You would bring judgment on him and free me of my pain.

Yet, thirty years later, I'm sitting here, and I'm asking You to free him of his pain and for his punishment to be rescinded. It's over. The case has been closed. It feels so unfair, yet it feels so freeing. How could I feel the same at once?

Thank You, Lord, for helping me through. Wait! I don't feel as if You're finished. Oh no. I know You aren't finished. This is when I want to close this journal and run. What is it, Lord?

I want you to go see him.

Go see who? Charles?

Jason . . .

Lord, please no. Please, please, no. You can't be asking me this. I can't. There is no way that I can.

Why? Why are You doing this? All I want is to come home, and You're asking me for more.

Go see him.

I don't even know where he is. Really, I don't even want to know where he is.

Yes, you do.

I was reflecting on the pain I used to be in and how happy I was that You saw me through it, only to continue on and find out You have another painful thing You're calling me to do. When will this stop? Haven't I been through enough?

Hello? Hello? I guess that means I get no answer.

Okay. I just said that I trust You, and I know that You're good. How do I take that back ten minutes later? I can't. So, I'll pray and process, and eventually do what You ask.

Please, help me.

All my love,
Glenda

~ Thirty-Five ~

CHARLOTTE

December 14, 2012

Dear Diary,

Here I am to unload on you again. Thanks for always being here for me to show you my hidden places.

I've been in mental turmoil after talking with Brett. Self-deprecation is taunting me. I met with Glenda, and I shared additional details. I told her specifics about my relationship with Brett and how I had hurt him, almost intentionally, for what I thought would be his own good. I just didn't realize it would cut me deeper.

I finally told her about my friendship with Joe and how we had gotten closer throughout college. I had told you about the night things changed between us. It was after that party I'd escaped from, when he came to my apartment knowing something was wrong but accepting that I didn't want to talk about it.

I shared with her what I could. The truth is that there is so much more than even what I told her.

When we said our goodbyes the next morning, I walked away with a slight tingling in my gut, a weaker form of proverbial "butterflies."

We talked a couple days later, and there was nothing strained after what had happened. We made plans to go to dinner that week at my favorite burger joint near campus.

We started with superficial conversation and ended up laughing so much that my mouth and stomach hurt.

The tone slightly changed when Joey turned and asked how I was doing after the party. . . . I really didn't want to share. He'd never been afraid to ask hard questions, but this time his look indicated he was more invested in the answer.

"I'm okay. It was just a crazy night, and I probably overexaggerated some. I just got worked up over nothing. I'm sorry that I dragged you into that."

He shifted his body forward and looked more serious than I'd expected.

"Charlie—really? That's what you're going with? You overexaggerated? I was there. I saw pain and fear in your eyes."

He was getting worked up and I couldn't understand why.

"You can ignore it if you need to, but don't lie to me. Tell me you don't want to talk about it. Tell me it's none of my business. But don't tell me it was nothing."

My throat started to close, and my eyes were ready to water again. I was pissed, but my heart also wrenched remembering that night again.

"Okay . . . then I'll go with the option of telling you that it's none of your business. Is that acceptable? Will it make a difference, or even stop you from asking again?"

"It probably won't. You're right. I've seen you put up walls for years. I've yet to grow tired of it, but you're starting to convince me it's what you want."

I couldn't figure out why he was so upset, but it was apparent that a new Joey was emerging.

"And what do you think it is that I want?"

"To be left alone. To isolate yourself so that you can continue to hide and hold on to something that has pulled you away from the person you used to be."

"Joey . . . why . . . ?"

"Why? What does that mean? Why what?"

"Why do you care? Why do you have to ask?"

I didn't want to be weak again. I didn't want to open up and cry and let him see all of me. I wanted to run.

"Because . . . truthfully . . . I like you."

"Well, I know that."

"No, Charlotte. I like you in a grade school type of way. As in, I like you–like you."

There it was. The bomb I didn't see coming.

"Uhm . . . I don't know what to say to that either."

"You don't have to respond. I just wanted to answer your question about why I cared. There it is."

"Okay. Good point. The room feels like it's starting to spin. Can we finish this conversation later?"

I tried all I could to leave as my heart was racing.

"There's nothing to finish. You asked me a question, and I answered it truthfully because I couldn't hide it anymore."

"Okay, you know what? Let's get out of here and go somewhere else. I don't want to be here anymore. I don't care where we go, but let's just go."

We left and headed to the baseball fields. There was a game going on, and we figured we would stop by and see a few innings. The walk was awkward. Once we got there, we stood down the right-field line, slightly leaning over the railing.

We stirred up a light conversation, but uncomfortable silence returned. The discussion at the restaurant caused tension between us.

I have no idea why, but everything he wanted to know jumped out of my mouth.

"Brett and I had sex before we left for college. It was spring break of our senior year."

There was my own bomb to drop.

"Wait—what?" Joey tried to interrupt, but I just kept talking over him.

"It was stupid of us. We promised ourselves never to let it get to that point, and fear sucked us in. We were scared we'd never be the same after we left for college.

"A few weeks passed, and we got news that we were both going to Vanderbilt. We were so excited, yet so disappointed in ourselves. After fearing the worst and acting on it, we neglected to see the best possibility. A couple weeks later, we got more news. I was pregnant."

Tears started to come. Joey put his arm around me and led me out of the stadium. We just started walking on campus, and I kept talking.

"Yes, I got pregnant. We got pregnant. However you want to say it or see it. We were shocked, panicked, scared, upset, disappointed, ashamed, guilty. All of it, rolled up into a huge, ugly mess, created a dark shadow over our relationship."

Joey was listening because his face showed it.

"With what we both had at stake, I decided it was best to have an abortion, but it wasn't what he wanted at all. When I made up my mind, I shut Brett out. I didn't want to see him. I didn't want to see his disappointment in me."

Streams of tears were now flowing down my face.

"He said we could work it out. He said we could change our plans and start our lives together sooner than expected. I couldn't stand to disappoint our parents. I couldn't bear thoughts of him passing up school for me. I couldn't think of disappointing my future coaches and turning down a scholarship. These were all stupid things in hindsight, but they were choices of a scared eighteen-year-old girl."

I stopped walking and just wiped my face. I had to take a deep breath.

"Sorry. This is a lot—I know."

"No, I'm glad you're finally sharing all this that you have been holding in. It all is starting to make more sense."

"Brett hated me for it. He took me to the office for the procedure, but still begged me not to go through with it. After it was all done, we cried the whole way home, but not with each other.

"I looked out my window and streamed tears. He looked ahead and did the same. He dropped me off, and I mustered up parting words to say to him.

"I apologized to him. I told him he'd find someone who'd love him enough to take away this pain, but it wasn't me. I made it clear we were over and that was it. We never spoke again."

As I was crying, Joey tried to comfort me. He rubbed my back and tried to hug me. I pushed away enough so I could finish my story.

"Fast-forward to the other night when I saw him with that someone. His body language told me he'd fallen in love with her. I was so happy for him, but that knowledge still stabbed me deeper than I expected. It was just that final cut."

"Charlotte, I've never been one to be at a loss for words, but I don't know what to say right now."

"I didn't share this with you for a response. I did it so you can understand why I've changed."

"I just want to say that I'm sorry that you went through all that. I wish I could've been there for you. I wish Brett would've told me so I could've been there for him. I hate to know that my friends went through something so devastating alone."

He seemed genuinely hurt that neither one of us trusted him enough to share.

"I can't speak for him, but I felt like I deserved the punishment of isolation. I was stupid. I made decisions that destroyed any dream I had.

"One thing I know now is every choice has consequences, and you have to live with them. There is no pity to be had. It was a conscious choice, and I knew what I was doing. I hold myself accountable."

"You were so young, though. You're being hard on yourself. Did your parents ever find out?"

"Yes. I guess my parents had a right to practically disown me. After all, they had not raised me to be that girl. They had raised the church-going young lady who loved youth group and considered ministry in her future. They raised the honors student and soccer star.

"They didn't raise the daughter who ended up having sex and an abortion in high school. And they didn't raise the child who would've had sex, given up her college scholarships, and had a baby instead. No one would know if I chose to end the pregnancy, so the abortion seemed to have been the least embarrassing option for them."

Tears wouldn't stop flowing as I was endlessly divulging memories.

"What you just said paralyzed me. You aren't believing that because of what you did, you aren't accepted by God anymore . . . are you?" He said it with such a slow and leveled tone that I knew he was shocked by what he heard.

"Joe, please don't go there. I don't want to go down that road."

"Charlotte, I think it is necessary to go there. What you're saying is a lie, and I'm stunned you'd believe it."

He was now focused on the point even more. His voice became firmer, and his inflection was more confrontational.

"Look, I understand that what I did was the most grotesque thing I could have ever done against God. I killed a life that belonged to Him. I destroyed a child conceived by having sex, not a miraculous, beautiful Mary moment. No, it was a moment of stupidity all on my own."

My voice cracked and I was getting more defensive as I went on.

"My mother made it clear that God was disgusted with me and He'd want nothing more to do with me. Her words still ring in my mind, and I believe her. I used to think nothing could separate me from Him, but I found something that did. All those years in church were for what? They couldn't keep me from sabotaging myself."

Joey just looked at me and took a while to respond. I looked right back at him.

"Charlotte, out of all you've said, those words are the saddest. You think that God wants nothing to do with you? You think He's turned from you? All those years in church weren't meant to make you perfect. They were for a time like this, when you lose your way."

"Lose my way? I killed a baby."

"Wait. That's not the point. Those times growing up were for you to know Him so well that you knew that no matter what you ever did, nothing could ever separate you from Him. It was so that you could always return to Him and know the truth of how much He loves you."

"Yeah, well, He and I will never be the same. I can't face God with what I did. I can't crawl back and expect our relationship to be like it was. He doesn't need me."

"He's not like your mom. He never shut you out. He never disowned you. That was her. That was your mom and dad. Don't let them change who you know God to be. Please."

"Just stop. What you fail to see is that I don't know any of them anymore—not my mom, not my dad and definitely not God. And that's okay for me. I don't want to face all of that again.

"Can we just end it there? I told you about the past, and now you don't have to wonder. I don't want to get into the psychology of it right now. My head hurts just from talking and revealing all of that."

Luckily, he listened.

After that night, we never discussed the issue for months. Our bond grew slowly. I believe we both knew it was heading toward a deeper relationship, one that came close to the line of romance.

We cared for each other. We knew what the other liked and would surprise each other occasionally. That is actually how the tide turned for us.

One night we were getting together to go to dinner. Joey picked me up, and on the way I pulled something out of my purse.

"Oh, Joey. I picked these up for you. I saw them at the gas station, and I figured I'd surprise you."

It was a simple, general statement made in a joking manner. I had gotten him purple-packaged Skittles. He laughed and was smiling in exchange. But then it went further.

"Charlie, that's why I love you. I was craving some of those yesterday. You always know what I like."

My face shifted immediately. He said it in a joking tone of voice, but it didn't feel like a joke. I tried to act like I didn't hear anything.

"I'm sorry. I didn't . . ."

His expression quickly changed to one of embarrassment. I quickly interrupted to try and save him.

"It's okay—no big deal." I shrugged and tried to offer a convincing smile, but I don't think I pulled it off. "So, where are we headed?" I had to change the subject as fast as possible. It was awkward, and I hated the shift in the space between us. Instantly, the elephant was sitting between us again, and it was pushing both of us out of the car.

This time it was his turn to remove it from between us.

Joe was staring down toward his lap and timidly lifted his face and turned in my direction. "Can I be honest with you for a minute, Charlie?"

Inside, I wanted to scream *no!* But I stifled that reaction. "I don't know. Your honesty scares me. Whenever you start a conversation that way, words that follow often sting."

"If this hurts, then I'm way off base. Charlotte, what I just said was a mistake. I didn't mean to say that."

"I know. We just covered that. I said it was no big deal—"

"I'm trying to say I didn't mean to say it just then. But I do. I *do* love you."

I just stared at him. My heart clenched. I knew we were flirting with romance, but I had been in denial that we were never going to cross over into more than friends. His statement tore the veil off my eyes.

I didn't want to address it. I didn't want to commit to telling him that I loved him and establish something intimate.

I had talked to him for over three years about my inability to be deeply personal, and here he was attempting to lead me into just that.

"Joe, why? Why are you doing this?"

"That wasn't the answer I would've put in the bucket of possible responses, but I'll try again. I love you. I love everything about you. I enjoy every moment we spend together. I look forward to every time we plan to see each other.

"I was somewhat attracted to you years ago, but I avoided even considering you in that way. I've known you since you were in elementary school, and you'd been my best friend's girlfriend."

"Joe, please . . ."

"Please let me finish. Our time together has forced my view of you to change. My original perception of you as that young girl or

Brett's girlfriend disappeared. In college, I began seeing you as my best friend, and I spent more time with you than anyone else.

"Each time we hung out, I fought seeing you that way. If you want me to be specific, the turning point came the night of that party. I knew then how much I cared for you."

Tears welled up in my eyes because I had felt how much he cared and knew how much I cared for him in return.

"You left and I had to find you. I had to know that you were okay. I saw your face, and I could read your body language. You were suffering, and I couldn't stay there knowing that.

"When I did, you were in pain. You didn't need me to listen, but I knew you needed me there. That is all I wanted for you."

"Joe, I know you cared about me. It meant a lot to me."

"You asked me to stay the night. I knew the invitation wasn't related to romance. It was a need to know that someone was there for you and you weren't alone. That is when I wanted to be that person for you. And equally, I wanted you to be that person for me. So, when you ask me why, that is why."

"Joe, this isn't how this was supposed to turn out. We were supposed to be friends and not shift into this complicated area."

I didn't know what to say nor how to pull it together. I was facing two of my greatest fears. On one hand, I feared that I couldn't enter another relationship. I was so scared to feel all those things again. I was scared of what I could do to him and what Joe could do to me. I trusted him, but I still hadn't trusted myself.

On the other hand, I feared losing him. If I told Joe I didn't feel the same, there was a good chance that our friendship was over. If it didn't end right then, it eventually would. Friendships never last long when one likes the other and feelings aren't mutual.

If our friendship ended, I would've been left with no one. I had gotten used to having fewer people in my daily life, but Joey was a main character. We did everything together. I was facing losing another person I cared for.

So, what was it going to be? Which fear was stronger? Was it going to be fear of getting hurt later, or fear of being all alone now?

The part that made me love him in the first place was present until the very end. He always saw through my wall of words. I could tell him things, trying to protect myself, and he would call me out and tell me I was lying to myself.

And the part I hated was that he was always right. He could read me like no other. And that night was no different. I told him I didn't want a relationship. I told him I didn't have feelings for him like that. I lied as best I could, and he saw through it again.

"Charlotte, I don't believe one word of what you're saying. I know you have feelings for me. I'm not an idiot. This isn't a scenario where I read your signals wrong. This is a scenario where you're scared of having a relationship because of things in your past, and it's easier for you to deny you like me at all. I cannot believe you're doing this."

"Doing what, Joe? All I'm saying is that I like you as a friend, but beyond that, there is nothing there. We have been friends forever, and that is how I intend to keep it. You have been one of my best friends, and over these last couple years, my only true friend. I've cherished that. I don't want to lose that."

"You know, this is interesting. Since college, I've realized that you always had a problem with denial. Being on the outside of your inability to open up was all right. When you were hurting and denied it, it was easy for me to see your pain and be patient for you to be honest with me.

"When I knew you were hiding something but saying that nothing was wrong, it was easy to wait and care for you through it.

"This time it isn't because your denial is personal. I love you and I care about you. I know you feel the same. If you tell me I'm wrong,

I won't believe you. I know you too well and know what you're doing right now."

"You think you know me? You think you're right? You have no idea who I am or what I feel."

"You're only trying to push me away. I know the truth. If you want to lie to yourself, I'll let you believe what you want."

He started up the car, then turned it around.

"Where are you going?"

"I would assume our night is over. I figured you'd want to go home and isolate."

How in the hell did he know that? It actually pissed me off.

A terrible feeling suddenly came over me when I thought that getting out of his car was going to be like many years before when I got out of Brett's car. He glanced at me long enough that I caught sadness in his eyes. We drove there in silence. There was no way to transition back into a superficial conversation.

We pulled into my apartment complex parking lot, and the rubble of my heart was being crushed further. I wanted to tell him I was lying. I wanted to take back what I'd said and feel the comfort of his arms around me. His sterile look made me think he was mad at me. I wanted to make him happy and give him what he wanted, but how long would that happiness last?

"I'm sorry. I'm really sorry. I don't think you understand. I know you think I'm rejecting you, but I'm not. I'm protecting you."

"Let's at least be honest. This isn't about me. This is about protecting yourself."

"No, really. I'll admit this. I'm a broken girl. I only have pieces of my heart left from these last painful years. That's all I have. Maybe you're right. I never want to feel what I felt back then, and no relationship can ever guarantee that I won't be hurt.

"You're right. There is a motive of self-preservation. You're an amazing guy. You deserve someone who is just as loving, caring, kind and encouraging as yourself, and I'll never be able to be that person."

"You can stop with excuses whenever you're ready to."

"They aren't excuses. Plus, I'm leaving after college. I'm going as far away from this place as I can. This town just reminds me of the worst of me. These last years here have been the loneliest times of my life. I just can't do it anymore. I've reached my limit of pain I can handle."

"I hardly have a response to that, except that you're wrong. You can't see what I see. You make me feel loved. You make me feel cared for. You're just as encouraging to me as I am to you, but you can't accept that. Your shame blocks any view of your goodness, and nothing can change that.

"I get you wanting to leave, but it won't help. You can run as far away from here as possible, but how you feel about yourself won't change. All that you're running from will eventually join you again."

His self-righteousness was getting hostile.

"Thanks. I appreciate your analysis."

"I love you, and I'll leave it at that. If you ever change your mind, I'll be here. If not, I wish you the best and hope that one day you can see that you're so much more than what you give yourself permission to believe."

Was he serious? Was he really willing to just leave it at that? I expected more of a resistance. I expected it to be me to tell him we couldn't be friends, but I never expected to hear it from him.

"So, this is it? We can't be friends either?"

"No. I can't. The same way that you want to protect yourself, I don't want to put myself out there to be temporarily used. You just said you want to run away and leave everything behind. That includes me. That includes our friendship. Does it matter to you if it ends a little sooner?"

His voice couldn't have been any firmer. Everything about him in that moment was stoic. The emotionless response crushed me more than I expected.

"I guess this is an unexpected goodbye. From the bottom of my heart, I want to thank you for all you have been to me these last few years. Without you, I don't know where I'd be. You're—you were—my best friend. Please know that this hurts me as much as it is hurting you. I-I-I'm sorry." Tears joined the goodbye party.

"Sadly, I enjoyed it just as much."

I opened the car door to get out and just sat there with it open. I began to get out, slowly letting one foot meet the ground and then the other. I turned to get out, but as I was about to lift myself out, I turned back toward him to look at him one more time.

Everything in me wanted to stay in that car. I didn't want to stand and watch him drive away. We stared at each other for a time that lasted seconds but felt like minutes. We both knew this was a terrible ending to a really good thing.

Speechless, I turned back toward the door and painstakingly lifted myself out. I got out and whispered, "Goodbye."

I shut the door and backed away from the car. He pulled out and only gave me a slight nod. I knew that was the last I would see of him.

After he drove far enough away, I sat on the curb in the dark night, trees swaying behind me. I hoped I blended in with the woods, because I was weeping. The building I didn't want to go back to was in front of me. I knew once I went into my apartment, it would hurt even more.

That was my best friend who drove away. He rescued me from the pit of hell and had brought me to a place where I could feel again.

But, when he asked me to feel more, I quit on him. All these years, he never quit on me. He never gave up on me, until I forced him to.

What the hell was wrong with me? I didn't think I could sabotage myself any more than I already had, but I was wrong. I was so tangled in a web of stupidity and terrible decision-making that there was no way out. I was caught.

I kept remembering Joe and his face as I left his car. I thought back about the last time I left Brett's car and his painful look, too. With each exit, I left possibilities behind me—and great guys who loved me more than I knew how to love myself. The only way to show that I loved them was to let them go and be loved by someone who could.

~ Thirty-Six ~

GLENDA

I've processed the things that we spoke about last time. I'll do as you have asked me to, but can you please lend me some grace concerning how fast I act on it? Please don't make me rip the bandage off, because I'm just not strong enough right now. Please show me the next step you want me to take.

I'm writing to talk to you about Charlotte. She called me, asking to meet with me. I think she wanted to shake off some residue from our last conversation.

We have met a few times since she told me about her abortion, but it seemed as if she wanted to keep it light. When she called this time, I didn't get that feeling, and I knew I was right when we met.

Charlotte wanted to talk to me about how she had been trying to forgive herself. She mentioned that during the course of working on it, she had realized there was so much more that was making her feel guilty. The sweet girl knew that most of it was a result of the abortion, but lately more had surfaced.

Charlotte talked about Brett and how she pushed him away intentionally. Loving him never stopped, but her guilt for what she was responsible for led her to believe that he deserved better than her.

She had given him up, not because she didn't love him, but because she loved him so much. That revelation has been painful for her. She still believes that she did the right thing for him but regrets pushing him away so callously.

Later into the conversation, she mentioned something I had never heard her talk about. There was another boy in college whom she'd had a relationship with.

Her parents had pushed away from her, friends didn't understand her anymore, and the man she thought she would be with forever seemed better off without her.

Her only comfort was this boy who had known Charlotte her entire life. The closer they got, the more fearful she became.

It was late in her last year in college when he confessed that he had tried hard to keep his feelings platonic, but as hard as he tried, it didn't stop him from falling in love with her. She was more shocked to realize that she had begun to fall in love with him also. She had formed this friendship to help her get out of the ruins of one relationship, only to begin another with the person she thought would save her.

On one hand, she was scared he'd be the last person to have a glimpse into who she was and love her anyway. On the other hand, she couldn't bear to hurt him as much as she had Brett. She couldn't stand the idea of disappointing another person emotionally, and that seemed to be the pattern with her over the past few years.

She thought she would be protecting him in the long run if she stopped the relationship then, but Charlotte ended up hurting him anyway. She lied and told him she didn't feel the same. This continued with telling him that she had only wanted to be friends, but she said his response stabbed her even deeper.

He told her that he loved her so much that being around her as a friend wasn't healthy for him any longer. She was all he thought about. He confessed she was everything he ever wanted in someone.

He admitted that being around her constantly—knowing that he couldn't have what was in front of him—would be too painful for him. But not having him in her life would probably give her more room to find someone she could love again.

His ending comments stung the most. He'd always thought that Brett was so lucky to have her, and he could never understand how Brett could let her go. He thought he'd won the lottery because of Brett's stupidity. He soon came to learn that Brett hadn't been stupid and that he hadn't been lucky at all. They had both just fallen in love with an amazing girl who refused to be loved.

Those words brought her to tears. She admitted that he was probably right.

She mentioned the second boy's name once, and I believe that I know him.

God, is this something You're up to? What are the chances that this man's the same one Charlotte was close to falling in love with over ten years ago? This couldn't possibly be. If it is, it will be another time in my life that You have awed me.

Back to Charlotte . . . She is really hurting. When she talked about Brett, she'd be on the verge of tears. When she talked about this second man, she'd have similar emotions on her face. When she talks about her parents, her shoulders drop and her face expresses exhaustion. There isn't much in her past that she talks about and smiles.

Really the only thing I've seen her smile about is when she talks about soccer—her teammates, her games, her awards, her coaches, her trainings. I asked her about soccer and why she loved it so much.

I was never a high-level athlete and never practiced or trained for anything the way she did. I didn't understand the thrill behind it.

When I asked, her face lit up and she sort of stared off. She said that when she stepped on the field, her focus shifted to what was in front of her. All her worries or concerns disappeared.

When she was younger, the sport thrilled her. It gave her butterflies. That changed when she went to college. Soccer was all she had. After her parents had cut her off and she left her life as she knew it, her only constant was the game itself.

The first summer's intense trainings helped her survive moving away from home. Games were the things she looked forward to in her everyday life. Practices were dreaded by some, but she welcomed them, as her thoughts stopped for those few hours of training. She has mentioned a couple times that she wishes she had that field to step onto now and escape from her pain.

You have given me this child to help. You have repetitively shown me that. I want to sit and listen to her so she can have someone to confide in, but when stories are over and the heartaches have been expressed, where do You want me to lead her?

Of course to You, but in what way? Do I wait for her to ask for help? Do I offer advice ahead of her asking? Do I continue to teach her about forgiveness?

It all seemed great at first. I could offer comfort and help to this girl—this young woman who reminded me of Sarah. It was going to give me a chance to connect and see what it might have been like as a mom. It seemed as if You were giving me a chance to heal my own heart.

But You flipped it on me. You threw in the fact that You wanted me to walk the same journey alongside of her. I wasn't just to talk about forgiveness. I was to walk it myself and give her the testimony of my experience rather than a sermon.

Lord, at first, I welcomed this idea of Yours to help her, but now that it's turned so personal and painful, old rebellious feelings are rising up inside. I don't want to be obedient. I don't want to walk the walk.

It's no coincidence that I just read Your Word the other day that referenced Jesus as the vine and You as the gardener. It says that You cut off every branch that bears no fruit, while every branch that does bear fruit, You prune so that it will be even more fruitful. It says to remain in You because no branch can bear fruit by itself.

So, here it is in the form of real-life application. I've always loved when You've brought Your Word to life and put skin on it for me to understand it clearly. But this particular application I could do without.

After all, I'm seventy-five years old. How much fruit do I have left to offer? Isn't my time here ready to be over? I would think at this age, my obedience would be automatic. I would think that I would've just done what You asked of me by now, but here I am, feeling like I'm a child resisting direction.

Lord, I want to do this because You told me to, but pain scares me so much that it feels like I would be willing to forsake You to avoid it. Yet my mind overrides my feelings and knows this is something I have to walk.

Lord, I love You, and at the same time, I don't understand Your ways. My trust is hidden behind the fear. I believe You're good, and I believe You're to be trusted, but please help my unbelief. Take my hand and help me take my first step. Please.

All my love,
Glenda

~ Thirty-Seven ~

BRETT

"Son, this is your dad. You know why I'm calling. When you're ready, give me a call."

That was the message my dad left me today.

I want to be ready. I want to hear his wisdom. I want him to tell me what an idiot I am. I want him to tell me that I need to be a better dad and husband. I want him to tell me that I should be ashamed of myself. I want him to tell me that I disappointed them then and now once again.

But I know what his answer will be. "This is between you and God." The truth is that there are galaxies separating God and me.

I wait for the day my parents give up on me, but nothing seems to shake them. They know my past. They know all that happened. They were gracious during those times.

"Dad, I don't even know what to say. I'm embarrassed, and I know I let you and Mom down. You raised me better than this."

I remember dropping to my knees and begging him to forgive me.

"I'm so sorry, Dad. Please forgive me. Please. I'll try and make it up to you guys. I swear."

All I remember is looking up and seeing him crying. At first, I thought he was ashamed of me or angry at me.

"Brett, you don't have to beg. I love you, son, and I know this is hard."

He was crying *for* me. He was crying *with* me. He could feel my pain.

"I love you no matter what you do and no matter what you could ever do."

"Dad, I know you will punish me, and I'll do whatever it is you want from me—"

He cut me off, and his response was memorable.

"Brett, you're a man now. You're eighteen years old. You have decisions that you have to make for yourself.

"If I punished you, it would almost be a double consequence. You're already punishing yourself. You're hurting inside more than I could ever hurt you outside.

"This is between you and God now. You have to confess to Him and let Him forgive you and pour His grace on you.

"The hardest part of this walk will be forgiving yourself. God will forgive you immediately, but with the amount of pain and shame you just shared with me, it will take you a lot longer."

My dad might be the wisest person I've ever met in my life. What he said was absolutely true. That was fourteen years ago, and I've never been able to even begin forgiving myself. I've dug myself even deeper by leaving my family because I couldn't face my demons.

Having a father like him is a blessing and a curse. He was an amazing dad and still is in so many ways. That part is a blessing.

But he also wears shoes that I could never come close to filling. I could never be the father he has been to me or the husband he has been to my mom.

I have to be such a disappointment to my parents. They always told me they didn't care what job title I ended up with. All they cared about was that I had a relationship with God.

They were never the religious type of people who had strict rules about what I watched or listened to. They just put choices in front of me and showed me right from wrong and then let me decide.

That could be another dagger in the situation. They'd trusted me so much, and I'd let them down. After eighteen years of them thinking I'd gotten to a place where they hoped I'd be, I ruined it. I think that was another reason I worked so hard to get through law school and begin a good career.

I hated who I was inside and who I failed to be, but if I could look put together externally, I could maybe get away with not appearing like a failure.

I think my mom always knew what I was doing. She would tell me that I didn't have to impress anyone. I never knew what she meant. I would always tell her that I was just working to have a good life.

The last time she mentioned it to me was a couple months ago. I got pretty frustrated and asked if she could see that I was working hard to support my family.

She simply said, "Brett, your family needs more than financial support. Be careful."

I was so pissed off at the time. How much more did she want me to give? She must have seen things way before I could. Maybe I was angry because deep inside, I knew she was right.

I can't call my dad right now. I wouldn't even know how to begin a conversation. If he had any questions, I wouldn't know how to respond either. I just need more time to figure myself out.

I wonder what will happen if they find out that I met with Charlotte. I'll see her for the first time in what seems to be a hundred years. I have a thousand thoughts running through my head, stirring up just as many emotions. I have a head full of questions.

There are major issues that are staring at me, but the one I'm avoiding most is God. I feel like He is going to punish me. The longer time goes on and I don't see any proof of His revenge, it scares me even more.

I think about my kids getting a terrible illness or killed in a car accident. I'm sure He has the right to one of mine. After all, I took one of His.

My wife could be another treasure He takes from me. The closer I get to her emotionally, the more I fear losing her.

That stupid counselor said I have "intimacy issues," but that's just a kinder way to say I'm a terrible husband and dad. Does Charlotte have the same thoughts? Does she avoid the same closeness with people?

I'd heard that she and Joe had started dating in college. I knew they were close because they were together all the time.

Whenever Cassidy and I weren't together, I'd call Joe to hang out. He was always out with Charlotte somewhere. He'd be over at her apartment or at her games.

Eventually, he and I drifted apart. He'd been my best friend, but Cassidy took his spot when she came into my life. Joe had always been close to Charlie too, so it makes sense that he looked to her for companionship. It's almost as if I pushed him in her direction.

I admit I was pretty upset when I found out they were spending time together. I knew that meant something was going on between them. I was even more pissed off when I found out I was right.

He and I both studied law for our undergraduate degree but went on to different law schools. I stayed at Vanderbilt, but Joe went on to Duke.

I always wondered if Charlotte went with him or not. Someone had mentioned she was dying to get out of Nashville, so I thought it was probably to follow him. I don't know why that image has always stung me.

I think of Cassidy and how she'd be crushed if she knew what I was doing. I haven't been able to connect with her in so long, yet I'm reaching out to someone else.

This may be the breaking point for Cass. I don't want to lose her. I don't want to lose the kids. But there's something telling me that I need to settle all this internal turmoil in order to keep them.

I can't believe my desire for answered questions would drive me to commit marital suicide. I know there's a chance to stumble over trip wire, but I'm willing to chance stepping on the mines in case I can make it to the other side.

The irony is that I'm meeting Charlotte at a cemetery. There are countless emotions I want to put to rest and leave behind. The truth is, I could be leaving more there than I think. I want to bury the past with Charlotte, but I could end up burying more than that. Is one burial plot worth three more?

~ Thirty-Eight ~

GLENDA

Good morning, Lord,

I have a few things to chat about. Just two, actually.

First, I did a little research. Charlotte told me about her friend Joe. She'd mentioned he went to Vanderbilt with her, but after he went on to Duke Law School, she never saw him again. She stated his family was from this area.

Bells in my head went off every time she mentioned his name. I thought you were drawing my attention to something, and I think I figured it out. He's Sheryl's son, Richard, my new estate attorney I met with.

When I went there to meet with him, I remember commenting on his beautifully displayed law degree from Duke.

Duke University was one school that Sarah had considered attending for nursing school, so that's why it stood out to me.

His office door read *J. Richard Gardner*, and the plate that sat on his desk read the same. But the degree said *Joseph Richard Gardner*.

Ironically, I asked him about his name and why he had changed it. He mentioned that his dad's name was also Joseph, so he used his middle name for professional purposes.

After I remembered all of this, I turned into a private eye. I love any chance to be a detective. I convinced another friend who knew Sheryl to ask her questions about her son—where he went to high school, where he went to get his undergraduate degree, and how old he was.

He attended Williamson County High School, he went to Vanderbilt for law school, and he graduated in 1998. I looked up the graduating class, and there they were—Joseph Gardner, Charlotte Madden and Brett McDonnell.

In my old age, and throughout my journey with You, I know that nothing in life is a coincidence. They are encounters that You place before us to get our attention. Recently, I heard the best explanation. Coincidence is Your way of staying anonymous. That was Albert Einstein. Who would've thought he was a theologian?

Here are the pieces I see. I have a recommended estate attorney. When I finally get to join You all up there, he'll be the one who makes sure that all my requests are done as I wish. Those are the first couple pieces.

Then we have You putting it on my heart to leave most of everything I have to Charlotte. I've not done so yet, but I love the idea. I have no other family, and I would hate to just have all my stuff turned into a fancy garage sale.

And the final piece: Charlotte once fell in love with the man who happens to be that estate attorney, the one she would have to interact with to settle my estate. That's amazing. I know You must have something waiting there for her.

This is too big for me to interfere. I'll keep my mouth closed as best as I can. I won't tell Charlotte, and when I go to his office to change my will and trust, I won't react when he realizes who will inherit my assets. This is so exciting.

Now to the not-so-great part of this conversation. I did do a little bit of research on Jason too. It definitely wasn't as exciting as looking up Joe, but nonetheless, I did it. He's at South Central Correctional Facility in Clifton, Tennessee.

The prison is about two hours from here. I hate driving, but when You ask me to do something, You always make it possible.

I already thought of Charlotte driving with me. My hesitation is that she doesn't know all that my past entails. But I'm open to bringing her, if that is what You would like.

If I'm going to face Jason where he's being held, I realized I needed to research how to get in as a visitor. It turns out that I can't just show up there, and I can't even make my own appointment ahead of time. I have to be placed on his visiting list. Not only am I having to do that, but now I have to ask him if he'd allow me to carry out what You've asked me to do.

I went with it. I wrote Jason a simple letter asking permission to visit him. I told him I was getting older and I had some last few things to share with him.

I made sure to let him know that it wasn't a visit to scold him or take any anger out on him, but a civil visit. I also asked if he could put Charlotte's name on the list in case I did end up asking her to come with me.

I sent the letter yesterday. Placing it in the mailbox was painfully humbling. I was asking the person who took the most from me if he would consider allowing me to visit him in jail.

I don't know how long his response will take or even if he will respond at all. All I know is that You asked me to do it, and so I did. I'll say that something in me healed a little more when I sent that letter. I see that no matter how old you are, there is always room for humbling and always time for healing.

So, those are two big things that are happening. As always, You already knew all of this, but I love sharing it with You anyway. You always change my perspective as I share my heartaches with You. You're so good to me.

All my love,
Glenda

~ Thirty-Nine ~

CASSIDY

The space between Brett and me is getting wider with each passing day. I've begun to adjust to him not being in our bed at night. The first few weeks were torturous. I slept a few nights in our guest room just so I wouldn't have to feel his absence.

When we first got married, we would hold each other every night, and we couldn't get close enough before we would fall asleep. As years went on, there would be an occasional touch of the hand or other gesture of affection.

Months before he left, we weren't even telling each other good night. We slept in a king-size bed, yet our hearts were oceans apart. I guess even knowing that he was distant was better than knowing he wasn't there at all.

Brett has seen the kids a few times and taken them with him for the day. He's never attempted to talk to me outside of logistics, as in what time to come, when to return them, and when he could see them again.

In my most honest admission, I cry every time I see them pull out the driveway. I watch the car carrying everything I love farther and farther away from me, while I stay behind, alone.

In the short time that Brett has been gone, that's what seems to happen every time he leaves—and we also get further and further away from each other in so many other ways.

I've made some changes since he's been gone. I started going to church with the kids. They love it. That's what encouraged me to keep going back.

When I'm in the sanctuary, I feel safe. I feel comforted. I feel vulnerable. I feel fragile. Last week, the pastor spoke about forgiveness. In the last fifteen minutes of him speaking, it hit me dead center of my forehead.

There was an element of forgiveness that I had to come to with Brett. I thought this whole time that he was the only one in the wrong, and I hated him for it. I didn't think that my reaction to how he had treated me required any personal responsibility.

But the truth is that I was harboring bitterness, resentment, hatred, anger and sadness, and I blamed it all on him. I had never heard the pastor's analogy about unforgiveness. "It is like lighting yourself on fire and waiting for the other person to die of smoke inhalation." The pain that was inside me wasn't hurting him. It was killing me.

Questions ran through my head, pleading to be answered.

Why, God? Why? Why do I have to forgive him? Why do I have to do the work? This man that I love has turned into stone and left his family because he couldn't face his past or future.

I've tried counseling. I've gone to Bible studies. I've recommitted my life to You a little more each day. I've sat in this church, week after week, while he lives some parallel life that doesn't intersect with ours any longer. Yet You're asking me to do more work? What are You asking him to do?

I wasn't only upset with Brett. I realized I was furious with God too. How does someone find themselves angry with the only real thing that is good in this world? But I'd managed to get to that place.

Days between that service and our next Bible study went by fast. My questions were still circling, and resentment toward Brett and God were swelling.

I went to the Bible study reluctantly. I didn't know where else to go to talk about these overwhelming emotions.

Michelle spoke on different fears we all experience—fear of failure, fear of loss, fear of intimacy, fear of abandonment, fear of insecurity, fear of death and fear of being alone.

Fear of being alone. Fear of being alone. Fear of . . .

Those words repetitively struck me. I was afraid of being alone. I was scared to not have Brett anymore. I was terrified of not being a wife, a partner, a half. I was angry at him for that too.

The teaching ended, and everyone shared their reaction. I finally had the courage to share.

"I'd like to share, but it's all jumbled around inside, so if I'm hard to understand, forgive me. You all know that my husband and I have been in a bad place. I've been on my own with the kids, and he has disappeared into a different life.

"I recently realized that I'm bitter. I'm resentful. I'm angry. I'm upset. I'm terribly sad. I'm lonely. And I blame him. I actually want to say I hate him, but I can't bring myself to speak that.

"Today, I realized that I'm afraid to be alone. I'm afraid that he isn't just going to leave our home, but our marriage altogether."

Tears streamed down my face, and I was slightly embarrassed, but I had to get this out.

"How can I have all these terrible emotions and still not want him to leave me? Is a failing marriage better than no marriage at all? Am I that desperate?"

I could see understanding in their faces. I felt safe to keep going.

"This weekend at church really upset me. I didn't think the message on forgiveness was for me, until the end. God showed me that even though Brett had done these things, I still had to find a way to forgive him. I felt like that was a joke. I'd gone there, not realizing how angry I was at Brett, then left angry at Brett *and* God."

They chuckled at my inserted humor, but it was only a mask to my pain.

"I was expected to pray for this man who wrecked me. . . . I was supposed to pray for our marriage. But how would that do me any good? Today you let me see what's in my heart.

"I'm mad at Brett. I'm mad at God. I don't want to pray for Brett. I don't want to pray for our marriage. I don't want to pray to God. I don't even know if God would listen anyway."

It was out there. I said it. I felt like I could breathe. All those feelings bundled inside of me were making me sick. Tears that emptied with the words felt like they carried emotional weight.

The group was silent, but I felt their affection. I looked around and noticed that some women had tears in their own eyes.

"Cassidy, I'm so sorry you're hurting." Michelle wiped tears off her face that had fallen. "I want to try to give you some relief. God isn't mad at you for being angry with Him. He knew you would be angry when you got to this point. The part that hurts Him is when we turn away from Him in anger.

"If we face Him and tell Him we're angry, we're still communicating with Him. We're still speaking to the One who can heal our pain. If dialogue continues, healing will eventually show up. I encourage you to not turn away from Him."

All I wanted to do was that—turn away from Him.

"And here's this. I understand that you can be so upset with your husband that you don't want to pray for him. I get the fact that you feel hopeless in your marriage and you feel like you're wasting your breath praying for it."

Someone else interrupted with, "We've all been there."

They had? It made me feel better for a moment.

Michelle continued, "I encourage you to do this. Pray about things you *can* pray for. Pray for your kids. Pray for your strength. Pray for your healing. Look back on times God's been good to you, and trust He'll see you through again.

"Then, allow us to pray for the rest. Allow us to stand beside you and pray for your husband. Allow us to pray for your marriage and believe there will be restoration for you both."

How were their prayers going to count as mine? Confused, I asked, "But isn't that me still not praying for him?"

"No. God showed us something in the Old Testament."

Old Testament—oh no. I knew almost nothing on that side of the book.

"Moses was leading the Israelites in war against a group of people that attacked them. . . ."

Okay. I had heard of Moses. I think he was the one with the Ten Commandments.

"During a war the Israelites had with a neighboring tribe, Moses went up on the mountain with the staff God had provided for him.

"When Moses's arms were raised, his people were winning. When his arms grew tired and he lowered them, they would start to lose. Two men with him made Moses a seat on a rock, then held up his arms for him in order to defeat what was against them.

"Apply that to yourself and to us as your friends. Your arms are tired—you're tired of fighting for your marriage. We want to stand in the gap and continue to lift your arms for you."

For lack of a better phrase, that morning cornered me. I had God telling me to move forward with Him. I had friends who were encouraging me to move toward God. And I was in a mental state that just wanted to turn and run from it all.

I didn't understand why those women wouldn't have sympathy for me. I needed them to feel bad for what Brett had done to me. I wanted them to say he was a jerk and he didn't deserve me. I expected them to say that if he wasn't making me happy, I should leave and move on to a life that would make me happy.

But they didn't. They felt bad for me from the point that I was missing out on what God had for me. They felt bad that I didn't want to fight for my marriage anymore. They didn't care one bit about my "happiness."

I left there feeling strange. I wanted to go home and have another temper tantrum.

Where was an advocate who would pity me? Didn't anyone feel bad for me? Didn't anyone see that I was in pain? Didn't I matter to anyone? Did God love Brett more than me? Did God even see the gaping hole that all of this has left in me?

I decided to pity myself. I felt bad for everything Brett had done to me. I resented how God was treating me and what He was asking me to do. I was disappointed that those women didn't support me.

I tried to self-medicate as best I could. I shopped online, shopped at the mall, and started exercising too much.

I tried to start drinking, but it always gave me a headache. I tried to go out with friends, but it was so hard with the little ones, especially when my main babysitter was Brett's mom.

What would I say?

Can you come and watch the kids so I can go out with my friends and try to do something stupid to get revenge on your son?

That wasn't a good approach.

So, I ate tons of desserts. Thankfully, exercise and sweets offset each other—otherwise, I would've gained forty pounds.

Then one night, I was on the couch, watching a romantic movie and crying. I was eating my favorite chocolate ice cream, snuggled in my favorite blanket, and wearing my cozy pajamas, which I believe might have been the second day of having them on.

My hair wasn't washed. My legs were unshaven. I definitely had not been in the midst of any perfume. I was depressed and allowing myself to wallow in it like a prized pig. I happened to take a good look at myself.

My own self-pity had left me paralyzed instead of comforted. It had allowed me to make excuses instead of changes. I had continued to be the victim instead of taking responsibility for how I moved forward.

Is this working for you?

I knew that was God speaking in my head. I don't feel He was shaming me. I think He was waking me up to see that His way is the best way, whether I agreed with it or not.

I was shocked that I was surrendering my opinion. I couldn't believe that I was giving up the last of my resistance. I was scared and completely insecure, but there was a sense of peace knowing that there was a chance for this to work because everything else I had tried failed.

Soon after this revelation, I went to coffee with Trish again, after a humbling call to see if she could meet. I had to go back to our first conversation, when she told me I had the wrong perspective of God.

I had opened my mind to the idea of learning more about Him and how much He loved me. What I was experiencing didn't feel like love at all. I had to have been doing something wrong.

I thought I was beginning to watch Him work in my life. At the few studies, the messages spoke to me clearly, as if a laser were pointed at me. The same happened at church services I'd been to. I began to feel cared for by God, but the minute He required something from me, I lost interest in going.

Trish and I met at the same place, and I promised myself I would not break down like the first time we met. We exchanged pleasantries, but I didn't hesitate to get right to the good stuff.

"Okay, so I have a lot of questions for you. I'm attempting to put pieces together before I feel like throwing away the entire puzzle."

"Give 'em to me, girl. I'm ready," she stated with a smile and excitement.

"Last time we met you spoke about me having the wrong perspective of God's love for me. At times, I've known you were right, and other times, I knew you had to be completely wrong.

"I wanted to press into God, then I wanted to push away from God. I like it when He comforts me, but I hate it when He asks something of me. It sounds childish, but it isn't this simple."

"Okay . . ." Her excitement seemed to get more intense as I spoke.

"Here is my timeline. The counselor shares with me that I have a confidence problem. He tells me that I gave it away years ago and I have to find out how to get it back. That is the starting piece.

"Unexpectedly, you and I met for the first time, and you state something similar. You share that I traded my confidence for lies about my worth or value. That was the next piece. I saw the bridge between the two observations."

Still engaged, Trish interrupted, "I could see that."

"Then, I went to Michelle's study. My first time, I felt like God met me in that living room, silencing roaring voices in my head. That was another piece.

"At the next study, the message was about the crippled man by the pool, and I was asked if I wanted to be well. Of course I said yes. Another beautiful piece. I felt like the answer to being well was soon to come.

"And then you know the rest of this story. I told you at the study about the sermon on forgiveness and how it upset me. That piece didn't go with the other messages. I wanted to throw that piece out."

Trish laughed at my attempt at humor.

"I was faced with the fact that I'm frightened to be alone. I realized that I'd rather have a terrible marriage than be alone. That piece didn't fit either. Between unforgiveness and fear, I've wanted to quit the puzzle altogether.

"I was on the verge of throwing it out, but the problem isn't that the pieces don't fit. The problem is that I can't see how they do."

I was ready for the answer, but all I got was another question.

"Your analogy is easy to follow, until the end." Trish cleared her throat with a slight smile, then looked me in the eyes. "When you say the pieces don't fit, why don't they?"

"You told me that I needed to change my perspective and see how much God loves me. Ones that don't fit don't let me experience that at all."

"So, you think if it doesn't feel like love, it can't be love?"

I knew it was a trick question, but I answered with my truth. "Yes. Love can't involve pain."

"But God doesn't operate on our level. We have that exact misconception that if you love someone, you make them feel cared for by tending to their needs. If they are hurting, love can take on the image of enabling. If they are struggling with something, love looks like helping them end the pain."

"Exactly."

"But what if we have the wrong interpretation of what love is? If your five-year-old child wanted to fly an airplane and was in deep pain over it, would you allow him to fly it anyway to make him feel loved? I would assume no."

"Of course not. But that's different." I was confused on how that related to what we were talking about.

"Pastor Marks said this once: 'When God hears our prayers, He sees the eternal effects of our prayers more than His children at the moment of their prayers. To give us what we want because we want it would be to put our fate in our own hands.'

"What if those pieces are part of what you're praying for? What if unforgiveness in your heart has nothing to do with Brett at all, but has to do with you and God?"

"So, you're saying they aren't necessarily related."

"Yes, possibly. Giving up unforgiveness toward him probably feels as if you're weakening and letting go of vengeance. But in reality, it is giving it to God and saying that you trust Him. You trust that He can protect your heart more than you ever could."

Trish leaned forward with her eyes filled with compassion. "Let's talk about the fear piece. God highlighting fear of losing Brett is what might be strangling you. Is showing you that unloving? If there were a bus coming toward me, would you not push me out of the way? Is your fear so tight that it is choking you? If so, perhaps God is trying to give you ability to see it, to move through it, and be able to breathe again."

"When you say it that way . . ." I really had no answer. She brought a different view that I would've never considered. Not only was I taken aback by what she said, but I immediately questioned my definition of love.

"Do you remember me telling you the first time we met to press into God so that you would know how much He loves you? There was more that went with that.

"I told you that I believed God was using these marriage struggles as a tool to bring you closer to Him. I said that it wasn't to hurt you, but the exact opposite. What you're experiencing right now is exactly what I warned you about."

"So, pain is a tool to come closer to him? Couldn't he have used something else?"

"We wish that were the way, right?" She laughed dismissively. I then knew she was serious about what she was saying.

"You have come to that point where the decision is yours. This pain will take you either to God or away from Him."

That statement was like an arrow shot in my heart. It was black-and-white.

"I can't tell you what to do, but I can tell you this from personal experience. Choosing to move forward in pain is frustrating, but faithfulness and frustration often go hand in hand."

She had so much wisdom, yet I wanted to reject it all. I thought life would be easy with God. I never thought it would be harder.

"The frustration means that you stayed, that you persevered, that you trusted God in ways you might not have wanted to. I can say that the fruit of staying—the fruit of obedience—is worth any pain endured on the way to get there."

Trish sipped her peppermint mocha, so I thought she was finished. I sat there thinking how we were going to transition into a lighter conversation. But she wiped the corners of her mouth with her napkin and kept going.

"Here is a relatable example. When you were pregnant, was it hard?"

"Yes, of course." Protective laughter returned.

"Did it get harder as you went on? At the very end, was it the most physical pain that you had ever experienced in your life?"

"Of course . . ."

"But, when that baby was laid in your arms, you hardly remembered the pain you had just endured. By the child's first birthday, those pains were hardly ever thought about. And soon after, you probably started thinking about having another child.

"Because of how precious your first child was, you were willing to endure all that pain you went through in order to experience the same blessings once again, right?"

As she was talking, I asked myself, *Why did I want to talk to her again?*

"That's the same pain you're going through now, only it's emotional and spiritual. I don't know what 'trimester' you're currently in. I don't know when you'll reap the fruit of your labor, but I know God is faithful."

She said that last phrase with love and conviction. But the words didn't seem warm, and they definitely didn't make me want to smile.

"Usually, when I feel confronted, it's the result of someone testing me or getting under my skin. It's almost competitive, and that alone drives me to fight back.

"But this is a different challenge. It's like standing at the starting line of a marathon with no training and arguing with myself on whether or not to start. What normal individual would jump in with enthusiasm, eager to take it on?"

She laughed again and I slightly resented her for that. She was enjoying herself as she stirred me up.

"I guess I can't stay where I am and remain stagnant. I've been upset that no one has given me any false comfort by telling me to leave him or that I deserve better than what he has put me through."

"I can completely understand that. You think no one is validating you and how you feel."

"Yes. They've all given me advice on how to survive and how to love him despite everything. I didn't want to hear that. So, I comforted myself and had my own pity party.

"I ate like I was pregnant. I watched romantic movies and felt sorry for myself because my marriage was so far from the romance on the screen. I even abandoned my shower for a couple days."

Funny . . . not funny.

"My lowest point was one night when I sat in my pajamas, watching more depressing movies. With ice cream in hand and tears running down my face, a terrible, sour odor saturated the air. I realized the foul smell was coming from me.

"It worked almost like a smelling salt because it made me ask myself, 'What the hell am I doing?' That was when I called you. I knew I needed to get out of whatever funk I'm in."

She started laughing again as if I were telling a joke, but I was sharing my most embarrassing moment. How could she laugh?

"I don't mean to laugh as if I'm dismissing what you're saying. I laugh because I've been there many times."

What did she just say? That she had been at this point many times? Her? Was there hope?

~ Forty ~

CHARLOTTE

December 14, 2012

Dear Diary,

I'm trying to calm down so I can gather my thoughts. My entire body feels like it's throbbing with adrenaline.

We met this morning. Brett and me. It happened. After all these years and all the struggles, we met.

I had expectations of how our time together would play out, but nothing I anticipated happened. It all took me by surprise.

I met him this morning at the Franklin Cemetery. I know it sounds terribly morbid, but it was the only place I could think of where we wouldn't risk anyone familiar running into us. The memorial cemetery for Civil War Confederate soldiers is usually only visited by tourists. With how cold it is, I thought there would be few visitors. I couldn't come up with anything else that offered the same privacy in a public place.

I don't know where to start. My knees are still weak from my encounter. My breath hasn't completely returned to a normal pace. My heartbeat hasn't settled either.

As you know, you're the only one I can share these details with. It's sad but true.

If I had spoken to Glenda before making my decision, I know she wouldn't have approved of me seeing him. She would've questioned what good could come from it. To which I would have to answer, "Nothing."

If I decide to confess to her now that I saw him, I think she would be even more disappointed.

So here I am with you.

On my way to the cemetery, the number of times I wanted to turn around was more than the miles I drove to get there. I resisted my hesitation and kept driving.

I pulled up and joined the few cars in the parking lot. I glanced around to see if Brett was waiting for me. I checked my watch to make sure I was on time. To make sure, I looked at my phone, but it told me the same thing.

I locked my car and made my way to the cemetery's entrance. I kept scanning the area as I worked my way toward the entrance. I wasn't only searching for Brett. I was afraid I would see someone who knew me.

I didn't see anyone, so it was clear for me to keep going. I turned straight ahead and found him. My heart plummeted to the ground. I'd usually say it had dropped to my stomach, but this was so much more dramatic. My legs went numb, and I could feel adrenaline rushing through them.

He was sitting on a bench under a huge oak tree, slightly leaning forward with his elbows resting on his knees. He wore jeans, a leather jacket and sunglasses.

I knew it was him by his body posture and shape of his face. As we recognized each other, we both slightly smiled. I approached him but didn't know how to greet him.

Should I shake his hand? Was I supposed to give him a hug? I couldn't make a decision fast enough, so I just stood there and gave him a slight schoolgirl wave.

I'm not even sure if I managed an actual wave. I think my hand lifted chest-high and returned to my side. My hands didn't know where to go. They were trying to make an attempt to hide—the same way I wanted to.

"Hey . . ." That was all I could say.

"Hey. How are you?"

Awkward laughs followed, then we diverted our focus to our surroundings, seeming not to know what the hell to say next.

How do you begin a conversation with someone you haven't talked to in ten years? Last time we spoke, it didn't end well, and we obviously couldn't restart there.

The silent tension got to us. I held out as long as I could. We began to talk at the same time. As we both were tripping over our words, he got his thoughts together first.

"Charlotte, I know this is strange. We don't have to fake that we're here just to exchange polite greetings and catch up. Do you want to go inside? We can walk around the cemetery and act as if we're tourists. How does that sound?"

"Perfect."

So, we turned toward the entrance and made our way into the cemetery. As odd as it was to be in a graveyard, it was great that we didn't have to talk face-to-face, since we were walking shoulder to shoulder. We could stare straight ahead or off into the distance, but we never had to look into each other's eyes.

Brett began to talk quickly and purposefully. I could tell he was on a mission, and it made me nervous.

"So here it is. Over the last ten years, I've had so many questions haunt me."

He had to clear his throat to keep going.

"Excuse me. Sorry. I'm sure this is painful for you, but please know that it is for me too." He shoved his hands into his jacket pockets. "So, do you mind if I ask you some?"

"No. That's why I'm here. I figured this wouldn't be easy."

"I just want to ask about the end, after we found out the news and everything flipped upside down.

"You shut me out," he said with a hint of sorrow. "You never let me be a part of any decision-making. You just decided how you wanted things to go, and that was it."

The words stung. I'd never heard him talk about this. I felt his pain as he spoke. I did shut him out. And I didn't have a response.

"You shut down. You became like stone. You acted as if you'd never had one feeling for me. You said all the right things as if you cared, but nothing that you did showed it."

I always thought that I was noble in letting him out of the relationship, but I remember when Joe told me that all I cared about was self-preservation. Joe was right then, and Brett was about to tell me the same.

Our walk started to slow a little, and his voice got more intense. His words had more emotion behind them than what I'd expected. They were beginning to make my heart quicken.

"I need to know, Charlotte." He said this while turning toward me and stopping where we were. "What did I do to make you treat me like that? Were you mad at me because we had sex? Did you think that it was all my fault because I initiated the idea?"

I stopped walking, but I couldn't turn and look at him. I kept looking straight. I tried to get lost looking at the trees, noticing they were bare. I stared up, noticing how cloudy and gray it was. But it didn't work for long. His upsetting voice had held my attention.

"I figured that you must have been mad at me for making you even consider breaking our pact to wait until we were married. That was the only thing that ever made sense. So, I must ask. Am I right?"

I was trying to avoid getting emotional, but tears were welling up in my eyes. My heart felt as if it were going to burst. "Give me one second."

"I didn't mean to upset you again—I just . . ."

"Okay. Here it goes. It wasn't you. I wasn't mad at you. I was stupid. I was scared as hell, and I didn't know what to do."

I wiped the escaped tear from my cheek. How could I explain? How could I make him understand? I couldn't come up with any words to explain what I'd felt back then. I had to at least try now. I took a deep breath.

"We had so many dreams in front of us, and at that point I felt that if we kept the baby, I would've been the reason you never went after them. Our parents would've been embarrassed. You would've missed out on the family tradition of Vanderbilt.

"Everything I would've given up wasn't as important as what you would have forfeit, but the options were all in the back of my mind, and the potential sacrifices confirmed my decision. I couldn't do that to everyone. I couldn't be responsible for ruining lives . . . including that child's."

Stray tears got away every now and then.

He took a deep breath to speak, and his whole body shifted. "Charlotte. Oh my God. I would've given it all up. I would've done anything for us to have made it. I didn't care about our parents at all.

"I would've fought for you every step of the way. I would've married you in a minute. I would've done whatever you needed. I would've worked three jobs to make it. We would've eventually followed our dreams—it just would've taken longer."

"I know you would've. That is why I had to act how I did. I knew you would've given it all up.

"You loved me. You truly loved me. You would've sacrificed all that you had ahead of you to make it work. But what you can't see is that I loved you too, but it just wasn't a love as virtuous as yours."

This is where I had to tell him that I loved him enough to let him go. I just couldn't tell him that I wish I wouldn't have.

"My love looked like giving you a chance at reaching all your dreams. My love looked like not holding you back. My love let you go. You made me weak. You would have made me change my mind and . . ." My voice cracked, and I tried to talk through my tears. "I could've never lived with that."

My face dropped. I couldn't look at him. I couldn't handle the disappointment in his face.

"If it was all an act, if you really cared about me but just didn't want to hold me back, why were you always so indifferent to me? You seemed to hate me."

He was getting more emphatic and questioning my answers. He was shaking his head and using his hands to emphasize what he was saying.

"You would stare at me coldly whenever you saw me. You know all the times our eyes would meet, and you wouldn't even acknowledge me?"

His voice cracked, and I could tell those moments must have hurt him as much as they hurt me. I thought he would've completely hated me by then.

"Brett, it wasn't just toward you. I hated myself. After we were through, I had nothing. I was dead inside."

I finally turned toward him and let him see my pain. I couldn't hold back tears and agony. I tried to keep talking through it.

"When I had the abortion, it didn't just take the baby. It took all of me. It took my ability to laugh or smile. It was the most torturous time of my life."

I stopped to cry. At this point, he had turned away. He didn't want to see me so upset, and he knew he couldn't comfort me.

"I'm not sure if you know or not, but my parents found out shortly after. They said some awful things. My mom wanted nothing to do with me, and my dad allowed her to completely cut me off. I knew he'd always been weak when it came to her, but I thought he would've fought to have a relationship with me."

Talking about my dad made the pain even worse. I started to stutter breathe. I had to catch my breath to even be able to keep talking.

"I was too broken to try to make them change their minds. It took my dad over a year to attempt to have a relationship with me. He begged me after a while.

"He would show up at school and ask me to consider seeing him and my mom, as if I had shut them out. As if I had told them that God wanted nothing to do with *them*. They were the ones who judged me and left me on my own."

I don't think he knew all that, because his face expressed surprise at that point.

"It wasn't just you. I was a bit frigid to everyone. If I were completely honest, I would say that I still am. At first it felt like an act. Now, it has turned into who I am."

"Was there anything I could've done to help you? Was there anything I could've done to make you change your mind?"

"No . . ."

"No? Just no?"

"Yes. Just no."

There wasn't anything he could've done. I was starting to realize that he had just as much agony left inside about our past as I did. I was starting to feel more responsible for his pain. I thought that because he had moved on, he had gotten over it all.

"Let me switch gears for a minute. Why did you disappear at the end of our senior year at Vanderbilt? Did you graduate early?"

"I'd rather not visit that subject, but a short answer is that I thought my life had reached another low, and I didn't know if I could survive there anymore. I figured if I stayed completely away from everyone I'd known, I'd avoid more heartache."

"I had heard that you and Joe had dated. Did it have anything to do with that?"

I didn't want to talk about this. I didn't want to visit this. I tried to not answer, but the pause was uncomfortable, so I gave in.

"We didn't really date. It began by him befriending me out of pity. He had seen me a few times around campus when we had all first gotten to school.

"He knew I wasn't myself after all you and I had been through. He challenged me, but he wouldn't let me keep isolating myself. He would show up to different games or trainings.

"Actually, he probably was the reason I made it through my time at school. He was just a friend, though. He had become friends with all my teammates. He hung out with them at times, mostly without me. I wasn't much for hanging out. You know that about me.

"There was something that happened. I don't remember exactly what, but something set me off emotionally. He was around and became concerned and was there for me at a rough time.

"There was something there, but it pretty much ended before anything really started. He liked me, and I probably liked him, but I wouldn't let myself admit it. I couldn't hurt anyone again, and I knew I was bound to."

"I think that was close to when I ran into you at that party." Brett stopped walking and faced me. "Was it around that time that everything happened? I know it was soon after that, because when I saw him next, he didn't seem like he wanted to talk about it."

How in the hell did he remember all that? Why did he have to bring up that night? I thought it would be best if I just played dumb.

"I don't remember. I don't remember a specific get-together or anything."

"You don't remember seeing me at that house party? You don't remember seeing me at that huge house with all your soccer friends? Let me jog your memory and see if you can recall.

"It was a huge house bash and people were all around, inside and out. I had shown up there with my girlfriend, and you were with your teammates. You all were hanging out, and then you realized I was there."

I couldn't figure out how to lie to get out of this one. As he was talking, I was trying to think of excuses.

"You gave me a look I'll never forget. If you could've killed me with your eyes, I would be dead. I tried not to bother you all. I think I accidentally crossed paths with you again, and that was the last I ever saw you.

"Your teammates were looking for you, and then Joey started searching. No one could find you. One girl said that you were going outside for a drink, but you never came back. Some people thought something had happened to you, but Joey thought he knew what was going on."

"I don't remember."

"Honestly?" he sarcastically commented and continued as if he knew I was lying. "He looked at me and said you were fine—just not okay to be there. I knew what he meant. You were upset that I was there.

"I wasn't sure if you were just mad that I was there, or mad that I was there with a girl. Do you remember any of that?"

"Now that you say that, I think I recall some of that."

"Why did you leave? Was it my fault?"

This is where it got hard. The truth had to come out.

"Okay. I remember bits and pieces. Was it your fault? No. Did I leave because of you? Yes."

"Really? You hated me that much?" He sounded genuinely surprised.

"No, I didn't hate you. But I shouldn't share any more with you. I know we wanted to clear the air, but some details I think are better left unsaid."

I couldn't tell him that after all that time, I was jealous that he was there with someone. That in that moment I wanted that someone to be me.

"I would like to know. I would appreciate anything you can give me. I'm so confused that I want to have some clarity so I can move past my guilt built up inside."

"Okay. It wasn't your fault. I was caught off guard. After we broke up, I didn't want to be near anyone. I didn't want to even think about having a boyfriend or even a friend who was a guy. But you had moved on.

"I'd seen you with different girls through the years. The very first time it shocked me, but I'd gotten used to it. I'd seen that you were happy, and that was enough for me. But that night—that night was different. I'd known you long enough to read your facial expressions, and I could tell you were in love."

My voice let on that it was sad for me. That it even stung a little.

"You weren't just there with another girlfriend. You were there with somebody special. I knew because you looked at her how you used to look at me. You attended to her the way you used to attend to me."

I looked around because I didn't want to show how upset I was.

"I knew someone had finally taken my place, and she was the one. I didn't think it would bother me as much as it did. I realized I had really lost you. I know that I pushed you away, and I know that it was all my fault that we weren't together, but that was the night I realized that our relationship was gone.

"I realized that even if you left her in that moment and asked me to get back together, I would've pushed you away again, so I didn't think that it was fair that I was upset. You were in love, and for that I should've been happy for you. It hurt more than I expected."

"You were hurt? How in the hell does that make any sense?"

"I know. I didn't get it either. It was then I knew I still loved you. But I also knew that I had given you up so you could find exactly what you had right next to you. I was pleased you had found it, but I had to leave. I had to get out of there. You had moved on. It was good. But it also made me realize that I never had."

"I wish I would've known. I didn't even have a clue. All these years I thought it was because you hated me. If I knew there was even a slight chance you'd let me back in, I would've run after you."

"It wasn't your fault. That moment helped me realize I needed more time to get over us. Ignoring my pain only paralyzed me. It never helped me move past it."

Surprisingly, I didn't cry while I was telling him. We had made our way to the middle of the cemetery, and we were continuing to walk.

It was hard—hard to confess that I had still loved him, hard to admit that it was my fault we didn't work.

"Charlotte, I don't understand. I would've done anything to have you back. I would've jumped through hoops to have you by my side. I cried at times, but only when no one was around, because I was embarrassed. Yet, I would've set my pride aside to have been able to fix us.

"I guess I just couldn't get to you. I just couldn't make you see how much I loved you and that I would've followed you anywhere, no matter what."

That was the truth. He would have. And I knew that. I don't know what the hell was wrong with me that I wouldn't let him.

"Maybe you have a point. You waited much longer than I did to try to move on. Maybe I gave up on you too fast. Maybe I should've waited you out.

"I wonder if I could've eventually broken you down or worn you down like Joey did. You think if I would've shown up at your trainings or classes or front door that you would've given in to me the same way?"

"Brett, there was nothing you could've done to make me love you more than what I already did. You missed the whole first part of this conversation. I did what I did because I *do* love you—I mean, I *did* love you.

"Please don't read into that mistake. I made difficult decisions because I wanted a different future for you. I knew I wouldn't be good for you.

"You asked if you could've done the same things as Joey, but look at what happened there. I pushed him away before anything had a chance to develop. It ended no better than we did."

"I have to ask—in hindsight—was it all worth it?"

"What do you mean? Pushing you both away?"

"No, the abortion. You said you went through with it so we could both follow dreams we'd set before us. You said you wanted to try and salvage any respect that our parents might lose if they knew. You said you wanted me to have that connection with my dad and grandfather, and you didn't want to pass up a soccer scholarship you'd worked so hard for.

"So, was it worth it? Was what you gained in the end worth us not being parents?"

"I can't say."

"You can't say? Or you don't want to say?"

"I can't say."

"Okay, then let me say this. Where my life has ended up is great. I've done things I wanted to do and followed dreams I created for myself. Not exactly the same dreams we'd talked about, but new dreams.

"But if you ever asked me if the gift that you intended to give me was worth the price, I would say no every time. The cost of that decision is one that I'll pay for the rest of my life."

That broke me into a hundred pieces. I couldn't hold back more tears. They just made their way out.

"I would've given up all that you intended to give me to be able to follow through with what I believed to be my responsibility. Even if you would've left me with the child alone, I could've handled that better than what I ended up with, which was neither of you."

His words stung like hell. I had worked through this guilt as best I could, and now it was rising all over again.

"I'm sorry. Maybe it was a bad decision, maybe it wasn't. I can't say. I can't go there." I tried to be matter-of-fact, but my emotions betrayed me.

"You can't go there?" He had a tone of entitlement in his question.

"You gave up every relationship you had in exchange for your decision, and you're still standing by it?"

"Yes, it ended up badly, but how will I ever know if it would've ended up worse or not? Nostalgia might lead you to believe that it would've been better and we would've lived happily ever after, but who says?"

"Who says we wouldn't have?"

"What if we would've resented each other for how our lives turned out and that this child ended up with screwed-up parents who would've probably wound up divorced? We can't say."

"And what if we didn't? What if we would've worked out the kinks and gone through life's hard times to find ourselves stronger and wiser on the other side? What if that?"

"We'll agree to disagree, but at least you can see now where I'm coming from. I see the glass half empty. You see the glass half full. It's always been that way.

"I admired that about you. You always gave me hope. But hope wasn't enough to get through that time."

"Hope? Hope had nothing to do with giving up on everything. Faith would've done that."

"But, Brett, let me ask you something. Why are you really here? Is it to get me to say that I made a mistake?"

~ Forty-One ~

BRETT

Why was I really there? Why was I desperately standing in a cemetery to talk to this woman in front of me? Charlotte's question spun in my head so fast.

"I just had some questions." How was I supposed to say that I wanted to speak to the woman I once thought would become my wife?

"You go through all that you went through to contact me, and it was just for a few questions? I find that terribly hard to believe."

She was right, and I had to find a way to ask for what I wanted to know.

"I do need answers, and I was hoping you could help. I married Cassidy a few years after college. She was the girl you saw me with at the party."

Charlotte's facial expressions changed from curiosity to making me think she didn't want to hear another word I had to say.

"She is amazing. She is the best thing that has ever happened to me."

That was the hardest part to tell her.

"We have two children, a boy and a girl. He is five and she is three. They mean everything to me. But something's happened in me, and I didn't realize it until she asked me to go to talk to a therapist with her. When we met with the counselor, he asked me if I was angry at God. That opened up some huge wounds for me."

"Okay. I'm not sure how I can help with that . . ."

"No . . . no. I hadn't consciously sat and thought about God or what He meant to me in quite a while. The first thing I wanted to say was that He was mad at me. How I felt about Him was irrelevant.

"I started asking myself if there would ever be a way that I could get back into God's good graces. I feel like I got rid of a gift that He had given us, so why would He ever want me back?"

"I get that part." She reluctantly offered a side comment.

"But it got worse. A few weeks later, Cassidy asked me if something traumatic had happened before she and I met. She asked because she was trying to figure out why I never wanted to have kids. I thought I did.

"Then this idea popped into my head that I was going to be punished for what we did. I believed that my child would be brain damaged or stillborn. I knew God would take revenge on me through my child. So, I just said I wasn't ready to be a dad."

"You said you had two children, right? So how did she get you to change your mind?"

"I gave in. She and I fought all the time about having kids. I couldn't tell her about my relationship with you, so I just distanced myself in the argument. If I was going to hide that from her, I had no valid reason to object any longer."

I was getting more uncomfortable sharing so much. Looking at her and talking about my marriage felt foreign.

"Colin came, and I was anxious during her entire pregnancy. I didn't want to go to doctor visits with her. I didn't want to be there when the doctor might say our child had something majorly wrong. I was terrified to hear what my actions had caused.

"The baby came, and he was perfectly normal. After his first birthday, I felt even more relieved. But I noticed that I was waiting for something else to happen to punish me.

"I pushed myself into more work to distract me. My excuse was that I thought I was going to be a terrible dad. It didn't stand to reason, because it wasn't as if I had a terrible role model. My dad was amazing.

"A couple years later, Cassidy asked to have another child. I was furious inside. I'd hardly made it through having Colin, and here she was wanting another baby. My fear doubled. I was certain she was going to reap my punishment, but nothing bad happened.

"I couldn't figure out when the hammer was going to drop. When was God going to finally punish me?"

"Did it ever go away?"

"No. But Cassidy kept asking me questions and pressing for answers about you and me. I didn't want to give in. I got nastier to her. I threatened to leave if she didn't stop asking me about us. I thought it would make her stop, but I was wrong."

"Wait, what? How could you do that?" Her face held so much disappointment.

"I don't freaking know. I misjudged how upset she was with me. I couldn't back down. I couldn't tell her the things I was ashamed of. So, I did what every coward does. I left."

I was ashamed of myself more as the story went on.

"Where the hell did you go? I'm sure not back to your parents." Her familiarity with them seemed canny.

"Of course not. I moved to a long-term hotel and tried to justify why I was there. I knew I was lying to myself. I couldn't figure out how to move on. I couldn't see straight. I didn't want to go back to that counselor. I didn't want to ask to go back home when I knew I still wasn't able to tell her anything."

"And you're still there? You haven't fixed it yet?" She seemed more surprised as her questions added up.

"Yeah. I thought if I could talk to you, I'd find some answers about how to get past this. I hoped you would know how to move on and you could tell me. Maybe I'd be able to see the whole picture clearer."

"I wish I had answers for you, but I don't." She seemed puzzled and slightly bothered by my explanation.

"No? I didn't come here to rekindle our relationship or revisit anything in that sort of way. I actually came here in hopes of saving my marriage."

That was the hardest thing that I had to say. I had to tell the girl that I'd been in love with that I was married. I had to tell her that my wife was the best thing that had ever happened to me. I had to tell her that I was there to save my marriage, not reconnect with her.

Clarifying my intentions was hard but necessary. She seemed more relaxed, and it felt platonic immediately.

"That all makes sense now. If she was the girl at the party, did she ever know about us? Did you ever talk to her about us?"

"She asked once, but I didn't want to answer. I'd told her some things, but I rarely brought it up. I think the only time I shared a bit too much was when we almost broke up early in our relationship.

"She told me she loved me, and I freaked out. I didn't want to have any of those feelings again. I pretty much shut her out for a few days, then realized I was a complete idiot.

"I wondered if I would ever let anyone into my life that way again. Realizing I was screwing things up, I decided I had to take a chance with her.

"When I went to repair things, I had told her about my last relationship—my relationship with you—but never mentioned your name. I explained that we'd tried to make it work, but there was nothing we could do to fix it. My apology was enough, and everything moved forward seamlessly. Until after the wedding, when conversations came up about children, and I unknowingly sabotaged things again."

"Did you expect your fears to disappear after we met today? Was I expected to have answers to get you past your concerns?"

Unknowingly, I thought I had come to her for answers, but I recognized I came to her to fix me.

"I guess I did. I thought maybe you would have some insight that I haven't found yet. I do have a question that I thought I'd ask you.

"My family hadn't been attending church before we moved to Franklin—until I met you. You were so involved with youth ministry that I knew if I wanted to spend more time with you, I had to get involved with the church myself.

"At first, it was for you, but then it began to be for me. My parents started to attend, and eventually it became their church too. I remember how much our family changed.

"My mom would pray with me, and I'd never heard her pray before. My parents seemed to get along better, and our home was more peaceful. I actually started to enjoy it and believe it.

"As they say, I wasn't just a believer—I was a follower. My life looked different. I was lucky to have you then. Our relationship looked much different than others our age.

"Our lives changed that one night, and we were no longer different. We had fallen into the same world most lived in.

"After our ordeal was over, I felt like I was never able to return to where I'd once been with God. I felt like I had traded in my faith for shame. I never went back to church.

"My parents still go, and Cassidy has a church that she likes us to attend on holidays.

"My parents know why and also know they can't help me. I have to get back on my own.

"Something inside of me is pulling me in that direction. Not toward the church, but for me to turn around and face God.

"Your faith always inspired me, so I figured maybe you knew something I didn't. So, my question is this—how have you been able to face Him?"

The wait for her answer was not just an extra-long pause. It was the type of silence that if you were holding on the phone, you would hang up and call back because you thought you must have gotten disconnected.

So, that's what I did—I called back.

"Did you hear me? I asked how you have been able to face—"

A tear was streaming down her cheek from under her sunglasses. I must've said something in all of that rambling that upset her. I'd been talking so long, I didn't know what had gotten to her.

"I'm sorry. I don't know what I said that upset you, but I didn't mean to."

"Brett, I haven't."

"You haven't . . . You haven't what?"

"I haven't faced Him. I've believed for a long time that He's wanted nothing to do with me. A huge part of me still believes that. The timing of you bringing this up is eerie to me.

"About two or three months ago, something happened to me. I can't say exactly what triggered it, but I remember looking around me and realizing that my life was so far from what I had ever dreamed it could be.

"I was alone. I had an indifferent relationship with my parents. I had a job that kept me busy but couldn't fulfill me. Every week started to look the same and blend together. I didn't know how I'd gotten there.

"Ironically, before this breakdown, a little white church on my way to work started to grab my attention. I would stare as I drove by, and when I did, my stomach seemed to warm inside. This strange feeling would work its way up to my throat. I couldn't explain it.

"I finally drove into the parking lot one day on my way to work. I'll spare you the details, but after some time, I became friends with a lady at the church. We've met a few times, and every time we do, I leave there with my mind spinning.

"I finally was able to share with her what had happened between us. I hardly ever told anyone, but something about her made me want to tell her everything.

"I didn't just tell her the events. I also told her about the emotional aftermath. I told her that I thought God wanted nothing to do with me. When I looked up, she was crying just as much as I was.

"I was so confused. I felt stupid for telling her. I put my head down and waited for her to tell me that I was a terrible human being—or worse. Instead, she said something that I haven't been able to shake.

"'When we think we're disqualified from having a relationship with God, that means Jesus's terrible death on the cross wasn't enough of a sacrifice for our sins. It completely negates the torture He suffered for us.'

"I've never been able to get that out of my head. I've vacillated between believing it and dismissing it, and every time I do, I can't land on either one. I can't rest at thinking He wants nothing to do with me, and I can't give in to believing He does. That slight chance that He does is what I've been holding on to lately."

I definitely thought she would have an answer, but after all of this, I realize she's just as broken as I am.

~ Forty-Two ~

CASSIDY

If I thought I'd hit bottom a couple months ago, I was wrong.

So many things combined had led me to believe that my confidence was returning and my life was finally moving forward.

And then, a bomb hit. It was a bigger explosion than the first one.

One night, I was scrolling through Facebook mindlessly to see how everyone else's lives were still pieced together. I hadn't posted in months. What was there to share? A picture of Brett's empty closet?

An alert came up while browsing, suggesting a list of people I'd be interested in "friending." There he was—Brett. Knots in my stomach formed immediately.

Hope held out that it wasn't him, but I started to dig. No picture was available, but the information lined up. The fictitious name he used made it even worse.

It was CharlieMac19. It stabbed me right away. His nickname in high school combined with her nickname—Charlie.

Charlotte was the girlfriend Brett refused to talk to me about, and I'd suspected what he's been hiding was about her. My discovery I was right was the match that had lit this fire. But the flames were much more damaging than I'd imagined.

I'd been assuming he was hiding something from his past, but grasping that he was actively betraying me made me physically sick.

Digging deeper, I found that "CharlieMac19" only had one friend—Charlotte herself. To most, Facebook was a social outlet. To my husband, it was a dating site.

What the hell was I supposed to do with that? Vengeance flooded all parts of my mind. Questions with no answers riled up the anger even more.

How long had this been going on? Had this started after we separated, or was this something that had been continuing over our entire marriage?

Were those details even important? Either way, we were married, together or not. My mind weakened, bouncing back and forth between him hurting me and me wondering why God would allow this to happen.

What else did I have to do for Him to protect me? I've been told repeatedly how much God loved me. Obviously, my expectations of what that looked like were completely wrong.

My spinning mind finally slept at about three o'clock in the morning. But by five in the morning, it was circling again.

Waking up to the memory of what I'd discovered hours earlier, pain and shock returned as if I were just discovering it for the first time.

Did she know he was married? She had to, right? I'm sure someone had to tell her at one point or another.

Could he flip past all that we had and pick up with her where they had left off? My bones ached wondering if he had regretted the last seven years.

What about his parents? How would I tell them? Was it my business to tell them or even their business to know?

Did I want them to know so they'd be pissed at him and feel sorry for me? Was I looking for allies? Had this now become a war?

I desperately needed to get control of myself.

The last time I'd met with my group, they expressed to me over and over again about how much God loved me. How would they explain this?

They said He had a plan for us. Was it His design for the kids and me to be alone while Brett moves on with his high school sweetheart?

They said God was always there for me. But where was He now? I'd been trying to do work to move past the pain, and then another boulder just knocked me over. This couldn't be a test of God's, right?

I wanted to reach out to Trish. I wanted to reach out to Michelle. I wanted to reach out to Nancy. But I couldn't.

They'd each tell me to hold on. They'd tell me to trust God. They knew I was in a crappy situation, but the impression I got was it was best that I push through it. I doubted this new situation would change their perspective.

They'd probably suggest I pray for Brett and the other woman's happiness. As much as I want to say that I'm kidding, most of me is not.

Giving up on God was more attractive after each unanswered question. What's holding me back are times when I knew God had pulled me closer to Him.

I know He found me that day in the window when I was washing dishes. I know He found me in the middle of that Bible study. And I know when I had read that devotional, He had called out to me. I couldn't deny those times and the way my heart and soul responded.

But what do I do now when that same heart and soul are crushed? Is revenge mine to have, or wait for?

I could send him a friend request, and that would immediately let him know that I see exactly what he is doing. Or I could wait and gather the information needed to confront him.

As much as I want to find him and throat punch him, I'll hold myself back and calculate the best approach.

~ Forty-Three ~

GLENDA

Good morning, Lord,

I'm listening. I know You have something to tell me. I was hoping that all I'd have to do is write the letter and Jason wouldn't respond. I trusted all You needed was my willingness. My hope died hard last night when I received his letter.

Dear Glenda,

Hello. I'm struggling to come up with words to use to write back to you. I got your letter this week. I was nervous to open it.

How could I not be? I saw the return address and thought it was going to be a letter that would rip me to shreds, so I waited days to open it. Curiosity got the best of me, and I read it anyway.

I was surprised by your request to visit me. I was surprised that you would even want to see my face ever again. It's been hard for me to look in the mirror through the years, knowing what I did and who I've hurt.

But your letter made me feel something I haven't felt, and I don't know what it is and I don't know why it happened. I wanted to say no to your request and throw it away, but I couldn't.

You have never been cruel to me, so I trust that you aren't wanting to come here for that. I have no reason to say no, other than selfish reasons of guilt and shame. I don't feel I have the right to say no for those reasons. If I can do this for you, I will. I don't know when you wish to come, but I'll be fine with whenever it is.

Truly,
Jason

So, there it is. You showed me that I need to go. I'll have to set it all up. I'll first have to ask Charlotte when she can spend a day with me. I don't want to tell her where we're going. I'll have to tell her it is a surprise.

Lord, I don't know what You're doing, and I don't know why. I know I keep repeating that phrase, but I only say it because I'm reluctant to go through this.

I know You're good. I know You love me. I know You want what is best for me, even when it stings. I know You gave me Your best, and I'll give You mine.

If that means doing what You ask me to do, I'll do it. All I ask is that You let me know that You're with me. I'm up in years and have been through many tragedies, yet I'm the most scared I've been in years.

As usual, I ask that You shower Charles and Sarah in Your love. Let them know that I love them so much and miss them even more. I'll keep waiting until I can see them again.

All my love,
Glenda

~ Forty-Four ~

CHARLOTTE

December 19, 2012

Dear Diary,

I met with Brett last week, and it ended up being intense. The conversation went differently than I'd expected.

He asked me some questions that stung. One particular question was breathtaking. He asked if it was worth it. I wanted to answer yes right away. I couldn't say that, because I knew it was a lie, but I tried not to give in to saying it was a mistake.

Of course, the abortion itself was tragic and emotionally painful. If I had decided not to have it, would that have been just as tragic or emotionally painful in the long run? We'll never know, and that was my answer.

It's easy to look back and think things would've been better if we had taken a different path. Don't we always look in the rearview mirror when we get to a bad spot? I could go back and say that I wish I would've never sat next to him in biology so then I wouldn't have been in any of this mess.

I gained something from loving him, and I lost something because of it as well. So, was any of it worth it? I'll never know. One day I might see how it impacted my life in the big picture, but it might not be until I'm Glenda's age. I'll have to live with that.

After we hit that bump in the conversation, he opened up. He told me about his marriage, the kids and fear of vengeance, which crippled him.

I could understand. I had thought about the same consequences over the years, but I didn't have to face the reality of it like he did. I couldn't imagine what it was like, or maybe I should say I don't want to imagine.

Then our conversation took a twist. We started talking about our faith. After all, that is what held us together for so long. We were both believers, and our teenage years looked different because of it. Looking back, we had a fire in us that I didn't recognize at the time.

We loved working with younger kids and encouraging their faith. We enjoyed listening to pastors and their experiences they shared.

It was most impactful when messages incorporated personal stories I could relate to, but no one ever got up and talked about how they would've handled finding out they were pregnant at the age of eighteen.

Brett asked how I've been able to face God. I'm not sure why he thought I'd been able to. I was still trying to find my own way back to God. I told him about the last few months and how something was pulling me to that church after passing it all those times.

All I could do was refer to things that Glenda had told me. She had said things to encourage me to turn my face back toward God and draw close to Him again, so I thought I'd pass that information on.

When I was repeating Glenda's wisdom, some of what she'd shared hit me deeper than it had before. The part about disqualifying myself from the cost of the cross especially sparked something in me.

I told Brett that I'd written to God one time in this journal and asked for forgiveness, but I didn't think that was enough. After I told Brett all those things, I wondered if I should write to God again, and maybe I will . . . soon.

What stuck out to me was something I would've never expected. My mom used to tell me to pick the bad strawberries out of the bunch because spoiled ones can ruin good ones so quickly. After meeting with Brett, I realized that is what my bad memories had done to the good ones.

All this time, I had focused on Brett and me, often thinking that I deserved an emotionless life for what I did. I go back and think how everything ended with Brett and me and with my parents, and as I do, the awful ending ruins good memories I've lost.

The bad feelings those relationships left made good memories more painful. Shaming thoughts overshadowed any good I'd ever felt about myself. Painful parts of my past and pain I caused in return were all I could see.

As we were going over things, Brett asked about Joey. His curiosity held a hint of betrayal, or possibly jealousy. I gave him small pieces of information to start, but then I pushed past my hesitation and went on to tell him about our friendship.

Something ignited in me as I was talking about Joey. I got distracted in my own thoughts as I was speaking. Shaking it off, I went on but knew that needed revisiting.

Our conversation ended on a light note, and that was the best thing that could've happened. He thought most of his questions were answered, but he wanted to make sure that he'd addressed them all. I sense he is struggling anxiously to get past this, desperately wanting to move on.

He thought I had the answer, but I can't even fix myself. Hearing him say he was married and had children was surreal. I still saw him as the kid I knew, and now he had kids of his own.

I'd expected to have an emotional encounter when I saw him, being tempted to fall back in love with him. Strangely, the only thing I missed was the girl I was when we were younger—and leaving there, I knew she was gone.

After leaving Brett at the cemetery, I thought for hours about what that shift in my thoughts could've been about. I racked my brain and couldn't get it. But when it hit, it hit hard.

As grueling as this is to write, Joe was the one I lost. He had loved me when I was unlovable, not just romantically. I mean the kind of love that cares about another's well-being without any benefit for themselves.

He reached into my pit of hell and purposefully lifted me out of it. He made me laugh and smile when I thought I had no joy left in me.

I started to remember all of our fun times, and they strung together like a movie. There were no bad times to edit out when it came to our friendship. There were bad times that I'd gone through alone, but every instance, he was there to lift my chin and help me smile again.

The bad part was that it had gotten too good. I had fallen in love with him unintentionally, and it terrified me because I knew he was perfect.

Too perfect. I was one thousand percent sure that I'd destroy it, and as all self-fulfilled prophecies end, I sabotaged it.

I'd always thought my biggest mistake was losing Brett, and Joey faded into the background. But as the depth of field in my mind opened up, Joey became the obvious focus.

My biggest mistake was getting into a relationship I couldn't sneak out of. The other side of the mistake was getting into a relationship where my heart couldn't go any further. But what the hell does that information do for me now?

Brett desperately searched for a way to talk to me—to get past his regrets and get answers to questions that haunted him. I'm happy he did. I wouldn't have distinguished what was paralyzing my heart had he not.

Do I do the same to Joe? Do I hunt him down and find him? What if he is married or has kids? I'm sure he does. He would've made an amazing husband and a fun dad.

I can't do that. I can't get myself worked up with regret and hope to repair things with him. I need to just look at my side of the fence and clean it up. I need to look at where I went wrong and not make those mistakes again. I don't need to stir up the past for him when I'm sure he's moved on.

I feel like a weight has been lifted off my shoulders, but I also feel a familiar sting in my heart thinking about Joe. I'm sure that will go away shortly. I've moved past it twice before, so a third time should be even easier.

~ Forty-Five ~

BRETT

"Cassidy, can I talk to you for a minute?"

She only stopped where she was and slightly turned toward me. I'd never seen that expression on her face. She could've burned me with the lasers coming out of her eyes.

I'd just picked up the kids and wanted to avoid a conversation, but I could tell that her usual kindness was absent.

"What, Brett? What can I do for you now?"

"Uh, I'm picking up that you're pissed at me. Have I done something all of a sudden?"

"Am I not responding how you would like me to? Am I not behaving like a good wife? Or am I not being a good friend?

"Or maybe you just have never seen how a woman acts when her husband decides to leave her. When he shuts down toward her and her kids but has an entire secret life. Maybe that is what is confusing you.

"Go ahead, Brett. Move out for good. Find a place for yourself and settle in. There's no room for you here anymore. I've tried to hang on. I've even tried to change my life and have hoped that God would save our marriage.

"The truth is that one person can't save a marriage. All they can do is pray that the other one might want to save it too. I've done that, and it hasn't worked, and I just want to give up.

"I don't want to hang on any longer. I don't want to do all the work anymore. I tried to tend to you. I tried to support you. I tried to make excuses for why you distanced yourself from the kids and me. I tried to take care of the kids with hardly any help from you. I've tried to hold it all together, and finally my strength ran out.

"You won. Brett—one. Cassidy—zero. So now, go for the things you wanted from the beginning. Our marriage doesn't have to hold you back anymore. You can look behind you, see all the things you missed out on since we got together, and go for it.

"I'll be happy for you and whomever that person is who can make you happy. Maybe you could even reach out to Charlotte, see what she's up to. Or maybe you already have—who knows?"

I stood there stunned as she walked away. How in the hell would Cassidy know that Charlotte and I met? She couldn't. I'd only talked to her a few times and seen her once.

It must be a coincidence that she would say that. Or was it? After all, her mood had drastically changed and she was obviously angry. Was my lack of response just another clue she was right?

I took the kids to the movies, and they loved the popcorn more than anything else. Who knew that taking a family to the movies had gotten so expensive?

The big lesson was that kids and 3-D glasses do not pair well with popcorn. They couldn't see out of their smudged glasses after their buttered fingers adjusted them so many times.

I looked at them differently this time. I'd tried to stay distant from them for so long because I was afraid of losing them, but I ended up fulfilling my worst fear myself. Except, it was more devastating than losing them to circumstance. I'd lost them intentionally.

I brought them back home after a few days, and Cassidy's disposition hadn't changed at all. I didn't want to ask any questions and make things worse, so I gave her the space she seemed to want. With that, I drove off, and my mind picked up where it had left off the last time I saw her.

It's been about a week since I met with Charlotte. I questioned her about the one thing I'd wanted to know.

Was it all worth it?

I couldn't say the word *abortion*, but she knew what I'd meant. I was agitated when she didn't have an answer for me. Was meeting with her even worth the potential damage to my marriage? Ironically, I have the same answer she gave me—I have no idea.

In some ways, I can say it was definitely worth it. I got questions resolved that I would've left answered with my own lies instead of hearing her truth.

In other ways, I can say it was the stupidest thing I could've done during this time because Cassidy will never understand why I needed to do that. She'll believe that I have feelings for Charlotte and that I've carried them since before Cassidy and I got together.

That couldn't be further from the truth. Charlotte has taken up space in my mind, but not my heart. Cassidy means everything to me, and that is why I needed to figure out how to move beyond my past.

I didn't want to be the terrible husband I'd become. Somehow, Charlotte and I had reminisced about all the plans we had made for our future together. I had this image in my head back then of how I would look and feel as a husband and dad. I envisioned myself laughing and smiling with my young family.

After I left our meeting, the memory of what I'd imagined left an impression on me. I'm so far from what I had dreamed. I'd forgotten about the man I'd wanted to become. The husband that Cassidy has right now is almost the complete opposite. It stung when I saw it so clearly.

Had I not met with Charlotte, would I have had that revelation? Maybe that in itself was good enough justification for seeing her—a huge and selfish stretch, I know.

But from all this chaos, have I learned anything that will actually get me anywhere? I've dug into my past. I've asked hard questions that I needed answers to. I've distanced myself from Cassidy so I can see things clearly. I've spent time alone to figure out what the hell is wrong with me.

But has rummaging through the ancient ruins of my past helped me at all? How does looking in the rearview mirror help you drive forward? I have to put Charlotte in the past and leave her there.

If I want to give Cassidy all that she deserves, I have to figure out how to clear some things out to make room to let her in.

Should I meet Charlotte again? Do I email her or message her? Or do I just never talk to her again? After I figure that out, how in the hell am I supposed to get Cassidy back?

***

As much as I didn't want to, I knew I had to call the one person who could put me in line. He was probably more disappointed than I could imagine, but I needed him. I was lost, and I didn't want to be in that place anymore.

I called my dad. It was one of the hardest phone calls I've ever had to make. It was humbling to admit what had been going on, and my voice was extremely weak. He answered the phone, and my throat tensed up.

What was I to say? *Hi, Dad, it's me, your screwed-up son. I was wondering if you could help me put back the pieces to my marriage that I sabotaged?*

As dumb as that sounds, that was pretty much what I was going to have to say.

The phone conversation actually went better than expected. That gave me some relief. He didn't seem angry at all. He acted as if I were calling to see if he wanted to go play golf or something. I was confused, but I figured I'd keep going. I asked him if we could get together that week for lunch or dinner to talk. Dad didn't seem surprised—more like he'd been waiting for the invitation.

It was initially awkward when we met, but I didn't care. He walked up, and I gave him a huge hug.

"Brett, it's going to be okay. No matter what's happened, it will all be okay." That's all he said.

I didn't deserve that reception. I deserved a cold shoulder. I deserved him asking me what the hell I wanted and telling me I was a mess of a man.

We got into all the superficial points of conversation—what was good to eat, what we'd eaten there before, what we were going to order to drink, and how good their appetizers were. I barely thought about the food but faked some answers for the sake of conversation.

All I could think about was what I was going to say.

"You called me with a purpose." Dad withdrew a warm dinner roll from a basket on the table and slathered it with butter. "I know we didn't come here just for the food, so talk to me. Tell me how you are."

"I've been better. I've also been worse." I cleared my throat, then took a drink of ice water. "I don't know where to begin, so I guess I'll start with the obvious."

"That's a good place." My dad gave me a relieving smile.

"At the time everything went haywire, I didn't know as much as I do now. I didn't realize Cassidy and I were a mess. I didn't understand what you had tried to warn me about—you know, letting my work interfere with our marriage."

"I could tell when we talked that you probably didn't want to hear what I had to say."

"Yeah, I thought I was being noble in providing for my family. I was trying to give them everything they wanted. I guess I realize now that I did just enough to give them what I thought they wanted, but not what they needed."

I was getting choked up and had to recompose.

"I knew something was off with Cass and me, but I didn't want to see it. I allowed it to get buried under work. It was an accepted justification and a welcome distraction at the same time.

"Cassidy has always been supportive. Even at times when I thought she shouldn't have been. I know I took advantage of it and probably lost respect for her in the process. She was hurt, and I didn't want to see it."

"Brett, she has been a great wife and mom. That's why my heart broke for you guys when I saw things going wrong."

"I know. That's why when she finally came to her breaking point and started asking questions about why I was pushing her and the kids away, it was hard to keep up the act. I justified it as her being irrational and overemotional. She accepted that response for a little while but finally fought back.

"She wanted me to go to counseling, and I thought I could appease her by going. The counselor hit some deep scars I hadn't seen. He pointed out that my perspective was wrong, and I shut down."

"Counselors can do that." My dad was comforting, even while I was telling him what an awful husband I'd been.

"Inside, I was furious. Everything he said was right, but I didn't want to acknowledge it out loud. I thought he was a quack, but he turned out to be a wise duck."

Laughing, my dad added, "That's often the worst part."

"The session resonated with me for a while. I got angrier and angrier that he'd seen through my pretenses. I was trapped. I couldn't move forward with the same excuses, and I couldn't go back and acknowledge my weaknesses.

"I hated myself more than anything else, but I took it out on Cass. She kept seeing him, but I refused to go again. She was getting stronger, and I was feeling weaker.

"One night, she started asking questions about my past. She asked if I'd ever been through something traumatic. She asked if it had to do with Charlotte. It felt like the trap got tighter."

"That had to have stung. I know how much pain that brought up for you."

My dad's empathy gave me the sinking feeling in my throat as if I could've cried.

"I'd already known that our past had played a role in what I thought of myself, and now it was creeping into my marriage. I was crueler to Cass than I've ever been to anyone. I shut her out completely. I eventually told her it was best that I left, and I did.

"I was a coward. I was escaping any pain or acknowledgment of the past. How could I tell her the truth after all this time?"

"Wait a minute."

My dad placed both palms on the table and leaned toward me to speak directly to me.

"Just so I'm clear. You aren't generally talking about your relationship with Charlotte. You're talking about what you went through with her at the end. The abortion, right?"

My stomach churned. "Just hearing you say the word makes me want to throw up."

"Okay, I get it." He nodded, then removed his hands from the table and settled back. "I just wanted to make sure I knew what you were talking about. Sorry to stop you. Go ahead."

"I left her. I checked into an extended-stay hotel. It sucked, but my pride wouldn't let me crawl back, especially when I still wasn't willing to share.

"I started to think about the questions the counselor had thrown at me. He asked about God and what my relationship was like with Him. He wanted to know if anything was holding me back from a relationship with Him. I knew the relationship itself was distant, but I also knew God was still there."

The admittance of being far from God was visibly obvious that it pained my dad. "Ugh, that is hard to hear as your dad, but I understand."

"I finally figured out that I've believed God has wanted nothing to do with me, and those feelings go back to when Charlotte and I were together, when we didn't keep the baby. I didn't want to tell Cass. I needed to talk to someone who would understand and who might have answers to my million questions.

"But this is where I'm expecting your deepest disappointment. I selfishly reached out to Charlotte."

I just sat there for a minute and looked at him. He only stared back. His expression didn't change. I was waiting for his body language to show me I was definitely an idiot.

Luckily, the waiter interrupted us when he brought us our meals. He asked a few questions and gave me enough time to muster up more courage to speak.

"Okay, keep going. I want to hear this." That's all he said, with no hint of condemnation in his tone.

"I told her I had some things I needed to work out and wondered if I could ask her some questions. I just needed some answers to things

I couldn't get past. I warned her that I wasn't requesting a meeting because of an emotional interest.

"Trust me when I say it wasn't a romantic encounter at all. I truly wanted to get past some residue that I believed was the reason I was trapped. She was the one who had me take an interest in my faith, and I thought if she had gone through the same event with similar feelings, maybe she could tell me how she got to the other side."

Dad raised his eyebrows. "And did she? Did she have the answers?"

"No, not really. She has struggled all these years with the same painful curse but in a different way. Charlotte said she'd believed God wanted nothing to do with her, and I completely understood. She personally had nothing to offer to me, but someone she knew had told her something that had her mind spinning."

"That is so hard to hear . . . how all of this has made the two of you forget who you were before this all happened."

"I couldn't understand what she was talking about, because she mentioned a mentor of hers that she met in some parking lot or something. The part I heard clearly was that she'd told the woman all about what we went through. She told this lady that she has left God alone as a favor to Him."

"Oh. That stings hearing you say that." My dad's eyes slightly closed as if it were physically hurting him as he listened.

"The woman cried while Charlotte told the story, responding with this: 'When we think that we have been disqualified from knowing God, we're saying that Jesus's death on the cross wasn't enough of a sacrifice for our sins.'"

"Wow . . . that's powerful. I love that." His excitement returned as his eyes lit up. I couldn't get as excited as he had.

"Yes. I was caught breathless but wasn't able to grasp the full concept. I've thought about that statement nonstop. I still feel disqualified, even after hearing that. I must not want to believe it, even though it makes perfect sense."

"I couldn't have said it any better than whoever this woman is. I've watched you pull away from God as far as you could over the years." Dad's voice hinted of emotions he hid beneath the surface. "Was there anything else you talked to her about? I'm sure that couldn't have been the only thing."

"We talked about a few more things. I asked what happened to her after it all. You know, she had turned so cold after the procedure, and I never understood why. It was ultimately her choice. She said it was to protect me. She knew that I would've changed my life to make things work in that situation, but she couldn't do that."

Slight tears built up in my eyes. I tried to unnoticeably wipe them away.

"That was hard to hear. Part of it was that her life would've been disrupted and then changed forever also. I asked her about Joe and whatever happened to them. I think you remember me telling you that they had been spending a lot of time together."

"Yeah, I do, now that you mention it."

"She didn't want to have to break things off with him the way she did with me, so she just ended the friendship altogether. After our mess, she changed. She wasn't the same in college, and she still isn't herself. She seems melancholy. She'd never been a big talker, but that day, she seemed even more reclusive."

The waiter interrupted again but could tell we were in an intense conversation. He just wanted to make sure the food was okay, since I'd hardly touched my steak. I hadn't even remembered there was food in front of me.

"Brett, she has been through a lot. You both have. She just hasn't moved past it all, and you've tried to avoid it. Both of you have been affected by it in your own way. It's sad to hear."

"I almost forgot to tell you. Did you know that her parents pretty much shut her out after finding out what had happened between us?"

"I think I do remember hearing that. I recall her mom had choice words about our family, but it never bothered your mom and me."

"Did you know that she basically went to college on her own? I think she said something about her dad finally showing up on campus near the end of her freshman year in college. He was asking for a chance to talk, and I guess she said no."

"That's shocking. I couldn't imagine things getting that bad over a mistake she made."

"I guess she and her dad tried to resolve things, but her relationship with her mom never changed after she left. She kind of just slowly started to come back around to talking to her. They still haven't ever discussed the fact that Charlotte's mom told her that God wanted nothing to do with Charlotte, and neither did she."

"That woman said that? Are you kidding? I didn't realize it was that bad. No wonder she's a mess. She was an only child, and her parents told her they were done with her? That upsets me more than the choice you two made."

"How does that upset you?"

"How? They shut their daughter out when she needed them the most. They told her God wanted nothing to do with her when she needed Him the most." My dad's eyes watered and showed how much it truly hurt him to hear it.

"Dad, how do you do it? How do you sit here and talk with me, so calm and compassionate?

"Didn't you feel similar things about me? Aren't you mad at me? Aren't you upset that I screwed up so bad? Aren't you embarrassed of me?"

My head dropped in shame, and my eyes filled up again.

"Dad, I broke your trust back then. I made a terrible decision back then, and now I sit here and tell you that I screwed up again. I left my wife and kids. I moved out.

"I couldn't protect that baby, and that has never left me. And now I can't protect what I do have. How do you even want to talk to me and hear all this?"

"I never felt those things. I had to check my pride at that time, but I realized I couldn't take it personally. I don't know how to explain it to you, but I love you more than you will ever know.

"I raised you the best I could. I tried to teach you all that I knew. I wondered if I had missed something. I wondered if I had failed to give you good advice, but I had to leave it right there. I had to believe that I'd done the best I could."

He reached across and laid his hand on top of mine. A touch I didn't know I so desperately needed. Although there were people around us talking and laughing with music playing in the background, it was all silenced while we talked.

"When I looked at you, I felt terrible for the pain you were going through. You had walked into a mess, and I saw you trying to get out of it. I had to realize that it was your life, your journey. I wanted to take the pain away for you, but I couldn't.

"All these years, I've prayed and prayed on your behalf, but that is all I've been able to do. It's hurt because it seemed the more I prayed, the further you moved away from God. Part of me is trying to figure out if this very moment is an answer to my prayers.

"I wonder if you've gotten to such a low place that pain is making you reconsider what God is to you. Or is this just another stop on the way to your bottom? I don't know. I hope this is the final drop for you, but only you know that.

"The bottom line is that either way, I'll love you the same. I've loved you at your best, and I'll love you at your worst. That will never change."

His statement was overwhelming. My eyes watered up again, as well as his. Grasping my hand even harder, he told me everything was going to be okay.

The conversation reached its end. Through an uncomfortable laugh, we wiped our faces and asked for the check.

Leaving the restaurant, my dad gave me a long, tight hug. I could feel how much he loved me, despite any way I disappointed him.

Settling into my car, the realization set in that he hadn't given me one piece of advice or offered one opinion. He just listened—to all of it.

I wondered if I had it in me to be as good of a dad as he is. I guess I would have to start by wanting to be.

~ Forty-Six ~

CHARLOTTE

December 27, 2012

Dear Diary,

I have two new things to tell you. The first one is interesting with a bit of excitement attached to it. Glenda asked me to spend a day with her because she needs my help with something, but mysteriously, she wouldn't tell me what it was.

I love spending time with her, so it doesn't matter. Maybe she's taking me to where she grew up. Maybe we're going to a party where I get to meet her family. Who knows? But I'm excited.

The second thing isn't quite as lighthearted. I got another message from Brett. This one was a lot more in-depth than the other messages. I thought it was just a follow-up email from our meeting. I expected him to ask more questions and want to meet again.

I was wrong.

Dear Charlotte,

I don't know exactly what I want to say, but I know I must write this. I want to thank you for all your help a couple weeks ago. I'd waited years to have answers to some of those questions.

I see now that I'd created some of the craziest lies in my head, so it was relieving to hear the truth. You were very honest and straightforward, and I've always appreciated that about you.

I had to have those questions answered because I was lost. I'd told you about my wife and how I didn't know how to go forward in my marriage when I was trapped by so much crap. I've been doing a lot of thinking since our meeting.

I saw that neither you nor I has gotten over what happened. We both still carry guilt and have a hard time moving forward in fear of revenge.

But what I realized is that I have to make a choice to move past it. I have to actively try to rid myself of guilt. I realized a lot just from what you told me about dismissing what Jesus had done for me on the cross.

That stung. I was stumped. How could I even get to a place where I could consider Him dying on that cross for me? I've spent hours thinking it through, and I finally see that I have a lot of work to do to get there. I have to try and see what He sees in me.

I have to work to get my wife back to a place where she can even stand to look at me. And I must start to be the dad that I've wanted to be all these years. You sparked something in me to make me see that I'd hit rock bottom, and I'd stay there if I didn't make a change.

I want to thank you for everything. I want to thank you for all that you've taught me over the years—the good and the bad. You brought me to know God in a way that I never had before. You believed in me when I didn't believe in myself. You let me experience love at such a young age. Your example truly changed my life back then.

Yes, there was so much hurt after that, but I want to thank you for the good. I want to thank you again for your answers. They were hard questions to answer, but you did. Once again, your words spurred on my desire to regain my faith. That is where this story ends.

I don't want to come across as cruel, so I hope I can say this the best way possible. I have to say goodbye to you for good. You had a special place in my heart for years, and I thought that I'd taken it back, but all I did was replace that spot with the pain we went through.

I have to let all that go. If I want to give all I have to Cassidy, I truly have to give it my all. It's not that I have any hard feelings toward you—I just know that a friendship with you would not work well in our marriage.

Again, I'm sorry to have to send a message like this, but I know that you'll understand. You've always said all you wanted was for me to be happy. You've helped me to go after that again, and I thank you for that.

I want the same for you, and I'm sure in time you'll find it. Until then, keep your chin up.

Truly,

Brett

That was a surprise. I cried, yet I was happy for him. I was happy that something sparked him to want to return to a normal life. I was happy he wanted to get his family back with such fervor.

But although I was happy for him, I was also envious of his zeal. A bit of loneliness washed over me in that moment reading about his joy. He hadn't been in my life for years and only returned for less than a month, yet his goodbye was painful.

I had to check if I had more feelings for him than what I'd thought, but I didn't.

Then, it hit me again. After all the questions and answers had settled, the memories of Joe kicked up. When Brett said goodbye, it was as if all of my experiences had come to an end again, including those with Joe. My pain came from realizing that I'd screwed that up.

Brett had found me and asked questions, but I'd never get that from Joe. We didn't have a painful history that'd lead him to search for answers.

The way our relationship ended would require me to find him, which my pride would never let me do. After all, I let him go to protect him. Why would I find Joe only to tell him the same thing when things got too intense?

That's it. I don't have much more to share. The letter took my breath away, and I'm still trying to process all the feelings that it left me.

I did write him back.

Brett,

Thank you as well. I wish you the best of luck with your family. You deserve to be happy.

Take care of yourself,

Charlotte

It was short and simple. It was all I could say. And just like that, he was gone again and I was all alone. My heart was anguished and I was confused. I thought I'd gotten used to being alone and I'd be okay, but knowing that our ending meant a beautiful beginning for him crushed me all over again.

~ Forty-Seven ~

CHARLOTTE

"Charlotte, today's not going to be anything that you could've possibly imagined. I have a lot to share with you. During all our times together, I've wanted to tell you some things about me, but I didn't think it was the right time.

"Now, I have to tell you. You asked if we're going to see my family?"

"Yes . . ."

"That's not the reason for this little adventure, but I do have a lot to tell you about my family. I have a husband and a daughter. His name is Charles, and his nickname is Charlie, like yours. My daughter's name is Sarah.

"They're the most precious things in my life. My husband's an amazing man, and my daughter loves me more than I deserve. But the truth is that I lost them a long time ago."

"What do you mean? What do you mean you lost them?"

"They were killed in a terrible car accident."

"Glenda, I'm so sorry. I had absolutely no idea."

"I know you didn't. It's okay. I never talked about it. In fact, I don't talk about it with many people."

"What happened?"

"It has the potential of a long story, but I'll try to stick to the point and not add in all the details."

"No, no, I want to hear it all. After all, I have no clue where we're heading, but I'm guessing we're in for a ride."

"We lived in Marietta, Georgia. Charles and I had grown up around there, and it was a beautiful place to have a family. We had Sarah, and life was wonderful. We wanted to have more children, but that wasn't in the cards for us.

"We treasured Sarah even more because she was the precious gift that God did allow us to have. She'd started into a graduate nursing program but realized that there were better ones out there for her to become a nurse practitioner. She started looking into schools that were generally close to us.

"Charles was an amazing husband. We met in high school, and he had my eye from the first time that I saw him. We started off a little rocky, and our personalities clashed at first, but it didn't take long for both of us to become smitten with each other.

"He had a good job and always took care of Sarah and me. If I could've picked Sarah's husband, I would've hoped he would've been just like Charles.

"I can't explain the romance we had. It was as if I'd fall in love with him more each day. He'd treat me to flowers every few weeks. He'd pick up about six blush roses.

"That was our thing. It's a super-long explanation that wouldn't make much sense, but the bottom line is that I had casually mentioned they were my favorite, and he showed up with a bouquet to ask me to our first high school dance together. After that, it was our thing."

There was a pause, and I thought her story was ending.

"I don't mean to pry, but can you tell me what happened?"

"Oh, yes. I'm sorry. My mind started thinking back, and I got lost in the memories. Okay, where was I? Oh, the accident.

"So, I told you Sarah had been wanting to look at some schools for her nursing dreams. Charles was going to take her to look at colleges, and I thought it was so special for the two of them. I kissed them both goodbye, gave them a long hug, and watched them leave.

"That was it. That was the last time I talked to them. That was the last time I touched them. That was the last time I kissed them both.

"I got a call a couple hours later telling me there had been an accident and I needed to go. I raced there. I just knew that they were okay and he was trying to save someone's life who'd been in the accident.

"I was completely wrong. The car that hit them was going so fast that the impact was too hard for them to survive. I saw white draped cloths over two bodies. A highway patrol officer informed me that they belonged to me.

"I hardly remember anything after that. I know that I collapsed into him. I know that I ended up at the hospital. I waited there for hours. Friends came one by one, but I had no idea who.

"People asked about funeral arrangements and which funeral home would be coming to collect their bodies. They said they had to wait twenty-four hours or something to release them, but I could collect their personal belongings.

"They asked me to go to the morgue downstairs to officially identify my husband and daughter. Even though I'd seen them at the accident's scene, it was protocol.

"I went down there, and it was horrifying. They were lying on these cold metal tables, but luckily there was a thin blanket underneath them. Thin shards of glass were still embedded in their faces, and I could see punctures where it looked as if they had tried to remove the larger pieces. There were cuts that had bled, and I could see the stain of blood coming from those wounds, as if they had tried to clean them up.

"I identified their bodies, and then they gave me some time alone with them. My face fell onto Charles's chest. I begged him not to leave. I begged him to wake up and stay with me.

"It was so irrational, but I didn't know what else to say. I didn't want to say goodbye. I didn't want it to be over.

"I walked over to Sarah, and I stroked her hair like I did when she was a baby, asleep in her crib. I asked her to come back. I told her she had so much left to live for.

"I sounded like a fool, but I didn't care. I couldn't leave. I couldn't get myself to turn and walk out that door. My friend had to walk me out, and I yelled at her for making me go.

"I begged them not to leave me. I was left all alone. I went back to the waiting room, and I just lay in my friend's lap. I waited for who knows how long, and they finally brought me two bags—one filled with my daughter's things and one with my husband's.

"I didn't want to look at what was inside. I waited until I got home. Seeing his wedding ring—I can't even describe how difficult—how painful that moment felt. Spots of blood still lingered inside the ring. It hit me then that our vows had been upheld—*'til death do us part.* And that was it. They were gone."

Tears streamed down my face. It was the most beautiful and tragic love story. Her words relayed how much she loved him. Her body language screamed how much she missed them.

"Glenda, I'm so sorry. This whole time I thought that you had a husband at home and older children somewhere."

"Nope. It's just me. My parents died about ten years ago within two years of each other. Each death brought different grief with it, but grief is grief. I learned that no matter how hard you try, you can't escape it. At that point, I was even lonelier."

"I don't think I could've gone through what you did and kept a sweet disposition. I imagine I would be bitter and haggard."

"You'd be surprised. I can say with all sincerity that the only thing that allowed me to survive was my faith. I wouldn't have made it without that."

"You mean God?"

"Of course."

"What about the other car? Whatever happened to them?"

"I was getting to that part. There was one driver. He had been drinking. As it usually goes, he survived.

"I later found out that he was taken to the same hospital as Sarah and Charlie. I'm lucky that I didn't know it at the time, because my rage would've been aimed at him.

"Later, the state contacted me. He'd been in jail since the accident, and they wanted to talk about bringing him up on charges. They let me know the trial date and mentioned I'd have to be a character witness if it came to sentencing.

"I went. I heard all of his excuses. His wife had left him. He was about to lose his job. None of it justified taking two lives.

"I had to get up and speak about what he took from me. I wanted to tell him to rot in hell, but my exchange with God before the trial changed my mind.

"God and I had this encounter about forgiveness, and I realized that the man's punishment wasn't up to me. All I could do was work on forgiving him in order to free myself. It took a long time, and I had to forgive him over and over again. That's when I realized that forgiveness comes in layers, like an onion."

"I'm speechless. I don't even know how I could ever consider forgiving him at all, not to mention just a little bit."

"That makes sense."

"What do you mean?"

"You're having the hardest time believing that God would ever forgive you. If you don't think that the God of the universe could ever forgive you, why would you think that anyone else deserves forgiveness either?"

"I guess that makes sense." I couldn't process that entirely, but she was right. I had no concept of forgiveness. How would I ever begin to understand how she could forgive the man who took her husband and child from her because he made a terrible decision to drink and drive?

"Here is what I have to tell you, and this is why we're here. When you came into my life, I prayed many times over for you. I told God that I'd do whatever it took to change your opinion of Him. You reminded me so much of what my Sarah might've been like that I was more than happy to oblige.

"You and I had some deep conversations, and every time I wanted to change the way you saw God. I wanted to change your perspective of how He saw you. I wanted to show you that He loved you beyond anything that you could think you deserved, because He loved you long before you made any mistakes at all."

I interrupted with a laugh. "You did that pretty well."

"I prayed and prayed and prayed. I talked to Charlie and Sarah about you. I told them how you had brought more joy into my life."

I was taken aback by everything she said. She loved me that much? She prayed for me that often? I didn't think anyone in my entire life had cared for me in that way. I didn't even know how to receive it.

"During all that time, I was worried about you and you never knowing the full concept of forgiveness. But as I was praying, the tables turned. God started to work on me and ask me about the full meaning of forgiveness myself.

"He asked me if I'd really forgiven the driver and turned it all over to Him. I knew I hadn't. There was one way that I knew. I read something that said, 'You know that you have completely forgiven someone when you ask God to withhold punishment for what they've done to you or someone you love.'"

"That's the hardest thing I've ever heard. Asking God to withhold punishment from someone who hurt you? I couldn't."

"Yeah, I thought the same thing. I sobbed. I knew what God was asking me to do. He was showing me that if I could ask Him to not take vengeance against the driver, I'd be fully free.

"I was mad. I was angry. I was shocked. All these years my solace had been that God would one day bring him to justice. That's why I hesitated in taking revenge myself.

"That justice I'd relied on would be erased by me asking for the driver to be let off the hook for what he did. I remember setting the book down. I was furious and stunned and mad and resistant.

"I went to the kitchen to clean. I thought keeping busy would get it off my mind. It only circled in my mind more and more and ran me ragged.

"I remember the moment when I pleaded with God but finally surrendered. I told Him that if He'd help me, I'd ask that the driver be set free. I dropped to my knees and said it, asking God to not hold him accountable for what he'd done. I stayed there and wept, but for how long? I don't know."

Tears were forming in my eyes as I was listening to her retell her experience, crying on that kitchen floor.

"I felt powerless—like I'd given away all my weapons. After my chest stopped heaving, I stood up and felt as if fifty pounds had been taken off of my shoulders. I literally felt free. Even though I'd asked for his freedom, it was offered to me as well."

"You're probably the strongest person I know. There's no one else I know who could've done that."

"I thought I was finished. But God asked me to take one more step. I tried to act like I didn't hear Him ask. I told Him no at first. I wanted to refuse.

"God wanted me to go see the man himself. He wanted me to tell him that I'd forgiven him. He wanted me to tell him that I'd pleaded with God to set him free for what he did."

"Go there? Like, visit him in prison?"

"Yes, and that's where we're going. We're on our way to where he's been since I saw him last."

"Are you kidding? How are we going in? Don't you have to have a badge and permission and special visiting days and times? What if showing up there doesn't end well?"

She paused, then took a deep breath and smiled. "You see, I had to get permission from him in order to visit. I looked up all the rules for visitation, and I followed them."

"So, you've had this planned for a bit? When we get there, will I wait in the parking lot? I'm perfectly okay with that. I'm just curious."

"No, actually, I asked if you could come too. You were the only one that I wanted to come with me. I had to apply for you. I'm sorry if it bothers you that I did."

Who would've thought a seventy-five-year-old woman could have so many sneaky tactics? It didn't bother me, but it definitely surprised me.

"No, it's fine. I don't mind at all. I'm honored that you'd want me to go with you. I don't know how well I'll handle the situation, but I'll go anyway."

The rest of the way, she talked about more details of what happened, and I asked more questions. She laughed at some of my inquiries. In response to others, she stared out the window as if she were watching a movie from long ago. Her eyes would tear occasionally, but she never broke down.

We found the prison and drove through four security gates. We stuck a tag on the window from inside my car to show that we'd been allowed to come in, then got out and walked to the entrance.

We waited in the lobby until an officer brought us into the visitation room. I was nervous, so I could only imagine what Glenda was feeling. Her head was bowed, and her mouth was moving slightly.

I was confused at first, but I realized that she was praying—fervently. I could see her body swaying a little bit and noticed her hands embracing themselves, with her eyes intermittently squinting shut. I couldn't help but feel terrible for her.

I prayed for the first time in ages. I couldn't do what she was about to do, and I admired her strength. I could only imagine what I was about to witness.

~ Forty-Eight ~

GLENDA

Dear Charlie,

I couldn't get to the cemetery today because of the weather, but I want to talk to you and write to you about yesterday. I'll just bring this to you when I can get back there.

I think I've finished repairing the shattered heart I've had for the past thirty years. My heart will always have fine cracks where the pieces don't perfectly fit back together, but I believe this is the best it's going to get in this world.

Yesterday, Charlotte came with me on my crazy journey. She thought we were going to do something simple, but I finally told her the purpose of our trip.

I told her about you and how we met. I told her about Sarah and how precious she was to us. I told her about the accident and all that entailed.

Then, I told her about Jason. I told her about the journey I've been on recently with forgiveness. She thought I was crazy, and I can't blame her. Had I met someone who was about to do what I had to do yesterday, I'd think they were insane.

There are many details leading up to us getting to the lobby of the prison visitation center, but I'll start with the part where I couldn't breathe.

The prison officer came to get us from the lobby and brought us to the visitation room. I knew Jason was coming any minute and I would have to follow through on why I went there. I squeezed Charlotte's hand, and she squeezed back, as if she were just as nervous.

I heard the door opening, and I lifted my head to see an aged version of him walking toward me. He meekly smiled, and I returned the same awkward smile. He sat down and we exchanged all the pleasantries.

After I introduced him to Charlotte, there was a long break, and it was a strange place to navigate from. Jason finally broke the silence.

"Glenda, I know you came for a purpose. I've spent a lot of time wondering what you might need to say to me. No matter what it is, I probably deserve it, so I'm ready to answer anything you have to ask me."

"Jason, this will be the hardest thing I've ever had to do. I came here to talk to you about the obvious—the accident."

"Go ahead. I'm ready. I know this might sting." His face grimaced as if he were about to get hit.

"When we were going through the trial process, it was hard for me to even look at you. Charles and Sarah were everything to me, and I wanted to blame you as the person who took them from me. I wanted to seek revenge. I wanted to do anything I could to make you feel the pain that I was feeling."

His face dropped, and he looked down at his clasped hands resting on the table.

"But my faith took over, and I knew I couldn't do that. I knew that I had to start trying to forgive you, and I thought it would be impossible. But God slowly softened my heart toward you.

"I saw you in the courtroom, and I didn't want to feel for you. I didn't want to sympathize for you. Sometimes I'd catch myself sympathizing anyway, and then I'd have to work my way back to being angry at you."

At that, he slightly peeked up at me. I could tell he had slight hope about what I had left to say.

"By the trial's end, I was ready to let it go. There was nothing I could do to bring Charles and Sarah back. The trial was close to over, and reliving the horror of that night would soon end.

"With it, I needed to forgive you. I asked God to help me. This is where my story turned. He didn't help me forgive you. He helped change my perspective of the end result."

"You don't have to forgive me. I don't deserve your forgiveness. I . . ."

"Wait. You might've been the one to drive the car in the accident that killed them, but God was the One who said it was time for them to return back to Him. He had the power of life and death, not you.

"I was mad at God for a while after I learned that hard lesson. My faith carried me through because I knew He was still good during all those years before the accident, and He wouldn't change in one circumstance. Still, I felt betrayed. I couldn't believe that the God I'd worshiped my whole life would allow me to be hurt in that way.

"God's ways are higher than ours and often beyond understanding. I had to learn to trust Him again. It took a long time for me to have the same kind of trust in God as I did before the accident, but the process healed me."

Jason interrupted with a cracked voice. "I don't even know what to say. . . ."

"Hold on, there's more. In all that time, I stopped holding you responsible for taking them from me. I was still mad, but I moved past it more each day. Here I am thirty years later, and I'm finally coming to see you. I'm finally letting you know that I forgive you."

All he could do was lower his head again and cry. He didn't say anything. I reached over and placed my hand on his forearm. His head then completely fell onto his arm and he continued sobbing.

"But, Jason, there is another part. This was the hardest part for me, but I know that it's the best thing I've ever done.

"A little while back, I went to visit them at their graves. I was upset again, and some resentment returned. God started dealing with me about it. Around the same time, I'd been encouraging a friend to forgive herself for mistakes in her past."

His head was still lowered, so I winked at Charlotte. She knew that friend I referenced was her.

"God showed me that I had work of my own to do with you. I told Him that I'd forgiven you and I was past that lesson. An old adage came to mind immediately.

"'The hardest lesson to learn is the one you thought you already knew.'

"He brought me back to a book I'd recently read and wanted to throw away. It said this: 'You know that you have completely forgiven someone when you ask God to withhold punishment for what they've done to you or someone you love.'

"I had a more intense argument with God. I couldn't believe that He was requiring so much of me after all these years. Then, He asked me to come here and tell you.

"So, here I am. I want to tell you that I've fully forgiven you. I've asked God to watch over you. I've asked Him to not hold you responsible for what you did."

I had to hold back from sobbing while I was saying these things to Jason. I felt like I was letting it go all over again. I was in my most humble moment, and I felt so weak.

All my defenses were gone. I was letting the guy who hurt you and Sarah go free—maybe not physically, but spiritually.

Jason couldn't stop weeping. I kept holding his arm, and I could feel his guilt and shame flooding from his eyes. It took us both a little while to stop crying.

"Glenda, I'm so sorry." Jason lifted his head and wiped the tears from his face, then looked at me with sorrow-filled eyes. "I'm so sorry. I didn't expect this at all. I thought you were coming to say the exact opposite. And I believed I deserved it.

"But you came and told me that you've fully forgiven me, and that's more than I can receive. I don't deserve the kindness you've shown me."

His words struck a chord on my heartstrings, and I wiped my eyes and nose with the tissue clutched in my hand. "None of us do, Jason. None of us deserve anything."

That reality had sunk in, and I gave silent thanks for the opportunity to be in that room in that moment.

"The only reason we do is because God loved us first. He loves me so much that I don't need to hang on to the rage I had for you. He can sustain me, and He is enough.

"He loves you so much, and even though you may not understand the depths of that love just yet, I pray you will."

"I can't. I can't believe that He even wants to acknowledge my existence."

"That's not true. That's probably one reason I'm here, to tell you that He sent Jesus here to die on that cross, not just for everyone else, but for you. He hung up there and suffered so that when you suffered, He could wipe it all away.

"He was whipped and beaten so that when you continually sinned, He would be able to continually forgive you. He isn't up there disappointed. He is waiting for you to come to Him with your pain and let Him help you with it. When you take a step toward Jesus, all He wants to say to you is, 'Welcome home, Jason. Welcome home.'"

He looked shocked, confused, perplexed. He couldn't wrap his head around it all. We talked a little longer, but I didn't want to tell him about God. I just wanted to encourage him to experience God for himself. Once I felt my purpose for being there was over, I wanted to leave.

"Jason, I'm going to get on my way home. It's a long drive back, and my driver is pretty expensive."

I was laughing, of course.

"But I want you to know that I'll be praying for you every day. God loves you so much, but I hope you come to know that for yourself."

And with that, we hugged, exchanged kind parting words, and his guard led him out of the room. After he left, Charlotte and I were allowed to leave. We returned our visitor badges while signing out. They returned our licenses to us, and we walked out the doors.

Once I heard the doors slam behind me, I took a deep breath and exhaled thirty years of bitterness, anger and grief. I felt free. I felt like I was literally let out of a jail of unforgiveness I didn't even know I was in.

I looked at Charlotte, and she was wiping away her own tears. I didn't ask what she was crying about. I just reached out to grab her hand, and we walked arm in arm on the way to the car without speaking. We remained silent until we got back on I-40.

Charlotte whispered, "I don't know how you just did that." Her face showed confusion. "I cannot believe what I just witnessed. It's as if I were watching a miracle happen right in front of me." She was so amazed, that I was worried she couldn't focus on driving.

She glanced in the rearview mirror as a car approached from behind, its lights shining through the back window. It passed and sped on. Charlotte took a deep breath so she could gain focus.

"I think I can finally understand. You offered him something he could've never attained on his own. And you didn't offer it because you had to. You offered it because you trusted God."

She had a hard time getting her words out, because she was emotional about it. "He couldn't understand, and I wonder how long it will take him until he can."

We seemed to revisit the same conversation many times. She said she felt like she wasn't even there, but just watching from outside. We would pause, and then she would say the same thing again, always starting with the phrase, "I can't believe . . ." After we wore out the conversation, I asked her a question.

"Do you think that if I could forgive the man who is responsible for killing my husband and only child that you could ever learn to forgive yourself?"

Her face softened as if she were in agony. She thought for a minute. "When we were sitting in that room, I kept sympathizing for him. At one point, I realized that it wasn't sympathy. It was empathy.

"I knew what it felt like not to be able to receive a gift of forgiveness. I understood how he felt undeserving. I understood his head lowering and his mouth quivering.

"My heart broke for him, and I was embarrassed to feel that way. I didn't understand why then, but I do now.

"I have to begin the journey. I have to learn how to forgive myself. I need to know this God you keep talking about.

"When you told Jason you wanted him to not just hear about God, but to experience God, it hit me that I was avoiding that very thing. Even when I did believe and try to follow God, I don't know if I *knew* Him or knew *of* Him. This is a whole new concept, and it's scary."

"Experiencing God at a deeper level is always frightening, no matter how long you've walked with Him. When I became a widow, I'd never trusted God with anything like that, but I had to walk through it with Him.

"Knowing that I had to forgive the person I hated the most, that was another trial I had to walk through. I had to choose God to be my only family after losing every family member that I'd ever known.

"I learned to trust Him all this time He has left me here instead of taking me home to be with Charles and Sarah. Every stage has been as hard as the one before, but every time it was for my good.

"We would walk through that fire, and He'd deliver me from that thing that had a hold on me. I ask you to experience Him because telling you these things is like explaining a mountain while only holding a rock."

"Wait, can I ask you something about what you said?"

"Of course. You can ask me anything."

"You said something about asking to go home to Charles and Sarah. Do you mean that? Do you really want to pass on to be with them?"

"Yes, Charlotte, I do. I'm weary and tired. I've done all the Lord's asked me to do, and I've never been able to understand why He keeps me here. My family's gone.

"My family's now you, Charlotte. You've been a light in my life for the past few months. I've loved every minute with you. I've loved your smiles and your tears. You've given me a glimpse of what Sarah and I might've had. You've softened me and allowed me to mother you.

"But even that has to come to an end at some point. I won't be here forever, and one day, I'll leave you as you move forward into the next part of your journey.

"But I need you to know that every spring is the hardest season for me because that's when Charles and Sarah passed away. The scent of spring flowers and the feel of a cool breeze take me right back to those days of grief and pain. I'd sit out on my porch and just cry, all alone. The sounds and smells of spring kept me company.

"I just don't know how many more springs I can take. I've told you that I have to trust the Lord at every stage I encounter. This is a new one. How many springs is He going to walk through with me?

"I'll trust Him, and I'll believe that He's given me you as a gift to help me endure it."

Charlotte was touched by the conversation. She went on to tell me how she felt as if I were the mother she wished she had. We had the same sentiment about each other, and it was a beautiful and intimate moment. She did ask me another question.

"Glenda, I've always wanted to know something. What's the meaning of the necklace you wear? I would've normally thought it was just a casual piece of jewelry, but I've seen you touch it in the past as if it were a treasure.

"Today, when we were waiting to go in, I saw you praying. I know you were struggling, but I saw you holding the necklace so close. If it were a cross, I would've thought it was part of your prayers, but it's a locket. Is it something that Charles gave you?"

"No, it's something my dad gave me right before he passed away. It was a treasure. The meaning behind it was special to me.

"He said he knew that Sarah and Charles had left empty spaces in my heart, and even though they might never be filled again, I could keep their pictures close to remind me of the love we shared.

"It's been around my neck ever since. I take it off occasionally, of course, but it's precious to me. Sometimes, when grief sneaks up and gives me an unbearable day, prayer and that necklace get me through."

Then, Charlotte brought up something that surprised me.

"Glenda, I have something to confess. I just need to talk to you about it."

"Okay, go for it."

"Brett contacted me. He said he had questions for me about the stuff from our past and asked if we could meet to talk. I wasn't sure it was a good idea, but I felt like I owed it to him."

"I thought he was married with kids?"

"He is. That's one reason he was reaching out. His marriage was in a ditch because he couldn't get past the guilt from the abortion. He thought he had but was realizing that it was haunting him. He felt like God was going to drop the hammer and get revenge by hurting one of his kids.

"He asked me some hard questions. Like, if there was anything he could've done to stop me. I think I helped him by telling him there was nothing he could've done. He wanted to know if I thought having the abortion was worth it. I couldn't answer. That is something God and I'll have to work on.

"He's wondered how I've been able to face God since that day. I told him that I was still figuring that out myself. I told him what you'd shared about Jesus on the cross, but that's all I could offer.

"It was the one and only meeting because he wrote and told me that he heard everything he needed and was on his way to getting his family back. It's sad to think that I'll never talk to him again, but it's the closure we both might've needed.

"I'd always wondered if I missed out on the relationship with the only person who'd ever loved me. But after talking to Brett that day, I realized that the one I'd shared the most with was Joe.

"Joe saw me suffer in ways Brett never had. Joe walked me through the darkest time in my life.

"When I tried to isolate myself, he'd pull me out of it. When I wanted to feel sorry for myself, he'd make me laugh until I forgot why I was sad in the first place. He lit up my life, whether I knew it then or not.

"All this time I thought I'd messed up letting Brett go, but in the end, Joe was the one I let slip away. He never had to tell me he loved me. He showed me in all the ways he cared for me. That was the treasure I overlooked."

The words almost came rushing out of my mouth. I almost slipped and told her I knew Joe. I wanted to tell her I knew his mother and knew he was single.

I wanted to tell her to go after him, but I listened to God and didn't say a word. It was hard to see her in pain and not give her information to ease her ache.

We continued home with many more topics of conversation. We pulled up at my house, and we were both emotionally exhausted.

"Thank you, Charlotte. You have no idea how much this meant to me. You were with me during the hardest thing God has ever asked me to do."

"It means more to me than you'll ever know. I got to witness a miracle."

"Charlotte, do you mind if we meet again soon? I'd love to spend more time with you."

"I'd love to."

It was probably the best day I've had in years. I would've never dreamed that the day I went to tell Jason I'd fully forgiven him would end up being the most spectacular day of all. How much more could God have for me?

Charlie, please kiss my Sarah. I love you, and I can't wait to see you. Until then, know that my heart still aches for you as if you'd just left me last week.

All my love,
Glenda

~ Forty-Nine ~

CHARLOTTE

Dear God,

It's me again. I know that You're there, and I think that You're listening. I want to talk to You about this week.

A few days ago, I went on that long journey with Glenda to the prison. On the way, she shared her horrific story. I had no idea that she'd been through so much.

All this time, I'd thought that Christians had the easiest lives because they always seemed so content. What I realized is they just handle situations with a completely different perspective.

If I'd gone through the pain she did, I wouldn't have made it. I would've given up at some point, maybe even given up on life. I definitely wouldn't be involved in a church, and I'd definitely not be telling people about Your unconditional and faithful love.

I learned all that she'd been through, yet in stark contrast, I knew how passionate she was about You and Your goodness. It was as if I were trying to figure out a quantitative math problem. Nothing made sense.

All the times she'd told me about You, I knew she was sincere, but I wasn't ready to believe it completely. Seeing her in that prison—forgiving Jason for everything, reaching out to console him as he wept in shame, and then telling him that she has prayed that God have mercy on him—that was as if I had seen You work a miracle right in front of me.

It was better than a thousand sermons I'd heard over the years. There was only one way that she could've done that with such composure and love. You. There is no other explanation.

On my way home, I began to think about Your concept of forgiveness and tried to block out the way the world teaches it. I watched Glenda offer all her forgiveness, and then I saw Jason have a hard time accepting it. I thought he was being blind.

This woman had given the most beautiful gift, but he was refusing to accept her offering because he didn't think he deserved it. It hit me. That's You and me. You've offered me the most beautiful gift of forgiveness, but I turn away from it because I don't feel worthy. If I weren't worthy, You wouldn't have offered it.

So, here I am. I'm asking for Your forgiveness, but this time, I believe that You want to give it to me. I'm still having a hard time feeling worthy of it, but I realize that's not for me to determine. You've decided that I'm deserving, and I can't resist that any longer.

It'll take me a while to get past the guilt and shame that I've been so used to wearing, but if I walk with You, I believe that You can help me shed those ugly garments.

Tonight, I'm writing in my new journal. My old one was used as a diary, but this is for my conversations with You. I've never felt so close to You as I do right now while writing to You. It is another gift to me.

I do have a few things to talk to You about. The first is my gratitude. I'm so grateful that You've given me the gift of Glenda. She's been more of a mom to me than anyone ever has.

She's loved me when I didn't think I'd ever love myself again. She invested her time and love to try to heal my pain. She's felt my pain so much that she has cried right along with me.

She hugs me as if I haven't seen her in years and she doesn't want to let me go. It was awkward at first, but now I look forward to it every time I see her.

The part that scares me is that she might be a temporary gift. She spoke of her weariness and wanting to go home. Please don't take her from me. She's changed my life in such a short time, and I need her. I have no one else like her in my life.

She spoke of missing her husband and daughter and how much she wanted to be with them. I wanted to tell her that it wouldn't be fair to leave me, but I had no right to say that.

God, please give me time with her. I want to learn more about her and how she has handled her storms. I want to feel loved for so much longer. I want to feel her hugs for years to come.

My request is selfish and a lot to ask, but she brought me to You. She made me see You in such a different light and from a different perspective. I don't think You would've given her to me, let her be such an influence on me, and then taken her away just as fast.

You know that I need her to help me through this journey with You. In the end, You'll do what You need to do, but I pray You let her stay here with me. I promise to help her get through her spring pain.

Another question is about work. Before meeting Glenda, I'd put in a request to transfer to another hotel. I wanted to move up in management, and I also wanted to get away from Tennessee.

At first, I applied to Paris and London, but realized either choice would be too drastic of a change. I'm willing to move, but I'm not that adventurous. I looked at the other cities available for the same type of training program, and there's a hotel in Seattle that could offer me the change I'm looking for.

Right before this encounter with Glenda, I applied. I haven't heard anything yet, but the date for the acceptance letter is coming soon.

I've been begging You to keep Glenda here, so I can't leave her if I get accepted. Please don't let me be accepted if I'm not supposed to go. If I'm accepted, I might have to decline their offer anyway.

Thank You for so much. I can't explain how much better I feel after this time with You. Thank You, thank You, thank You.

I love You,
Charlotte

~ Fifty ~

CASSIDY

"I'd always thought that if I caught my husband cheating, that I'd be done. There would be no excuses. And here I am in that exact position. I found out that Brett has been seeing someone."

I was sitting across from Trish, and I wanted to tell her everything. I was in the situation that I'd dreaded, and I'd already predetermined how I'd respond.

"I just don't know what to do. I want to quit. I want out. I've spent enough time feeling as if I'm not enough for him."

"Cassidy, I'm sorry. This is awful, and it's so hard to see you having to deal with this. I wish I had a way to make it easier for you."

She just listened. She didn't give me any advice. It caught me off guard because I was expecting her to try to change my mind. I wanted her opinion.

"Do you think it's okay for me to quit at this point? Haven't I held out long enough?"

Trish took a long pause. I could tell she was ruminating. She finally spoke, and I was ready for her answer.

"Have you prayed about it?" That was all she came back with. That was all she asked.

"No."

"If you pray about it and feel it's the thing God wants for you, then it's the right thing to do."

"I should pray whether or not to leave after he cheated on me? Isn't that understood? Doesn't the Bible say that I can leave if the spouse has been unfaithful?"

"God knows what you can handle. I don't. You might not even know what you can handle. God is the only One who has the answer to whether you should end the marriage or not.

"Some women can forgive their husbands four or five times after they've been unfaithful. Some can only handle it once. I never know why some stay so long and others leave so fast.

"It isn't my business, but if you're asking me what I'd do, I wouldn't make a move until God tells you to move."

That was a great answer for someone else to hear, but not me. I didn't know what else to say. We ended our lunch, and I set out for home.

I felt terrible. I didn't have that powerful feeling of revenge that I expected to come home with. I felt weak. I wanted Brett to feel the pain that I felt.

Going out to my porch the next morning, I sat in the same seat I'd sat in last fall when I'd realized our marriage was worse than what I'd thought. Shortly after, Brett decided to leave, and I thought that was going to be the hardest time of my life.

I didn't expect it to get worse, but it did. I wanted to ignore God, or at least not listen to His answer for me to go or stay.

I cried until I thought I'd run out of tears. When they stopped falling from my chin, I realized I had to let go. God knew so much more than I did. I hadn't learned much in the short time back at church, but I did know that His ways were often harder but better.

So, I surrendered. I said that I'd stay still until I got a clear answer from Him. I also said that I'd pray for Brett. I told God that I couldn't pray past his name but asked Him to do whatever He needed to do.

I met up with Trish again a few weeks later. Sliding into the seat opposite mine at a table in our favorite coffee shop, she started with a simple, "So, how is it going?"

"I'm struggling with lies and pictures in my head. I imagine the two of them having a romance I envy. I picture them at candlelit dinners, walking through parks holding hands.

"The images that sicken me most are those picturing them intimate with each other. I throw up in my mouth each time I think about it. My imagination's holding me captive."

"That's an awful place to be, but you know your thoughts aren't factual, right? You're making up scenarios in your mind and letting them stay for as long as they'd like."

"I think about them less the busier I am, but at night the images run rampant. They return when my mind is free."

"You could be completely wrong about the entire thing. Remember, this all started by you assuming the worst."

"You're right. The advice you gave me last time helped. I surrendered to the idea of waiting on God.

"I held on during the weeks after. I worked hard to not be mean to Brett every time we met to exchange the kids.

"He'd leave, I'd cry, and then I'd ask God to help me because not saying anything was extremely painful. I kept telling God that I trusted Him over and over and over again. I know He has something good for me, whether Brett is part of it or not."

And I was right. When I got home from our coffee date, I received a letter. It was a beautiful, formal postcard-like invitation. I had no idea who it was from. All the details made me pay closer attention.

I'd been invited to a long weekend in Destin Beach. It detailed reservations at the same bed-and-breakfast we stayed at in October, which was highly suspicious. It also stated that I didn't need to RSVP, but my attendance was *greatly desired.*

On the schedule, there were two dinner reservations at exquisite restaurants, both on the water, and a reservation for a couple's massage at a local spa.

As I looked at the envelope again, I noticed a round-trip airline ticket was slid, along with an additional note, confirming transportation from the airport to the bed-and-breakfast.

A range of emotions assailed and overwhelmed me. Of course, I knew it was Brett. I could tell he was attempting something to brush things over. Of course I wanted to see him and be treated to a wonderful weekend, but last time, my books ended up to be my best friends. Would things be any different?

Did I consider going because I wanted to see him, or did I want to stand him up out of revenge? I had great thoughts of us getting back together, then my thoughts would shift to being angry that he thought that all he had to do was charm me to fix things.

For the first time, I asked God what I should do—without anyone suggesting it. I'd always loved to ask my friends for advice, and I'd gotten used to which ones to ask for certain topics. This was new for me.

As suspected, He nudged me to go. I had to humble myself and have an open mind about what the invitation could lead to. Brett's parents knew about the plan because they were watching the kids. When I dropped them off, our exchange was brief, but all three of us were smirking. It was one of those conversations that didn't need words, because you knew you were all thinking the same thing.

I'd planned to rehearse what I wanted to say to Brett before I landed, but the flight was short, and the descent snuck up on me. I gathered all my belongings to get off the plane. My mind and stomach spun out of control. I took the escalator and allowed it to lower me down as slowly as possible. I was buying time to try to compose myself.

As soon as I could see the baggage claim area, I saw Brett standing there, waiting. He held a sign, as if he were a limo driver, that said, "I'M SORRY," with a dozen white roses. I couldn't keep from crying.

I could go on and on about the weekend, but it was the most amazing time of my life. I couldn't believe that he planned it all on his own this time. All the things he'd arranged for us to do were dreamlike, but the first thing he did meant the most to me.

He wanted to go walk on the beach so we could talk. Brett asking to talk was a big deal in itself. He ended up sharing his deepest secrets that he'd been trying to hide.

He was sincere. He was broken. He was emotional. He was honest. He told me why he'd been drifting away from me. He told me why he was scared to get close to the kids. He told me that he tried all he could to stop Charlotte from getting the abortion, but all his attempts had failed.

I remembered back in college when he spoke about not being able to fix someone, and it all came together for me. He'd been in pain since the day I'd met him. But, unaware of what he was going through, there was nothing I could've done to help him.

He admitted to me every detail about his attempt to resolve things with Charlotte. All this time I thought it was for romance. He showed me all the message history on his account. He was going to delete the account but knew I wouldn't believe him if he didn't show me everything.

Brett laid it all out on the table. He validated every concern or suspicion of mine. How could I not forgive him? How could I resist us getting back together? After the talk we had, everything fell into place. I was as happy as a schoolgirl, and he seemed just as happy.

We held hands, and he would kiss me for no reason. It was as if we were on a second honeymoon. We fell back in love in a matter of days.

Our last night, we went back on the beach. He said he wanted to watch one more sunset before we went home. We were facing the beautiful sky washed in pink, purple and orange hues, when he suddenly bent over.

I'd thought he'd found a shell or something. I shockingly realized he'd gotten down on one knee. What he said was even more remarkable.

"Charlotte, will you please take me back? I promise I'll never hurt you again. This ring is a symbol of that."

The gesture itself was heart-stopping. And to make it even better, the ring was gorgeous, a diamond-filled anniversary band.

My eyes were watered, and my hand immediately covered my mouth in shock.

"What do I say? I have no words. Of course I will."

He jumped to his feet and kissed me with more intention than I'd ever felt before. He held me close, and I could tell something was different in his heart.

And that was it. The closeness I felt in that moment never faded that weekend. It was the most jaw-dropping experience I'd ever had. I don't know if I had ever felt so loved.

Ironically, I'm sitting in that same chair on my porch where I thought my marriage was in ruins. I'm looking at the scenery I'd stared at when I thought my heart was going to break open. I'd sat in this chair when I cried, thinking he was having an affair and leaving me.

Now, I sit in the same chair and thank God for all that He did. I thank Him for all the friends He brought into my life to support me when I didn't know what I needed. I surprised myself when I thanked Him for the husband He gave me and the in-laws that had been so good to me through everything.

Then, I thanked Him for being Him. I couldn't believe that I was praising God for not letting me quit. I expressed gratitude for Him stretching my faith further than what I thought I was capable of.

I thanked Him for finding me through that window when I was doing dishes. I'll never forget Him shining the sun on my face and allowing me to feel His love and grace. Of all the relationships I've had in my life, none mean as much to me as the one I've begun with Him.

~ Fifty-One ~

GLENDA

Good morning, Lord,

Thank You for another beautiful morning. The sun is just rising, and birds are just starting to chirp. It's cold as can be, but it's gorgeous already.

I just want to thank You for all the beautiful mornings You've given me over the course of my life. You've always shown me Your brilliance when I opened my eyes to it. I'm just sitting here, remembering all the times You've walked with me through my fires and my times in the wilderness.

I'm remembering all the times I sat on the mountaintop and never wanted to come down. But I couldn't stay there. I had to go through all the peaks and valleys to experience all of who You are. I'm in awe of You.

My visit with Jason the other day . . . I did what you asked—all of what you asked. I told him about our conversation, and I brought Charlotte with me.

I accomplished it all while fighting the belief that I wouldn't be able to. I was sure it was going to destroy me. I was convinced it was beyond what I could do.

On the other hand, I knew You'd never led me astray. I remembered You had always been good to me. I recognized that when You asked for something that was beyond difficult, it was more for me than it was for You.

Once again, You were right. I loved talking with Charlotte. I felt like I was sharing my heart with her.

I enjoyed talking to Jason. It felt like one hundred pounds were lifted off my shoulders when I left that room where we spent time together. I loved telling him about You and Your never-ending love.

I enjoyed my ride home with Charlotte. I could see the change in her after witnessing my exchange with Jason. She no longer had an excuse for not forgiving herself.

When I got home that night, I realized it'd been one amazing day. I would've never expected my description of that day to be as such, but it brought me joy that I hadn't felt in some time.

So, I wanted to tell You that I trust You with everything. I thought that I had, but I realized that I still didn't believe it was in my best interest to stay here on earth for as long as I have. In the back of my mind, it felt like torture or punishment.

I thought I needed to be here for Charlotte. I thought that my time with her and my talks with her were all You needed me for. Then, You let me see the lesson I had to learn about forgiveness. I didn't realize how much anger I still had deep within my heart.

I thought for sure that talking with Jason was the last thing You needed me to do, but on the way home, I heard the sincerity in Charlotte's voice when she said she needed me here. Her eyes had so much pain in them when I told her I wanted to return home to You.

It broke my heart because I knew how she was feeling. I know what it's like when the one person who means so much to you is taken away. I almost wish I hadn't mentioned that I desired to go to heaven, because it hurt her. I didn't want Charlotte to think I didn't enjoy every bit of my time with her.

So, I've decided to let You know that I officially surrender it all to You. When You decide to take me home, I know that'll be the perfect time. If You need me to stay here to do more of Your work, I'm happy to do it. I can make it through another spring. It won't be fun, but I'm trusting You through all of it.

I love You, and I'm grateful to be Your child. Thank You for loving me unconditionally all the days of my life. Thank You for the time I did have with Charles and Sarah. I'll cherish that and the memories and know that when You're ready, I'll see them again.

Please kiss them and hug them for me and let them know I'll be seeing them soon.

All my love,
Glenda

~ Fifty-Two ~

CHARLOTTE

January 12, 2013

Dear God,

Why? All I can ask is why? I don't understand why this is happening. I don't understand why You thought this was a good time to take her from me.

She was my rock and my guiding light throughout this last year, and just like that, she's gone. Like a wind that swept quickly through my life, leaving everything in me changed.

I know she was ready to go home to You, but, God, You know I wasn't ready for her to leave. She introduced me to You. She led me to connect with You. She led me to press into You.

Glenda showed me unconditional love. She loved me despite my scars and in spite of my missteps. I glance back and wonder what my life would look like had I not taken that turn into the church parking lot that morning. I wonder what my life would be like had she not come to my car and asked if I was okay. Her love drew me to her and ultimately back to You.

I'd just seen her two weeks ago. I'd become closer to her than ever. I'd heard her story and felt her heart.

I got to experience what I believe to be a miracle between her and Jason. I got to witness forgiveness firsthand. I'd just reached the point where I was ready to trust that You did forgive me and that You weren't out to hurt me at all.

Then, two days ago, I got the call that she'd passed away, and I can't see how that isn't punishing me. As much as I've come to believe that You love me, this is where my unbelief rises.

I'm angry with You. I'm upset with You. I feel guilty for saying as much, because look at all You've done for me and forgiven me for.

Yet, Glenda told me once, "Pain can either bring you closer to God or further away. If you're upset with Him, tell Him. If you're angry with Him, tell Him. He is God. He can handle your anger. It is when you stop talking to Him that you withdraw yourself because of pain."

So, I'm saying it. Why'd You do this to me? What did I do wrong? Were my prayers not strong enough to keep her here? Did You not hear me?

I told You that I wasn't ready for her to leave, and You took her anyway. I begged You not to take her. I begged her not to want to go. Do my prayers and pleading mean nothing?

Have I not reached the point of You listening to my prayers? I didn't think there was a threshold to pass through for You to hear me, but I can't explain or find another reason that You would allow this. It was You who decided now was the perfect time to take her.

I'll say that I'm grateful that You took her in her sleep, the way that so many of us would like to go. I can thank You for that, but the rest of my emotion is just anger.

I know she'd said she didn't want to go through another spring alone, but I'd planned to help her this spring. I was going to be there for her.

Who's going to be my rock? Who's going to continue to lead me to You? Who's going to encourage me to press into You? Who's going to show me unconditional love?

I am.

My venting stopped. Was that really God's voice? I sat in complete awe. I didn't move. I looked around to see if I was losing my mind.

"I am? God, was that You? What did You just say?"

I am.

Right then, through the tears and pain of losing Glenda, I saw the silver lining. She hadn't been my source, she'd been my vessel—a vessel that God used to draw me closer to Him.

My mind was brought back to a sermon my pastor had once shared about learning to go forward. He had talked about a baby eagle and its nest. He said the baby eagle is warm and cozy in its nest, and the food is brought to it by the parents.

One day, the parents decide it's time for the eagle to start flying, but the baby eagle doesn't want to leave. They stop bringing food to the baby. They start to make the nest less comfortable by pulling the feathers and soft roughage from its sanctuary.

Eventually, the eaglet's left on a bed of sticks with no food. It has no choice but to leave the nest to survive. The mother then pulls the eaglet to the nest's edge, and it's then time to fly.

Glenda wasn't my rock—she was my nest. And then God believed it was time for me to fly. He made me uncomfortable. He answered her prayer and couldn't answer mine. He let her go home.

Now it's my turn to fly. I'm supposed to experience His unconditional love for myself. But if this is what it feels like, I don't know if I want to. He left me here in my discomfort and sorrow. How do I know he won't lead me to more pain?

I just want to sit here for now and grieve over what I lost. I can't see a way to move forward without her. I've had so many people cut off from my life, but this empty space is going to be the deepest and sting the most.

Love,
Charlotte

~ Fifty-Three ~

CHARLOTTE

The hardest part was that moment when I woke up, devastatingly remembering I'd lost her. The tears immediately started, and my heart broke all over again, as if I'd just found out for the first time.

I wanted to go back to sleep and deny it'd happened. I didn't want to start another day without her. I didn't want to get dressed. I didn't want to do my hair or put on makeup. But I did it all through tears.

Appropriately, it was raining outside. It was patient, slow and steady. I'd always loved this type of rain—the kind that slowly tapped on the windows, made ripples in the puddles, and required minimal windshield wipers while driving in it. It always made me want to cuddle up with a blanket or put on an oversized sweatshirt.

On this day, it meant more to me. It was a comfort. It helped me grieve. It paralleled my sadness and almost wept with me.

The rain softly hit my bathroom window as I looked into the mirror and watched endless tears stream down my face. How was I supposed to stop crying long enough to put makeup on? I dried my face and eyelashes so I could put on my waterproof mascara and twenty-four-hour lipstick. That was going to have to be enough.

I went out to my kitchen and just sat at the table. I fixed my eyes on the small drops hitting the pane. Each tap on the window soothed me. I stared out the glass at the rain falling farther away, and my heart felt just as far.

I knew I needed to look at the silver linings of these clouds. Glenda was where she wanted to be. She wanted to go home to be with *her* Jesus. She wanted to see her Charles and hold him again. She wanted to wrap her arms around her Sarah and make up for all the years she'd lost with her. She didn't want to be lonely without them anymore.

But, as those words roll around in my head, pain is gouging me deeply. What about me? Now I'm all alone. I have other people around me, but I don't have her.

This is selfish in comparison to the statements I just made, but I have to ask. Was I not enough for her to want to stay? Didn't she know she was more of a mother to me than I'd ever known?

I need to refocus my thoughts and consider how happy she must be. After all, I love her so much that I should be rejoicing for God answering her prayers after waiting so long.

Yet, the wound within is still throbbing, and the anguish just began. This was the final day of a long goodbye. I had to wish my Glenda my ultimate farewell. The woman who changed my life was gone.

Riding to the funeral home was a blur. All I remember are windshield wipers and blurry traffic lights. Turning into the empty lot, I saw the hearse, and it paralyzed me. She was really gone.

I had the honor of arranging her service. I got to pick the dress she wore, how her hair was prepared, and how her makeup was applied. I searched through some of her picture albums for when she looked the happiest, and those were the photos I gave them to replicate.

Her glowing smile grabbed me as I walked into the empty seating area of the funeral home. I stared at her joyful face in the enlarged picture placed in the middle of the altar. Her smile was so genuine that her eyes were smiling.

Picking the color of flowers was easy. Of course, I chose blush roses. She would've loved that.

Wanting to honor her love of the Bible, I wanted to choose the Scriptures I thought would honor her. Yes, me, the one who barely knew the Bible. But I researched and did the best I could.

Pastor Marks was grateful to be able to give the eulogy. I was planning to get up and speak, but I didn't know if I'd make it through and hold myself together.

We went through the motions after I admired the setup. The guest book was put out for people to sign, and there were beautiful cards created with her name, date of birth and date of death. Those dates are just the parentheses around the time that Glenda's life made the world around her a more loving place to be.

People started flowing in, one by one. There were people from the church. There were friends of hers she had throughout the years, many of whom I'd never met. There were people young and old to celebrate her.

The most impressive of all was the number of teenagers from church that had come and sat together. You could tell they truly mourned for her. That scene alone spoke more precious words than any of us could say to honor her.

Slowly, each person went to her casket and paid respect. Some kissed their fingers before touching her face or her heart. Others stood back, admiring her. There were those who couldn't look for long, and those who needed to lean over and kiss her face.

Pastor Marks gave an exceptional eulogy—revering her perfectly. He mentioned the first time they'd met and what an impact she'd made in his life. He spoke of her dedication to our church. And he talked about the pain she'd endured and her understated strength to prevail through it.

He passionately explained how many of us would use her situation as a platform for sympathy and excuses of a self-centered life, but she did the opposite. She lived her life in a way to show God's faithfulness, by exampling that you can be a light regardless of your circumstances. Everything he said was tear-jerking for me—and many times for him as well.

I was the last one to leave the funeral home. Bringing myself to speak the final goodbye was merely impossible. I couldn't go out the doors. I sat and just stared at her. I asked the director to just give me a minute.

I finally got the chance to ask Glenda, "What do I do now? What do I do without you? Who else do I have to turn to? I know you had to go. I know you've wanted to go. I'm happy you don't have to grieve another day for Sarah and Charles.

"On the other side of this same coin is the fact that I'll spend my time left here grieving for you. I realize there is nothing that will change that. The only way this pain wouldn't exist is if I'd never known you at all.

"I'm trying to look at this grief as a gift because it's a result of knowing you so well—a gift of our friendship and our bond.

"You'll always be the most important woman in my life. You're someone I would've been honored to have been able to call 'Mom.' In my heart, you were my mother—the one who loved me, supported me, encouraged me, believed in me, always looked past my weaknesses and saw who I was inside.

"You showed me how to love and receive love. You even taught me how to love myself. Most importantly, you introduced me to a God I'd never known. You showed me His goodness, His kindness, His forgiveness, His grace, His unfaltering love and His relentless pursuit of my heart. That is the most precious gift in my life. And to me, that sums up everything I would want in a mom.

"All that's left for me to do is say goodbye. And I don't want to. This is the last time I'll see your face, and that tortures me. But I know I can't sit here forever.

"I have to make a choice to go forward. I must take the pieces of my broken heart, along with the lessons I've learned from you, and keep going. I have to let it be enough.

"I'll try to carry on your legacy in my life. I'll hold on to all that you've taught me and all you've demonstrated for me. Glenda, you're the most precious person I've ever had in my life, and I'll miss you every day I live. May God's face shine upon you forever. All my love . . ."

And with that, I stood up and walked away. I couldn't see one thing in front of me. Tears were saturating my eyes and face, and my heart was pounding out of my chest. The back of my jaws tensed, and I felt like I couldn't breathe.

I couldn't watch them shut the casket. I had to just walk straight out the strong oak doors. I was greeted with a slightly moist wind from the rain continuing to fall. I saw the hearse to my left, waiting to receive the casket and drive my friend to her final resting place. She was to be buried in Brentwood, at the place she had waiting for her—next to her Charles and Sarah.

That day was the hardest day I've ever faced. It went beyond any pain I've experienced before. This felt like a part of me was gone. My heart wasn't broken. It was shattered.

I somehow got through the burial. There were so many people, but I had no desire to look at anyone. I wouldn't have been able to make out their faces with my tear-filled sunglasses anyway. I couldn't bring myself to lift my face.

My mind must have been on automatic pilot to drive me home because I don't remember my trip home either. When I got there, I went directly to my room and just lay in my bed.

I called into work and told them I needed a few days off because a close relative had passed away. I was honest. She was more of a relative to me than anyone else.

I hadn't checked my mail in days, so the mailman put the overflowing letters on my doorstep. There was a thick package that stood out, and I opened it. It was my acceptance letter into the management program out in Seattle. With the blur of circumstances, I had forgotten all about it and couldn't muster up any emotion about being admitted.

I asked God to show me what He wanted me to do. I begged for Him to be clear. Yet, I told Him that I'd decline the offer in order to stay with Glenda. That obviously wasn't necessary anymore. I had nothing holding me back.

I was going to need some time to think about it. I couldn't even decide if I wanted to eat or not, much less move across the country. Eventually I had to decide.

A week later, something prompted me to accept the offer to enter the program. I couldn't stay here and continue the life I had before I met Glenda, and I didn't know yet what to do without her. I didn't want to go back to the way things were, so I needed a change.

I made the decision to move across the country. I let my work know that I'd been accepted, and I gave my notice to the landlord. Once I told my parents and made flight reservations, I became conscious that it was really happening.

There were living arrangements the program had offered. For the first couple months, I'd be put up in an apartment-type suite in the hotel, but after that, I'd be on my own for housing.

All I had left to do was pack and figure out what to do with what was left over. What did I want to put in storage, and what did I want to get rid of? When I looked at the storage pile, I wondered if I'd ever be back to get it.

While I was finishing up deciding what goes and what stays, the doorbell rang. It was my mailman again bringing me the mail, but this time he came to the door with a package.

One cream-colored manila envelope looked formal and stood out to me. The return address was from a law firm in town—Bagwell & Campbell. I immediately thought I was in trouble. But the letter read,

Dear Ms. Madden:

We're writing you on behalf of Mrs. Glenda Ryan. We're the law firm that handled her estate matters.

We're so very sorry for your loss. We're sure you're terribly upset and grieving.

Before she'd passed, she'd given us some things that she requested us to do. One of them was to send you the enclosed letter. The other request is for you to come to the office and collect some things of hers.

We hope you're able to come by our office at your earliest convenience to go over her personal matters. We look forward to meeting you and helping you through this difficult time.

Sincerely,
J. Richard Gardner
Bagwell & Campbell
- Encl: Letter from Glenda Ryan

I was taken aback. I wasn't expecting to hear anything about her estate or will. I knew that she had no living family, but I believed that the church and her friends would be handling all the concerns of her estate. I went on to read the letter.

My dearest Charlotte,

If you're reading this letter, it means that God has taken me home. I wanted to write it in case I was taken before I had a chance to tell you these things in person.

Charlotte, you're one of the greatest treasures to me. From the moment I saw you in the parking lot, I knew you were going to be special in my heart. I even knew when you drove away that you'd be back again.

After we got to know each other, you were even more precious than I'd imagined. Your heart is so sweet and so heartfelt. You shared your story with me without reservation. Your transparency allowed me to look in and see all the pain you had gone through. Those talks we had were some of the most meaningful times I ever had.

When I was with you, I thought God was giving me a way to experience what Sarah may have been like. And, of course, your nickname of Charlie always reminded me of my Charles.

The ride we took to see Jason in prison was the closest I've felt to anyone in over twenty years. Ironically, sharing my pain with you brought me so much comfort. Your compassionate eyes alone showed how much you cared for me. I was so grateful you were the one with me that day.

That was the hardest thing I've ever had to do, and I don't think that I could've done it alone. Your presence allowed me to feel supported and encouraged, and the drive home was even more intimate.

I spoke about how much you meant to me, and you shared the same sentiment. The part that broke my heart was when I told you that I wanted to go home to see Charles and Sarah.

Your face looked like I'd shared something upsetting. You asked me to change my mind. I knew that I shouldn't have said that in front of you, because it would make it seem like being with you wasn't enough for me.

After your expression of how much you loved me and your belief that you needed me, I told God that I'd surrender to His time in taking me. I'd been impatiently waiting for years, but after our ride, I was willing to wait. I was willing to bear another spring just so I could be with you.

So, in case I didn't get the chance, here is more of what I wanted to tell you. Charlotte, you're an amazing woman. You have a fight in you that I admire. You're tenacious, and you don't give up. You might've felt that you'd given up for a few years, but you were only taking a rest for the next stage of the battle.

You have a huge heart. You opened up and showed me who you were, and it was beautiful. I know you have made some mistakes that changed your perspective of yourself, but we all make mistakes. We all make ones we regret. But all that needs to change is your perspective.

I'm confident that in time, God will help you do that. There are some relationships in your past that you can't bring with you into your future. There are some relationships in your past that you might be able to repair. Do the hard work. Repair them. It will be worth it to you.

If you can only remember one thing, remember this. I loved you as if you were my second daughter. I cherished you as if you were a treasure. I'll always have you in my heart wherever I am. You were the best ending to a life that I thought was finished.

All my love . . . all my love,
Glenda

She'd taken the time to write that letter to me and meant for me to receive it in my saddest moments. She'd told me things that I couldn't believe she saw in me. She loved me more than I knew how to love myself. How do you recover from losing a love like that? I don't know if you ever can.

~ Fifty-Four ~

CHARLOTTE

A few days after receiving Glenda's letter, I called the attorney's office. I asked if I needed to make an appointment in order to come in about her estate, and I set up a time for the following day.

I thought I should look a little more put together that day, since I was going to see the attorney. It had been weeks since I did more than shower. It was as if looking like crap made me feel better.

I even wore a little bit of makeup. I still had to use the waterproof mascara because I could break down at any moment. I'd jump into a tailspin in seconds if certain songs came on or I saw specific commercials.

The law office was beautiful. I arrived a little early, so sitting in the waiting room was fascinating with the beautiful architecture and furniture. The receptionist made some small talk as she mentioned that Mr. Gardner was ready to see me. Walking in, I went to shake his hand, and . . .

"Hello, Charlotte."

My eyes widened and I held my breath. My heart dropped and adrenaline shot through my legs. Shocked and embarrassed, I wanted to run and hide.

It wasn't Richard Gardner. It was J. Richard Gardner, who was also Joey Gardner.

The one I'd let get away was standing right in front of me. I was at a disadvantage because he'd been expecting to see me, but I was in shock and couldn't speak.

Come on, Charlotte, you can't just stand here and stare at him. I reached down inside and pulled myself together.

"Oh, my God, I can't believe I'm standing here in front of you. Pardon my disbelief. How are you?"

I had no clue what to say.

"I'm great. How are you?"

Still, nothing intelligent came to mind.

"Um, I've been better. I'm here because someone close to me passed away, so not that great."

"Yes, Glenda. She was an amazing woman. I've known her since I was a teenager. She was special to me too. She and my mom have been close for years."

Joe gave me a warm smile, and my shoulders began to relax. "It seems as if you were just as special to her. She would talk about you all the time—telling me how much she loved you and that you were like a daughter to her. . . ."

I don't remember what he said after that, because all I could think about was holding back tears. I made a good call on wearing the right mascara.

"Oh no, Charlotte. I'm sorry. I didn't mean to upset you. Let me stop talking. I have some tissues somewhere."

"No, no. It's not your fault. It's just still fresh, and I get like this often, sometimes out of nowhere."

"I have the stuff here that she wanted me to pass on to you." He rummaged for a package in his bottom drawer.

"So, wait . . . You knew that she was talking about me all along?"

"Yeah," he replied with a slow-forming smirk.

"You never told her that you knew me?"

"No."

"Why?"

"I was talking to her professionally. I never like to talk about myself when I'm helping a client."

"But you said she was an old friend of your mom's and you'd known her for a long time. It never came up?"

"I guess I should've expected these questions."

"I guess I'm just surprised at how much you didn't want to associate yourself with me."

"That's ridiculous. I just didn't want her to tell you that it was me who was helping her. I didn't know what you'd say about me . . . or us. I didn't know if you wanted her to know anything at all."

"I'm sorry. I'm just shocked by all of this. Anyway, so what did she have?" I started to get aggravated.

"Yes, yes, back to where we were. I sent you the letter. Then I was supposed to tell you about her property and her remaining funds in her accounts. She has them all written over to you upon her death. It's right here in her will."

"*What?* Are you kidding me? Why would she—no—no way!"

There came the next layer of shock. First, it was seeing Joe for the first time in years. Then, it was that he was her attorney, and he'd never told her he knew me. Now, she wanted me to have her entire estate.

"What am I supposed to do next?" Stunned was an understatement.

"We'll get the death certificate. In the meantime, you'll sign some paperwork. After all the information is received, we'll transfer all her property over into your name. Then, it's all yours—to do with it whatever you wish."

"I don't even know what to say or how to react. I never even expected to be in her will at all, and now I'm sitting here trying to understand why it's been given to me."

"It's a lot to take in. Especially if you weren't expecting it."

"I wasn't expecting any of this. I wasn't expecting to see you either. So, my world feels like it is spinning and eras are clashing."

"Oh, there is one more thing that she wanted me to give you. It is in this small envelope."

Crying began again immediately as I opened it. It was her long necklace with the locket on the end. It was gorgeous, but the meaning behind it meant more than its beauty.

There was another small note in the envelope.

Charlotte,

Make sure to hold those who are special to you as close to your heart as you can. Don't let this locket stay empty for long.

All my love,

Glenda

P.S. He is very cute, isn't he?

I laughed out loud. "*Uhhh...* have you seen this necklace and note?"

"No, she had brought it in sealed."

Thank God. This was awkward enough without him reading that.

"So, Charlotte, just sign these papers and you'll be finished. I'll call you in a couple days when we get the death certificate to make the transfer of property official and in your name."

"So, that's it?"

"Yes, unless you have any other questions?" He seemed slightly guarded and professional suddenly, as if he wanted the meeting to end and not get into a personal conversation.

"Thank you for everything. It was good to see you, Joe, or Richard. I don't know what I should call you at work. But it was good to see you."

Looking at him as if I didn't want to leave, he didn't react.

"Yes, it was good seeing you again too. I'm glad I can help you sort all this out."

That was it. Nothing more was said, and I awkwardly turned and left his office.

A few days later, I received word that all the paperwork was ready, and I returned to the office. He was just as professional and superficial as the first time.

I tried to break the ice, but he wasn't budging.

"So, Joe, how is your family?"

"My family seems to only be my co-workers these days, since I'm here so much."

He laughed but didn't offer much more than that.

I wanted to ask if he had a girlfriend, but that would've been so obvious that I was looking for more than just the answer.

We finished up the paperwork, and nothing about his disposition had changed. I'd try to make eye contact with him, and he seemed to try to avoid it. I was getting the picture that he was upset with me, and I could see that I'd hurt him. If he didn't care, he would've been friendlier, right?

Was this the relationship from my past that Glenda had mentioned about being able to repair? I'd thought she meant my parents or God, but it didn't hit me that she could've meant Joe.

When we were finished, I gave him a casual hug. "I appreciate all your help. You've made this easy for me."

I started to walk to the door, and when I got there, I slightly turned around. He was already about to sit back into his chair. I couldn't leave without saying something.

"Joe, I'm sorry . . . really sorry. I know what I did was wrong, and I've regretted it ever since.

"This might seem like it's coming out of nowhere, but ironically I've recently realized that out of all the things in my life I've done wrong, pushing you away is at the top of my list. I just needed to tell you before I left and then possibly didn't see you for another ten years." I turned to walk away.

"Thank you, Charlotte. I appreciate you letting me know."

He even said it with a superficial expression on his face. I was happy I'd said something, but I was also disappointed in his response. That was it.

It just added to the loss. I'd just signed all the paperwork that made Glenda officially deceased—gone. Her death certificate was officially submitted, and all her things were transferred over to me. How does one inherit so much and lose so much all in the same day?

~ Fifty-Five ~

CHARLOTTE

A few days later, more surprises showed up on my doorstep. My place was practically empty, as I was doing some of my final packing before leaving.

The doorbell rang, and I tried to remember the last time I'd gotten my mail. The mailman was going to stop delivering my mail if I continued to let it overflow from not picking it up. I was scared to open the door, but when I did, I froze. It was Joe.

"Hey, Charlotte."

"Hey . . . ?"

"Listen. I just wanted to stop by and apologize. After you left the office, I felt terrible that I didn't say anything more that day. You'd put yourself out there and apologized, and I left you hanging. I thought about how hard it'd been for you to share your feelings before, so I knew it took a lot for you to bring it up."

"I understand. How I ended things was terrible, and you have every right to be upset with me. I would probably be the same way."

I expected that'd be enough to end the conversation, but I could tell he wasn't finished.

"There is more, though. I'm sorry too."

"What do you have to be sorry for?"

I wasn't expecting an apology from him. But he glanced away from me as if he had something shameful to share.

"I gave up too fast. I knew that you'd been through a lot before college and even after. When we were friends, I knew when to push past your defenses. You'd always come around eventually. I just had to show you that you could trust me."

His eyes emitted pain when he looked at me.

"But, when I put my feelings out to you as more than a friend, I was too hurt to keep pursuing you. I regret that. I know that at the time, you did care for me. I know that you really did love me.

"I thought back and saw all the ways in which you showed me. I should've tried again. I should've explained that you could've trusted me, and I would've done anything to make you feel safe."

"Joe, look . . ." He wouldn't let me interrupt.

"Let me finish. I didn't try harder, and I regretted that for the longest time. I always thought back to the fun we had in college. I don't know if it was as fun for you at the time, but it was for me. I just wanted to come and tell you that I was sorry too."

"Joe . . . I don't think you have anything to be sorry for, but I appreciate you sharing all that you did or wanted to do for me. I'm sorry for the way it ended. It's really not your fault."

Then the bigger surprise came. He pulled back his shoulders and looked at me directly.

"This might be out of line or premature, but could I make it up to you? Could I take you out to dinner this week? Unless you can't or have someone . . ."

I was stunned and paralyzed. Words were hard to find. After an exaggerated pause, I realized how happy I was that he was asking.

"I would love that. Any night works for me. I have nothing going on. What were you thinking?"

I waited in anticipation and hoped it'd be as soon as possible.

"I'm going to take a wild chance, but are you available tonight?"

"Actually, yes! I'm up for it. I could throw something on, and we could go now, unless . . . I mean . . . maybe you needed to go later."

I was fumbling over my words in excitement. I would've left immediately to go anywhere with him.

"Sure. Now works great. I'll just wait while you get changed."

He came in the house and went to sit down, then gave me a confused look.

"Are you moving out? Are you going to move to Glenda's place or something? It's a beautiful home."

"No. It's a long story. I can tell you at dinner."

The drive there was filled with simple talk. We just went to an upscale pizza place. We asked each other what we did after college. I needed to see what his life was like now, though.

"So, I have to ask. Is there a special lady in your life right now?"

He bashfully laughed. "No. I've dated a few girls here and there, but nothing serious. How about you?"

"No. Believe it or not, I haven't dated anyone since . . . since college."

There was a pause as he came to realize I meant I hadn't dated anyone since him.

The conversation quickly turned toward college memories. At times we laughed so loud that we interrupted the people around us. Half of the things we laughed at seemed so serious at the time it happened.

We did start to slip into the more serious memories here and there, but neither of us wanted to dive in all the way. I asked about his time in law school and how he'd worked his way to where he was.

He brought up Brett once, and it was almost as if he knew not to mention the name again. I wanted to tell him it was okay and that I had seen Brett. I wanted to tell Joe everything, but it was too soon, so I let him think it was still a sensitive subject.

He then asked the obvious question about why my apartment was empty.

"Let me see. There are so many details that are personal, they might not make sense to you. I'll put myself out there, though.

"I've been back in Franklin since I left college. I wanted to move away, but it never seemed to be the right time or place. I applied all around, and the best place with the opportunity for growth was the Gaylord.

"It was exciting at first. I loved all the events they had there. The Christmas season was spectacular. The lights and the atrium were gorgeous. I loved driving onto the property to see all the trees lit up.

"The wedding season was just as beautiful. There were blooming flowers everywhere, gold and silver accents, and sparkling décor that met every little girl's expectations.

"After some time, the excitement wore off. Going to work became just work. Christmas season became more of a heavy load than a time to enjoy the scenery. I don't know if my perspective changed or if the newness wore off, but it turned into *Groundhog Day*. The seasons and events all blended together.

"I had a few promotions along the way, but after my last one, I stopped trying to take on any more work. I've pretty much coasted for the last few years.

"Finally, it hit me that I was stagnant. I desperately wanted a change. I applied to a program through the hotel chain that offered hands-on management training with the guarantee of management placement. It sounded perfect.

"After I applied, I met Glenda and had the chance to go through so much with her. She's changed my life in ways I can't explain. Right after she passed, I found out I was accepted into the program.

"I decided it was a good time to leave. I have nothing tying me here anymore. I was going to decline the training to stay with Glenda, but that's not an option.

"So, I went for it. I'm a little intimidated to move across the entire country alone, but I know it's a good opportunity."

His facial expressions paused a bit.

"It sounds great. Seattle is beautiful and so different from around here. You'll enjoy the city. Pike Place Market is unique, and all the scenery is one of a kind. The couple times I've visited, I've loved it. You're very lucky."

Although he was saying all the right words, I couldn't tell if his answers were genuine. His facial expressions seemed confused, as if he didn't know if he should be happy for me or not.

I got a strange feeling that he wasn't pleased to hear that I was leaving, but I could've just been hoping for that to be the case. I hadn't talked to him in ten years, so his body language could've changed a thousand times since then.

I turned the conversation around and asked about the times he'd visited Seattle and his favorite parts, and the tension left.

We finished up, and I couldn't get over how good the time together had felt. The food was amazing, and I had great company.

It was the first time I'd sat across from someone at dinner and laughed so much. I don't think I had this much fun with him when I was in college. He was always entertaining, wanting to get me to laugh, but I hardly gave in.

We got the check, and I automatically went to my purse.

"Are you kidding me? Don't even think about it. I'm paying for this. It will always be on me, so no need to try that again."

Always? Did that mean we'd be going to dinner again?

He laughed, but you could tell he really meant what he was saying. He was emphatic to grab the black leather book with the bill in it.

He drove me back home, and we went back in my place, where we had another light conversation.

"Thank you so much for dinner. That had to be the best pizza I've had in ages."

I settled into the corner of the couch—the only piece of furniture not covered with boxes—then tucked my legs underneath me and faced him.

"Listen, Joey, it's great to see you again. I'm glad that you came over. I had one of the best nights that I've had in a while. It was great to sit across from you and laugh. I know I wasn't too good at that in college, but it came naturally tonight."

"Joey? No one has called me that in ages." He laughed. "I enjoyed it too. I love that place. I have to admit that the company made it much better.

"I should let you go. It's probably getting late for you. I could stay here and talk all night, but both of us have to get up pretty early, I assume."

"You're right. I have to go to work early, and morning seems to come quickly."

"I'm curious. When do you leave for Seattle?"

"In about a week. This is my last week at work. Then, I have to get all sorts of things worked out. I have to make sure my storage is taken care of.

"I have to make sure all's well with Glenda's things. That's probably my most stressful piece. She just handed over all the things that she had to me, and I'm leaving them in the hands of a stranger."

"Did you need any help with that? I know you have a management company, but I wouldn't mind checking on it for you periodically so you can rest easy knowing it's all okay."

"Would you really? I feel bad saying yes, but I would trust your help. Things have changed so fast, and I feel overwhelmed. Your help would be great."

As I was exhaling with relief, I saw a mischievous smile appear on his face that made me curious about what he was going to say next.

"I guess I shouldn't have offered that easily. I do have some stipulations."

"What? Stipulations? Was that a trap?" I surprised myself as I flirted with him.

"I'm willing to help you under one condition. You have to promise me that you'll go to dinner with me again before you leave, except this time we can do a little bit better than pizza."

His teasing was more than welcome. I was so happy he asked to go out again and I didn't have to endure the wait to hear from him.

"I would love to! But, tonight was pretty good, so I don't know if we can top it."

"We can try. I'll give you a call soon, and we can figure out a good time. Are there any nights that are better than others?"

I wanted to say tomorrow, but that would've been slightly aggressive.

"I'm pretty much wide-open. I don't have any plans before I leave."

"Perfect."

I loved seeing his smile again. I missed him more than I realized.

Our conversation ended, and we both were unsure how to end the night. We simultaneously decided to end with a hug. Our embrace felt so comfortable. There was no awkwardness, and I actually allowed myself to enjoy it. It wasn't extremely long or anything dramatic—it was perfect.

I was kept from going to sleep because I kept replaying scenes from that night over and over again. I couldn't stop thinking about all he'd said and overanalyzing each word.

I recalled his smiles and his laugh. I knew he was the one I let get away, and there I was sitting across from him. The day went by pretty fast because I was thinking about the night before all day long.

His feelings must've been similar because he called me after work and asked if he could take me to dinner a few nights later. I accepted and was on cloud nine after I hung up. I turned the music up in my car, and the phone rang. It was him again.

"I had such a great time, and I know I asked you to dinner in a few nights, but is there any way we could grab a simple bite together tonight?

"If not, I understand. I don't mean to be aggressive. I just know that you're leaving in a matter of days, and we don't have much time to catch up."

"You know? I'd love that. Something simple again sounds great. How about the great taco place on Hillsborough?"

"I can pick you up in about an hour, at about six. Is that enough time?"

I could feel the whirlwind coming. I could tell our feelings were climbing fast. I couldn't believe he was willing to give me another chance.

Almost every night after, we had dinner together. Each time was better than the night before. I was the happiest I'd ever been and didn't want it to end.

Reality hit that it was going to have to, and I hated it. I'd committed to the program. I'd moved all my stuff already. I'd been dying to get out of that town and start a new adventure. And I finally had the chance.

I considered giving up the training in Seattle, but what if Joe and I didn't work out? I would've been in the same situation I was in months ago. I'd be all alone with nothing to look forward to.

On our last night together, we finally had to face that I was leaving. I started the awful conversation.

"This really stinks that I'm leaving. The timing is awful."

Every time I was with him, I didn't want to leave. I wished I could stay and spend every evening with him. I hoped he'd felt the same, but that was selfish. How fair was it that I desired him to care enough to want me to stay, even though I'd made up my mind to leave?

"I haven't wanted to think about you leaving. I knew it was coming, but denial was working fine until tonight."

He went to grab for my hand but stopped himself. I wanted him to keep going, but I couldn't tell him that. I had to make the conversation simpler.

"At least it has been nice getting to catch up this week. And you said you liked Seattle. You can come visit me?"

But his response wouldn't let it stay shallow. "Do you think that's all it was?"

The tone of his voice changed to the same one he had the night we ended our friendship. I didn't expect that direct of a question, nor that pitch. Luckily, he kept talking because I had no idea how to respond.

"I mean, us hanging out together. Did it seem like just catching up for you?"

The extra time he took to speak did nothing to help me find my own words.

"This is kind of a strange question to answer. I don't know exactly what to say."

Joe started to get more assertive with the conversation out of frustration with my evasive answers.

"Let me say my part, then. This has been one of my best weeks. I've enjoyed our time together, even more than I did when we were in college. . . ."

I was thinking the same thing.

"I had expected both of us to have nothing in common after all these years, but it seems I enjoy being around you even more than I did before, and that was when I was in love with you."

I completely agreed but still didn't know how to tell him the truth.

"It was great for me too. I knew that I'd messed up, pushing you away and letting you leave that night. I knew that I missed you, but I never imagined us having the time we've had. . ."

He interrupted me.

"Don't go. Don't go to Seattle. Change everything and stay."

My breath stopped when he boldly asked me to stay. I'd wanted to stay myself, but I'd talked myself out of it. Wouldn't that be immature and irresponsible to do?

But here was one of the most responsible people I'd ever known, and he was asking me to do exactly what I'd talked myself out of.

"Charlotte, I know it has only been a little over a week. I know that we haven't seen each other in ten years. But I'm willing to say it—I still love you—I've always loved you.

"Even after we stopped talking to each other, I was torn up. I thought I'd lost you for good. I didn't want to date anyone after that. And I've never really tried to find anyone.

"I've met really nice women over the years, but none have kept my attention. Unknowingly, I still missed you. Then, I saw you at the funeral . . ."

"You saw me at the funeral? You were there?"

"Yes, of course. But let me finish. I'd talked to Glenda about you all this time, but when I saw you there, I was drawn to you, and I knew I still loved you."

It was hard to absorb all he was currently sharing emotionally while I was trying to piece together things he told me about before we saw each other in his office.

"I anticipated your call to go over Glenda's things. When I knew you were coming in, I was torn. I didn't know if I should act like I wanted nothing to do with you, or if I should be just as friendly as I'd always been. I picked the wrong answer.

"When you left my office, you were so kind. I never remembered you putting yourself out there like that, so I knew it took a lot to say what you did. I knew I had to at least try to see if there was anything left between us . . . and there is."

He was getting more intense with every sentence, and I wanted to say whatever he needed to hear.

"If you leave, then I lose you again, and I don't want to do that without a fight. So, I'll ask again. Please don't go."

I wanted to stay. I wanted to say I would stay, but I couldn't. The only thing I could do was finally tell him how I felt.

"I know you're right, but I want to share something I've been waiting to tell you. Let me finish the whole story before you jump to conclusions.

"Brett contacted me about a month ago. He said he'd been struggling with some things from our past. He wanted to ask some things about the pregnancy and all the mess that surrounded it. We resolved quite a few things through the awkwardness.

"The best part is that he got what he needed to work things out in his marriage. Please keep that between you and me, because that isn't the kind of thing that's good for people to know.

"The only reason I tell you is this. All these years, I've had my attention on things I regretted in my past. He was such a big part of my mistakes, that I focused on him more than anything else.

"I'd always thought I'd messed things up between us. But when I thought about you and me, it was like icing on the cake of my mistakes.

"When I met with Brett, something happened. We talked about so many things, but there was one thing that stunned me. He asked if you and I had dated.

"I began to tell him that you and I were great friends but I'd messed it up when it started to get more intense. I felt something stir in me as I was saying it.

"After I left our meeting, I realized it was *you* I let get away. You'd been the one who'd carried me through the hardest times of my life—not just for a part of it, but for three and a half years. No one had ever cared for me that way, but I didn't see it until it was horribly too late."

The pain from hurting him surfaced as I was talking to him and brought up regretful tears. I tried wiping them away, but more followed.

"Joey, I just want you to know how I feel. I don't want to hide it anymore. I've been hiding my feelings for years, and all they do is haunt me."

I finally had gotten out all that I'd been storing inside and breathed out as much guilt as I could.

"Wow, I would've never expected you to say all that. I'm slightly speechless because I don't understand. If you feel the same way, I don't know why you'd leave now. Don't you want to wait and see what happens?"

He gave every effort he could to make me want to postpone my trip.

"My heart wants to stay. It does. But my mind won't let me. I've been trapped in my own shame and regret since college. Glenda finally started to help me make my way out of that prison. I could stand to stay here if she were here.

"But then she was taken from me. Just thinking of the pain of remaining here without her is indescribable.

"I have a chance now to leave all the agony behind. I want to stay, I really do. But what happens if you and I don't work out? What happens if this dies down just as fast as it's started? Then what?

"I'd end up in the same exact spot that I've found myself in for years, except I'd add in the pain of losing you again to the pain of losing Glenda."

Having to feel more pain than I already had was what I feared—and that fear was not letting me trust Joe enough to cancel my plans.

"I wish I could let you see how much I don't want to lose you again. If there's anything I could do or say to change your mind . . ."

"Joe, I can't. I need to go. I've admitted that I feel the same as you do—it's just that the timing is terrible."

I had to remain strong and remember what was at stake if I stayed.

"I won't push you, but I'm going to hold on to hope that you'll change your mind. You heard everything I said, and I meant every word. I hope this isn't the start of you pushing me away again."

We had a hard time lightening the conversation after that, so we wrapped it up and he drove me home. He walked me up to the door, and we said all our goodbyes again.

I could see that he was upset. His pained expression was similar to what I'd seen that awful night in my apartment complex parking lot. I knew that was the worst mistake, yet I was justifying making it again. I wanted to cry but couldn't mislead him.

We shared a long embrace, and he leaned in for a goodbye kiss. Touching his lips gave me chills on my skin and butterflies in my stomach. I wish I would've changed my mind right there, but I didn't.

We said our last goodbye, and I had to turn and go inside. Once the door shut, I let out all the emotions I was holding in throughout the night. I'd found myself with an amazing high followed by a painful low, twice within the same month. Between Glenda and Joe, my world had been flipped upside down, and I didn't know what to do besides try to gain control by leaving it behind. Old habits die hard.

The next morning, I still wanted to stay, but I did what I had to do. I got on the plane in Nashville and took off toward Atlanta for my layover. Catching my flight for the trip's next leg, I headed to Seattle.

When we were taking off, I stared out the window. I was leaving with so many emotions. A week earlier, I would've left nothing except grief for Glenda. Now I'm leaving with regret for leaving Joe all over again.

I thought about the necklace that I had on. I'd put a picture of Glenda in it already. She had told me not to leave it empty for long, so I started with her.

For one week, I thought I might have someone's picture to put next to hers, but after saying goodbye to Joe again, it remained empty.

~ Fifty-Six ~

CHARLOTTE

The air felt cool and crisp when I walked out of the Seattle airport. The breeze's smell was captivating as I waited outside for the car service taking me to the hotel.

I was excited to start this new chapter. I had so much that I looked forward to experiencing. The hotel was captivating as we pulled up. Gratitude that this would be my new home exuded out of my smile.

The lobby was exquisite, and the room they gave me was like a high-end apartment, complete with a full kitchen and a luxurious bathroom. I knew I could get used to the accommodations.

A few days later, the demanding program started. There were prolonged days of teaching followed by exhausting days of training. It was grueling at times and questioned what I was thinking when I applied.

One week turned into two. Two weeks turned into four. It had been a month since I'd started, and I finally felt like I was learning what I needed to learn. I have to admit that I was beginning to miss Tennessee, but I still loved Seattle.

I talked to Joe every now and then. He'd call to say hello and let me know how Glenda's house was doing. Our conversations didn't last more than five to ten minutes. We'd talk about work and some other things here and there, but our exchange was always short. I think we both knew there was no point in trying to create more of a relationship when I was thousands of miles away.

A few months in, I had started to get used to Seattle, but didn't think that it was where I would end up long-term. I enjoyed its eclectic mix of people and places. Just going to the grocery store was an adventure.

There was the organic mom who wanted everything pure so her children didn't become toxic. You had the grungy rocker who had just woken up but needed to get a few things to eat. Elderly couples would hold hands while going through their grocery lists.

I flashed back to the time in the Nashville coffee shop when I realized my life was stagnant. Watching all the people enter in, I'd theorized about all their lives, and those assumptions were so much better than my own.

A year later, I was in a Seattle grocery store doing the same exact thing. But I was in such a better place than when I was in the coffee shop. It was the first time I had something to measure how far I'd come.

I came home and was excited, as if I'd accomplished something. I wanted to call Glenda but realized I couldn't. It happened a lot. The thrill of something would automatically make me want to share it with her, and I'd have to remember she was gone.

The next automatic thought would be to want to call Joe. I couldn't do that either because that wasn't right to do. Plus, we've talked less and less over the year, and lately he's been the one pushing me away. I can be hurt, but I can't be mad at him. After all, I probably forced him to.

But it doesn't mean I didn't desperately want to call him. I missed him. I pined for him at times. We'd only shared that one week after all those years, but I'd fallen in love with him all over again. There I was, across the country, missing the guy who had begged me to stay—again.

He'd almost promised me that it would've worked out between us, but how would I have held him to that? When he'd decide to break up with me, would I pull out a contract that said he wouldn't let that happen? There was no guarantee.

I do have one small secret. I call him often to ask about Glenda's estate even though I don't need anything. I think he did the same at first, but it didn't last as long as my unnecessary queries.

The same night as the exciting grocery trip, I brought takeout back home to eat. I can remember that night clearly. I bought three beef empanadas and a side of black beans and rice.

I grabbed my plate and sat down in front of the television in my cozy sweatpants and sweatshirt. I put on a movie and was winding down for the night, when I got a surprise call from Joe.

He'd been asking me questions about Glenda's house and certain details that had been overlooked by the management company. He seemed happier, so I was hopeful he might've resumed calling for needless reports again.

I was so happy he called and I could hear his voice. Yet, it made me yearn for his presence even more. I told him I'd follow up and call the company the next day. I was curious if he was missing me as much as I was missing him.

Right after we hung up, I got a call from the front desk on the hotel phone. A fax had come in for me. They asked if I'd come down and get it because all the bellmen and hotel attendants were busy.

I was aggravated because I just got out of presentable clothes, but I tried to make myself look decent so I didn't embarrass the hotel. Making my way to the front desk through the crowd of people, I asked for my fax. My friend behind the desk smiled.

"I'm sorry. A fax came in, but we contacted the wrong room. Sorry to make you come down here."

She kept smirking, and I suspected they were playing a prank on me. It only made me more annoyed for having to get dressed and come down after I was finally eating dinner.

My friend finally laughed, then looked past me, nodding her head as if I should turn around. Curious to see the full hoax, I spun around. And I froze after what I saw.

"Charlotte Elizabeth Madden, I've flown all this way to talk you into coming home with me. I've missed you since the day you left. I've tried to talk myself out of coming here, but no reasoning could make me stop.

"Ten years ago, I told you how I felt and you ran away. I never went after you, and it's one of the biggest regrets in my life.

"So, that's what I'm doing now. I'm coming after you. I'm not leaving here without you. I'll stay here as long as I have to in order for you to come home with me. I love you, and I want you to be my wife."

He'd gotten down on his knee with the most gorgeous ring. As special as all that was, there was one other thing that brought me to an ugly cry. He had brought me a dozen roses—blush roses.

It was as if all things had fallen into place in that moment. The man who had gotten away proposed to me. He brought flowers that showed he knew me and understood what mattered to me.

I immediately said, "Yes!" I said yes a thousand times. But I had a hard time with the idea of leaving the program prematurely.

He stayed in Seattle for three days before I caved and told him that I'd leave with him. I couldn't push past my feelings this time. I spoke to my supervisor, and he understood. I was close to finishing, so I didn't leave him without help.

I packed up all my stuff, and we walked out of that hotel together, hand in hand, with my ring finger sparkling. I flew home with my *fiancé* and could hardly believe how much had changed in my life within a year.

Glenda had done more for me than I could put into words. She knew my darkest secrets but loved me anyway. She knew how to show me a genuine kindness I'd never experienced before.

She offered me an example of true forgiveness that I'll never forget. Her humility and authenticity inspired me to see the good in myself and offer that to those around me.

And I dreamed to have a love story like her and Charles. With blush and white roses surrounding us, Joe and I got married six months later, hoping that was the start to something timeless.

I thought of her every time I saw one of those blooms. I would smile because I knew that so much of what I had was a result of her help.

In the end, I know that all the help came from God. I was in a place where I didn't recognize myself, and He called me to Him. He was luring me back, starting with the pull into the church parking lot. I know He specifically sent Glenda there to help me.

She was tenacious and didn't give up on me. I know that only God could've given her that desire, because I didn't want to let anyone in. He knew I'd gotten so good at beating myself up, that I could go on the rest of my life continuing on the same path.

God knew me in high school when I was at my best. He knew me shortly after when I was at my worst. He knew me when I withdrew as far away from Him as possible. He knew me when I came close and pleaded with Him to forgive me.

I had a terribly hard time even considering forgiving myself. Glenda gave me example after example of why I should, but it wasn't until witnessing the miracle of her forgiving Jason that I knew I had no more excuses. That was the most humbling act I've ever witnessed—and probably ever will.

Although I would've wanted my time with Glenda to last forever, I know God gave her to me for the perfect amount of time. He gives you what you need more often than what you want. I wanted her to stay, but He needed her to go.

When she left, it opened up the door for me to see Joe again. God had orchestrated the entire thing. The one man who I had confessed I'd messed up with was placed there to rescue me in one of my saddest moments.

He gave me a gift at the same time He took one away. But through them both, He restored my hope, saved my life, and filled every empty space in my heart.

The End

CPSIA information can be obtained
at www.ICGtesting.com
Printed in the USA
FSHW012326230421
80592FS